The Alexandrite

a novel by
Rick Lenz

CHROMODROID PRESS

Lenz, Rick, author.
The alexandrite : a novel / by Rick Lenz – Second Edition

ISBN 978-0-9996953-5-7 (softcover)
ISBN 978-0-9996953-3-3 (eBook)
ISBN 978-0-9848442-7-2 (audiobook)

1. Monroe, Marilyn, 1926-1962--Fiction.
2. Actors--Fiction. 3. Performing arts--Fiction.
4. Time travel--Fiction. 5. Noir fiction. 6. Science fiction.
I. Title.

PS3612.E557A44 2015   813'.6
QBI15-600138

Printed in the United States of America

***

Cover by Foster Covers
Interior by Polgarus Studio
Editing by My Two Cents Editing
Consulting by Outrider Literary

***

ALSO BY RICK LENZ
North of Hollywood

For more about the author and his books, please visit
http://ricklenz.com/

Chromodroid Press
Los Angeles

Praise for *North of Hollywood*

First Place Memoir—Los Angeles Book Festival
A Performing Arts Book of the Year—Foreword Reviews

"A touching bittersweet remembrance… breathtaking…"

—KIRKUS REVIEWS

"Applause? Standing ovation! …masterful…"

—WRITERS DIGEST

"Most people don't know the simple truth that Lenz reveals in this captivating autobiography: Actors are real people, and acting is a real job… We're enthralled by the glamour, but Lenz helps us focus on the real point: The hardest part of a glamorous life, of any life, is to find one's feet and stay standing. Lenz is still standing, and *North of Hollywood* is a warm, credible account of how he found his place in and out of the limelight… The earned wisdom of a seasoned veteran.

—US REVIEW OF BOOKS;
a Recommended Review

"… An overwhelming sense of peace… poetic prose… The effect is beautiful."

—FOREWORD BOOK REVIEWS

"An actor's intimate, sometimes hilarious, sometimes touching, and always honest account of making a living while living next to Hollywood legends."

—PUBLISHERS WEEKLY

"A poetical, quirky, and heartwarming read."

—*G. L. BLANCHARD,*
author of THE MAN WHO TRADED HIS WIFE
FOR WOODWORKING TOOLS

"An essential book for anyone who has ever said they want to be an actor and anyone who was lucky enough not to. Compulsively readable! ...perceptive and poignant wisdom…"

—*MICHAEL KAHN,*
artistic director of the Shakespeare Theater in Washington D.C.;
former head of drama at The Juilliard School

"Talent to burn."

—*LAUREN BACALL*

"I love this book! Insightful, honest, wise, and charming!"

—*BERNARD SLADE,*
author of "SAME TIME, NEXT YEAR"

"I greatly admired Rick Lenz's thoughtful and well written book."

—*PETER BART,*
VARIETY

"*North of Hollywood* should be required reading for anyone who aspires to the acting life in New York and the City of Angels. Enchantingly written with a sure hand and a knowing eye, Rick Lenz reveals with enormous poignancy and gleeful insight what it has taken to make one real life work while pursuing the Hollywood dream."

—*ELIZABETH FORSYTHE HAILEY,*
New York Times Best Selling Author of
A WOMAN OF INDEPENDENT MEANS

"What a book!! I respected this actor's work and wanted to read anecdotes of his career, etc., and what a surprise! I got more. A superb writer who can so articulate his feelings—his emotional and mental journey through his life and career with ironic and witty humor and a piercing honesty—an actor's internal memoir with none of the ego we connect with an actor's recounting. No self-pity. He lets us into who he is by how he tells his story. It will inspire. Not just a showbiz story, but a universal one. I couldn't put it down.

—*JOSEPH R. SICARI,*
actor

"Raises the genre of the Hollywood Memoir to an art form."

—*MICHAEL NORELL,*
Writers Guild of America Award winner;
two-time Christopher Award winner

"I was totally engaged with *North of Hollywood*, start to finish. Sometimes it felt like Rick Lenz wasn't just 'opening the kimono,' as they say in business, but was actually peeling off his skin. I admire his courage in telling it."

—*SCOTT CAMPBELL,*
author of TOUCHED *and* AFTERMATH

"*North of Hollywood* is an often funny, sometimes gut wrenching, and immensely engaging true tale of one actor's journey … If you want to believe happy endings are possible in real life, even when real life is show business, take a look at *North of Hollywood.*"

—*TOMMY KENDRICK,*
ACTORS TALK podcast

This book is dedicated to Aaron, Riley, and Frances

and, always, Linda

"(Time) goes backward to an instant so ancient that it is beyond all memory, and past even the possibility of remembering. Yet because it is an instant that is relived again and again and still again, it seems to be now.

Those who are to meet will meet."

— A Course in Miracles

"How do you find your way back in the dark?"

—Marilyn Monroe, *The Misfits,*
screenplay by Arthur Miller

1

Alexandrite: a gem variety of chrysoberyl
that appears green in daylight
and red in artificial light.

TUESDAY, OCTOBER 8, 1996

At some unidentified point during the first time I live through the following events, it becomes as clear as my muddled brain has ever experienced clarity that most of us do not see what we see or hear what we hear; in fact, we can't tell what's going on right in front of us. As a result, few of us understand that life runs in a circle, that it's forever changing, but always, always in a circle. And the reason for this is, if it wasn't in a circle, if life went out in a straight line, it would take us away from each other. And that wouldn't work because we are all connected, made of the same stuff. Most of us, to one degree or another, are terrified of the end of the path we're on, never understanding that our path is a circle, and that it won't end—because it can't.

Curiously—or at least I think it's curious—what I have just said is something I've yet to learn, yet I already know it.

Go figure.

I know this is an odd way to start a story like this—if there is another story like this—but I am experiencing a lot of odd moments lately, and am having a new and alarming sensation of the (forgive me, psychobabble haters) Now in my life. Everything that happens to me is happening as it occurs—not a few minutes ago, not yesterday, not last year, but now.

My name is Jack Cade. I'm a forty-year-old actor, and going through a rough patch in my work life. My marriage is not doing well either, which is entirely my fault. Sophie is the most wonderful thing that ever happened to me.

Also, if I want to be totally honest (and what's the point of writing a journal if you don't plan to be honest), my career is in the process of falling to pieces.

WEDNESDAY, OCTOBER 9, 1996

I go to an audition today—four lines for a cable television movie. It's for one of those TV characters who knows what he knows with absurd confidence. When I get to the casting studio, I feel pins and needles up and down my spine, and my stomach is dripping acid as if I've just taken part in a black-coffee-drinking contest. There are four other actors who look just like me but confident waiting in the outer office. On the walls hang photographs of Cagney, Garbo, Rita Hayworth, Henry Fonda, Bette Davis, and as always in my life, it seems wherever I go, Marilyn Monroe.

Inside, I jump all my cues, reading the answers before the character I'm auditioning for has a chance to hear the questions. By then, perspiration is causing my shirt to stick to my chest and back, and it's clear the producers are not about to hire an actor whose clothing is pasted to him, who looks like he's just run a marathon and is about to, as the first marathoner did, drop dead.

The producers, who seem knowing and sophisticated beyond their years in their supercasual clothes and three-hundred-dollar haircuts, are disappointed. Who can blame them? They ask for devil-may-care and wised-up—kind of like they are—but I don't have that on my menu today. I have worried. I have unsure. I have bleeding actor's ego. Almost immediately, I notice that these foolishly confident TV guys are all wearing Rolexes, except for the doughty TV gal, who sports a large Mickey Mouse watch. I'm wearing a Timex that stopped working last year.

My mother, Rita, looms up in my mind like Gypsy Rose Lee's mama. She looks disappointed in me. I hate that look.

Passing through the outer office as I leave the audition, I glance at the picture of Spencer Tracy on the wall and wonder if there is anything generous, anything un-ego-bound behind his eyes, anything that, even with the ultimate actor and movie star, one could hang onto that isn't just part of "The Spencer Tracy Show."

THURSDAY, OCTOBER 10, 1996

I didn't sleep much last night. I've been having a recurring nightmare that I'm in a darkened hallway, standing at the top of a flight of stairs, trying to work up the guts to go down to the first floor. I'm terrified to start down, but there's a relentless pounding in my brain, and it leaves me no choice. I can see light at the bottom of the stairs coming through a short passageway from the next room.

I'm gripped constantly by two fears: that I am a perverse exception to the larger circle of life I sense in my gut that my life is running in a grinding and infinite loop with no means of changing its course; and that the only way I can possibly escape is to jump from the frying pan into the fire—leap free of the rut I'm stuck in and walk through that passageway into, for all I know, something even more sinister.

I wake up in a cold sweat just before I have to start down the stairs. I'm up for hours sometimes before I'm able to fall back into an uneasy sleep, but Sophie sleeps heavily. She gets up early and goes to work as a private care nurse at the Beverly Vue Apartments for a gentleman she calls "the old boy." Except for the times I gaze at her as I'm falling asleep, I hardly ever see her lately except in the evenings, and not always then.

Today, the telephone wakes me. It's the director of a play I've been working on, a five-character *Hamlet* at a tiny nonpaying workshop theatre in West Hollywood. I'm playing Polonius and alternating with the other supporting actors to do the narration. When you do a five-character *Hamlet*, a lot of things need to be explained.

An actor in his late thirties named Douglas Crossley is playing Hamlet. He is also directing. I was told Crossley almost became a star several years ago, having done nice roles in four big films when he was a young man, but evidently he didn't quite click, because after that he was once again, like most actors, struggling to get by. He's counting on this production to finally do it for him. I have my doubts.

On the telephone, Crossley says, "Hey, listen, Jack, rehearsal's canceled today. I'm making a couple of cuts. We're running too long."

"Oh, yeah? What are you cutting?"

"Nothing of yours. I'll see you tomorrow. Three o'clock."

I hang up, trying to ignore my usual paranoia at such moments. I turn my electric clock toward me and see that it's five, which is impossible in either direction—the sun is high in the sky. It has to be a Department of Water and Power problem. The people in the San Fernando Valley lose power quite often. It gets too hot, or it floods, or fires sweep through driven by Santa Ana winds which, even if there's nothing burning, can do plenty of damage, blowing down trees and high-tension lines and tossing huge truck trailers off roads. Sometimes the power sources seem to collapse for no reason at all.

It was windy last night. The Santa Anas have sucked the heat out of the desert and pushed it across the Valley and the LA basin to the sea. Tree branches are strewn across all the yards in our neighborhood and on the street in front of our house. I call up the automated time lady on the telephone (a decades-long sacrament) and reset my clock to 11:45, feeling depressed that so much of the day is already gone.

Looking out the front window, I hardly notice the pretty postal carrier as she drops my mail in the letterbox and moves off to the bungalow next door.

Sipping my coffee, I open an envelope that has no return address. Inside is a pawn ticket. I have no idea what it's about, and for a fraction of a second, I feel an eruption of déjà vu—a volcano locked up inside me with no vent for its energy, no way for it to identify and explain itself to me. I look at the ticket again, grateful for something to take my mind off my nightmare and show business.

I dress, get into my sun-faded, pale green 1984 Jaguar convertible, and drive the Hollywood Freeway from the San Fernando Valley into the central megalopolitan ooze of Los Angeles. Exiting on Vermont, I make my way to Morgan's Gifts on a seedy part of Oxford Street in the Wilshire District.

The inside of the pawn shop looks like it's been put together by a Hollywood scenic designer, from the careful layer of dust on the long file of guitars to the shiny, age-worn wooden counter outside the cage and a bad acrylic painting (there she is again) of Marilyn Monroe visible through the front window.

I've never been able to fully account for what feels like my lifelong connection with Marilyn. Staring at this crude rendering now, I know it isn't a sexual fixation I have on her. Okay, a little sexual, but mostly it's romantic, something like the sentimental feelings I had toward the girl I gave a bottle of perfume to in the seventh grade. The girl was a beautiful, delicate waif with a sad smile and a look in her eyes that transfigured my awakening teenage passions into something between fascination and obsession. I picked her name in the class drawing for an exchange of Christmas gifts and bought her a bottle of Shalimar that cost me every penny I had. When she thanked me for it, I know I turned crimson; I was unable to say a word to her. It felt like a triumph anyway; I knew from the way she smiled at me that she understood the magnitude of my gift.

On the second of January, the day after Christmas vacation ended, my father died.

Rita sold the house and we moved from Jackson, Michigan, to Los Angeles where, if Rita had her way, I would one day become a movie star. I have no idea what caused her to hatch this notion. Madness is my guess.

But this waif, Marilyn, goes on and on in the back of my mind, always there, as needful of something in me as I am of whatever it is in her. It's as if we have a subcutaneous interdependence, despite the fact that she departed the world almost thirty-five years ago. There's something upsetting about the artlessness of this depiction of her. It's as garish as any paint-by-number piece, but without the saving grace of guilelessness. This artist thought he knew what he was doing, but he had no clue.

The only thing to distinguish Morgan's Gifts from most other pawnbrokers is a tiny but stoutish woman with a hairline about as high as the first Queen Elizabeth's after she'd had smallpox. She has a pinkish complexion and is fast asleep in a chintz-covered wing chair near the front window. A strip of midday sunlight creeps up her shins toward her pudgy knees and she breathes evenly through her mouth.

I gaze at her for several seconds and am startled when she abruptly opens her eyes and catches me at it. I look away quickly, as if I'm browsing the shop. By the time I glance back, her eyes are closed again.

Afraid to wake her—if she actually is asleep—I don't ring the bell at the cage. I whisper hello a couple of times.

A loose-jointed young man with no hair on the sides of his oblong head unfolds himself into position inside the cage.

"Help ya?"

I hand him the ticket. He frowns at it, looks at me, sniffs, then hitches himself around the corner, where I hear him rustling through layers of other people's lives.

He reappears holding a small brown velvet jewelry box. "Here ya go." He pushes it out to me.

"How much do I owe you?"

"Been paid for."

"By whom?"

"Don't know. You'd have to ask Mrs. Hightower." He points at the woman in the wing chair.

I look at her, wondering if she's overheard us, but her eyes are still closed and she's again breathing rhythmically through her mouth.

"Was it paid by check?"

The young man shrugs.

"Do you know when it was paid?"

"Dunno." He turns up the palms of his hands.

I thank him and start to leave.

"Hey, you got to look at what's in there before you take it."

"Oh, sorry." I snap open the box.

It is an antique-looking ring with a roundish, faceted stone, murky purplish in color. "It's a ring." I move back to the window and hold it out. "Is this an amethyst?"

He takes it from me, gives it a perfunctory inspection, then hands it back. "Could be." He shrugs and disappears into the rear of the shop the way he came.

I stuff the ring in its box into a front jeans pocket and, with another glance at the plump little woman, go back out onto Oxford Street.

When the box starts hurting my leg on the freeway as I'm driving home, I wiggle it out of the pocket and open it up with my left hand. At first I think the kid has played some trick on me. It's a different ring. The stone is now a bright bluish-green, clear, with almost the fire of a diamond. But it's the same ring. The kid only held it for a moment then gave it back to me. I try it on the ring finger of my right hand.

It fits as if it's been sized for me.

Later, at our little house in North Hollywood, Sophie gets home from work in Beverly Hills and finds me asleep under the influence of about half of a family-size bottle of Deer Valley Chardonnay. I complain about what's going on—or not going on—in my work life. She listens as much as she's able to as I enlighten her about the ways in which reality television, already scourging through the European market, is about to start robbing me of my living, et cetera, et cetera. I quote some dire warnings from *Variety* and the *Hollywood*

Reporter.

I look at her out of the corner of my eye and see she's under some kind of stress of her own. Sophie is pretty, open, and unguarded; so unguarded that I can tell now that something is definitely bothering her. She can be brusque and sometimes, frankly, a little cold, and she picks now, when I'm feeling shitty like this, as one of those times.

To be fair, she isn't usually cold or brusque. I met her at a lecture on "Taking Care of the Elderly after a Hip Fracture" at UCLA. My mother had broken her hip and I wanted to know how to take care of her. (It turned out her fall had been a freak thing. Rita has bones as hard as Bakelite, and nothing like that ever happened to her again.) After the lecture, Sophie and I struck up a conversation, and she invited me over for coffee. She didn't say, "Let's go out and have coffee." She invited me to her apartment. I couldn't believe this knockout girl was being so forward. (I'm not saying I minded.) I accepted her invitation, went over to her place, and we talked until dawn. We didn't mess around or anything. That came the next time. After that, we messed around a lot.

Just short of two months later, we got married.

I have my nightmare again and shudder awake, terrified as always. Sophie is asleep next to me. I know if I wake her up to tell her about it, she will do her best to comfort me, but I also know that won't fix anything.

Looking at her, I think about getting up and maybe reading a little until I get drowsy again. But her face is so beautiful—not in the usual way, but confiding, in her sleep, a heartbreaking vulnerability. I have a badly timed urge to nestle into her, burrow into that place on the pillow next to where she's adrift in whatever dream world she's in. I want to inhale her, get lost in her, be as close as I can, not from the fear of my nightmare anymore, but from this fanatical tenderness that multiplies in me watching her sleep. I think of the Leonard Cohen lyric, "Your hair upon the pillow like a sleepy golden storm." I want to enter into her storm and keep her warm and safe.

A while later, I remember the ring. I had taken it off and put it in the pocket of my windbreaker. I slip out of bed and go out to the front closet to get it out. I sit down on the sofa, turn on a lamp, open the box and take it out. I hold it closer to the light. The stone is a deep raspberry red.

I wonder what whoever left it for me wants.

I look into the deep red and feel the same sense of dread I feel in my nightmare. But this is concrete. It's a thing. I'm holding it in my hand, which takes it out of the realm of fantasy; this is *real*.

FRIDAY, OCTOBER 11, 1996

I wake to Sophie sitting on the arm of the overstuffed chair I fell asleep in.

"I'm going to work. What's this?" She's holding my right hand, looking at the ring, green in the morning sunlight streaming through the window. "Is this an emerald?"

I rub my eyes. "I don't know. I don't think so."

I tell her about the pawn ticket and Morgan's Gifts.

"Aren't you curious to know what it is?"

"I guess."

"For someone in the arts, you certainly can act like a cement salesman."

"Okay. I would definitely like to know."

"Can you meet me outside the old boy's apartment building at eleven thirty?"

"I guess."

I go to Ralph's Grocery to pick up a few things we need. On the way back, just north of Carmine's Carwash on Tujunga (advertising *FREE PSYCHIATRIC HELP WITH HOT WAX*), every gear but second on my Jaguar becomes unusable. I make it to our mechanic's shop on Lankershim expecting it to cost five hundred dollars or more. I've known trouble was coming but I hoped it wouldn't happen for a while.

It takes ten minutes to fix. Parts and labor came to fifty-three dollars.

When I get home, there's a message from my agent, Gordon, scolding me for not having a pager and telling me I have an audition at 10:30 in Beverly Hills for an independent film. There won't be time to do more than quickly read over the scene before I go in. The director is in town from New York for only one day.

I change clothes, head over to Laurel Canyon and turn right on Sunset just west of what used to be Schwab's Pharmacy, the one-time highly publicized actor hangout where, according to some forgotten gossip columnist, Lana Turner was discovered by a talent scout. I've heard that Turner said that story was a fable. To my right and up a short, steep hill is the Chateau Marmont hotel, where during her post-Hollywood period, Greta Garbo used to check in occasionally under the name of Harriet Brown, and where John Belushi died of an overdose.

Driving west through West Hollywood, I pass the sleek, deco-style Saint James Club, formerly the Sunset Towers Apartments and featured in at least a dozen film noirs; the Rainbow Bar and Grill, where Marilyn Monroe and Joe DiMaggio met on a blind date; the Roxy, where almost every rock star has played at least once; and the Comedy Store, previously known as Ciro's, where the studios used to send movie-star "couples" to be photographed together before they escaped out the back to their real-life partners—other or same-gendered.

I learned most of this from Rita.

My palms are sweating by the time I get to my audition. I have ten minutes to look at the scene. I can't make much sense of it. Evidently, there are several other scenes that are about the same. It's a character who doesn't say much, just "reacts."

The director, a muddy-featured lump of a man chewing on a thick wet cigar, says with an unlikely lateral lisp, *"I'd jusht like to shee you lishen sshum,"* and the casting director reads some of the star's speeches, and I pretend they are the most riveting words I've ever heard—could ever imagine hearing.

When the audition is over, the director makes a sucking sound with his tongue and front teeth, shakes his head and says, *"The feeling musht flow up from within or there will be no beauty on the canvash."* He continues shaking his head.

Somehow this self-important humpty with what looks and sounds like a turd in his mouth, shaking his head in condescension, opens up the place inside me where the homicidal little boy lives, the potential assassin: petrified, wounded.

A few blocks from the Beverly Vue Apartments where Sophie works is a fancy Beverly Hills jewelry store on Rodeo Drive called Jewels By Jaxon. Sophie and I are buzzed through wrought iron security gates into an intimidating space with plush sage-green carpeting, walls covered with elegant green and gold paper, floor-to-ceiling panels of mirror, and rich, dark walnut showcases full of expensive-looking jewelry.

An attractive ash blonde in her early forties wearing a simple pink silk dress and only a strand of pearls and tiny pearl earrings for jewelry approaches us and says in a near whisper, "May I show you something?"

"Actually, we'd like to show you something," I say. "I was given a ring. I wondered if you could tell me what it's worth."

She stiffens slightly. "Did you want an appraisal for insurance purposes?"

"No, we just want to find out … what this is—just to have a rough idea."

"May I see it, please?"

I take off the ring and hand it to her. She holds it to the light and makes a faint humming sound in the back of her throat. "This may be an alexandrite. I'm not an expert, but I'll let you speak with Mr. Parsons. He's our gemologist and appraiser."

She returns the ring to me, disappears into a back room and very shortly returns with a slender gentleman dressed in what looks to be a Forties-style Savile Row double-breasted suit like Adolphe Menjou used to wear, or Herbert Hoover. He is fine-featured, gray-haired, and appears to be in his early sixties. He takes us to a small immaculate room filled with books and gem-testing instruments.

"Won't you have a seat?" He speaks in a firm, friendly voice that's high, almost feminine. As Sophie and I settle into comfortable armless leather chairs, he says, "Let's see what we have here."

I hand him the ring.

Parsons examines it with a jeweler's loupe that springs miraculously to his right eye. He turns the ring over and back again.

"Do you know what it is?" says Sophie.

He looks up at her, startled by the interruption. "Yes, I know this stone. It's an alexandrite. May I ask how you came by it?"

"It was given to me," I say.

"And how did the giver acquire it?"

"I don't know. Is it valuable?"

"It's about seven carats. I'll measure it in a minute. I'd judge the retail value to be about fifty thousand. It has a small feather-shaped inclusion that would lower its market value, but it's an exceptional stone." He flips a switch on a matte black high-tech lamp. "This is a full-spectrum light source—the same range of illumination as the sun."

He holds the ring under it. The alexandrite is now a deep bluish emerald green, as it was when I looked at it driving home on the freeway from Morgan's Gifts.

"The changes in hue are due to the delicate balance maintained in the absorption color; a change in the color of the light transmitted is all it takes to produce a change in the color of the stone." He turns it and studies it from several angles. "This is extraordinary."

"Did you …? Was that fifty … *thousand*?" I say, glancing at Sophie.

She gives me the strangest look, as if she's happy and sad at the same time.

Parsons looks off into the distance. "Depends on the buyer. It could be more." He shakes his head slowly like a wine taster clearing his palate and returns his attention to the ring.

"Alexandrite is remarkable in the first place. It's a twinned crystal, as unmatched in its way as diamond. But the color in this stone is unusually deep." He puts the ring in the clip of a microscope, adjusts the focus and examines it again. "Here, take a look."

Sophie looks at it. I follow. It's a velvety green stone with a flat top ringed by triangular and kite-shaped facets that sparkle as the stone absorbs and reflects the light. Near the bottom and off to one side is a tiny floating feather that's a little lighter than the surrounding crystal. Gazing at it, I feel as if I'm in danger of falling, like I'm standing on the edge of a cliff, and for a half second, I have the notion that I might, without meaning to, step off and drop into some bottomless abyss I'd never be able to climb out of.

I stare at it for a long time. "That's … um, uh … that's really … fascinating." As I look up, congratulating myself on such sophisticated patter, Sophie purses her lips, frowns at me, then looks through the microscope again.

Next, Parsons puts the ring in something he calls a Leveridge gauge and measures the stone. "It's just over seven and a quarter carats. Who gave it to you?"

"I don't know."

Parsons looks puzzled, almost annoyed. "If I were you, I'd try to figure out where this came from." He puts an index finger to his forehead and massages lightly, as if trying to soothe a sore spot. "Plato believed that precious stones were living beings. And this is an alexandrite. This could be your friend."

Sitting with Sophie in Roxbury Park between Olympic and Pico in Beverly Hills, I say, "I won't be home till late tonight. I'm having dinner with Rita."

She isn't listening. "Somebody pawned the ring. All you have to do is go down there and ask that woman."

"She probably doesn't know either." I'm thinking how much better I'd feel if we had the fifty thousand in cash.

"Yes, but she might. Maybe it was paid for in person when the boy wasn't there. Aren't you dying of curiosity?"

"Actually, I don't think I want to know anything more about it."

She looks at me as if she's never seen me before. "Why?"

"I don't know. It blows my mind that this thing has … been given to me—anonymously, but it feels like there's something maybe in the stone itself that I really … don't want to know about." She's staring at me, and I realize she looks deeply sad. "I don't have any idea what I'm saying," I say.

"Maybe it's the fact that it changes color, and you'd never expect that. Maybe it's the crystal itself. When I saw it under the microscope, I felt … Didn't it make you feel strange—as if you were about to pitch off into the depths of somewhere you knew you didn't want to be?"

She's frowning.

"Never mind. It's me. I know it is. I just don't like change … I realize you can't avoid it, but … sometimes I feel as if I'm barely holding it together."

Seeing that I'm disappointing her, I say, "Okay, okay, I'll go." I'm gazing off toward the west. For some reason, I'm seeing in my mind the Pico Avenue gate of Twentieth Century Fox Studios, where Marilyn Monroe shot twenty of her twenty-nine completed movies. "Anyway, she's probably cashed the check by now."

Sophie looks at me like Rita used to when I was a kid and she was driving me home from acting class and I'd just told her I wasn't so sure I wanted to be an actor.

"But the customer would have been given a receipt," says Sophie. "And the woman would have a copy of it. You want to drive over there right now?"

"I don't think so. Maybe tomorrow … or next week."

She looks over my shoulder, off in the other direction toward Hollywood, and shakes her head. "I hoped this would work out to be something nice for you. You need something nice. But you don't seem to court nice things anymore. You don't even reach out for them when they're offered to you. You court unhappiness. You don't give as if you expect anything good in return. It's as if you expect only *bad* to come your way."

"What are you talking about?" I hold up the alexandrite. "I just got this thing."

She doesn't answer. "I don't know how to say this …" She looks shaken. "I think we need some time … away from each other."

I stare at her. "What do you mean?"

"We aren't … nice to each other anymore."

I'm numb. "Sure we are. It's just kind of a bad time is all."

"It's been a bad time for five years. And it's getting worse." She looks more pained than I've ever seen her. "You're sinking, Jack. I love you, but you're sinking." She shakes her head. "And I'm not going down with you." She looks at the grass beneath our feet.

"Something's going to break for me. I'll get a job, a better attitude. I really will. I'm making an effort to tap into the good parts of me, into my thoughtful, selfless parts, into my … you know, my generosity."

"I don't see how that goes along with continuing to do something that—as you pursue it, anyway—seems to be turning you into the opposite of what you're saying." She shakes her head again. "I don't think, when you tap into the deepest parts of yourself, you get what you want; I think you get what you are."

"That's a really shitty thing to say."

"I can't let myself go under because you're determined to. This has been going on way too long."

I don't even defend myself. I can't even speak up for my marriage to a woman who is without question the best thing that's ever come into my life. I think of her asleep on her pillow. I want to go back and be with her in a more loving, transfigured way, but I don't have the tools for something like that.

When I get home, there are two messages on my machine. The first voice says, "Jack, it's Gordon. They think your look is perfect, but you weren't there with your reading. Sorry, babe." Click.

The second caller is a woman. "This is Friday, ten thirty in the morning. My name is Maggie Partridge. I'm a psychophysicist."

I snort at the machine.

"I've come across something in my work that you may be very interested in. Could you meet me today? Say three o'clock? The address is 1833 Shoemaker Drive in La Vieja. It's extremely important." She has left her telephone number.

"What the hell's a"—the phone rings—"psychophysicist?" I pick it up.

"Hiya, Jack. I'm afraid I've got some bad news."

I don't say a word; just wait for more bad news.

"It's not going to work out," says Doug Crossley. "I have to replace you."

"But we're into dress rehearsals."

"The guy who was going to play it before I hired you has suddenly become available, and I owe it to him. He's played the role before."

"You *owe* it to him? That's not a reason. What about me?" It feels as if this is the second red-hot skewer I've had plunged into my guts in an hour. "You can't do this to me, Doug. It's just not decent. You weren't making cuts yesterday, were you?"

"Whoever said show business was decent, Jack? Hey, listen, buddy, there'll be other parts. Polonius isn't much of a role anyway. This is no comment on your talent."

I hang up, take several deliberate, deep breaths, gobble a couple of pills, wonder why Sophie doesn't love me anymore, force myself to stop thinking about her, then mechanically telephone Morgan's Gifts and ask to speak to Mrs. Hightower.

The young man tells me she's out and won't be back until late in the afternoon. I tell him I'll call back later.

I lie down, try to straighten out my tangled thoughts, whimper for a while, and fall asleep.

In our backyard, next to my faux Zen garden that's not feng shui the way I'd pictured it, but crowded with grasses that looked perfect at the nursery, I practice the ritual training moves of judo but can't concentrate.

My attempt at mind control melts into blind rage: *"Shit, fuck, shitty cock fuck!"* It's not enough that I've been dismissed by my wife. Now, I'm fired from a job I was doing for fucking free. How can someone fire you when you're working for fucking nothing? And how can my wife, who promised "for better or worse," leave me when all that's happening is I'm going through a little rough patch? It's not permanent. I'll get a better fucking attitude.

I sink to my knees as if I'm going to pray, but instead I shout, "WHEN I'M GOOD AND FUCKING READY!"

Like a rabbit in high weeds, my instincts tell me I'd better be alert for predators, monsters in my own backyard. It doesn't matter how well I think I've hidden myself. I have to watch out for everything—my own crazy impulses, for example.

For a few seconds I feel a wash of serenity. I stand up, and with my right knee bent, my left leg stretched back and my right hand reaching toward the sky, I gaze upward, avoiding looking at the sun.

I see it anyway, reflected brilliant green in my alexandrite.

I am changing too, into an angry man I don't recognize but also do. I don't know why this is—that I've lost all perspective. I have been telling myself lately that I am getting more tolerant of change, but my wife has left me with no warning at all—and for no fucking reason—and I feel like a pathetic fraud.

I guess that's a reason.

Maybe—it occurs to me—my real problem is that until now, the characters I've played have been at least a little under my control and that that's something I've come to need. Now, the world seems to be acting root and branch on me, randomly shifting my colors and the colors around me. Considering my ghastly breakdown of confidence and my nightmares, I wonder again if I've finally gone the whole tree and am now entirely insane.

But I don't necessarily want to do anything about it. To be honest, I've always been a little afraid of that part of me that I don't know—that thing that goes on underneath in people, the ghost in the machine, I think it's called. I don't trust the ghost in my machine.

I have an image of my new life, living by myself, no wife, no children, no work, no interests; and it crosses my mind that it wouldn't necessarily be such an awful thing if I went to sleep tonight and didn't wake up.

Then it strikes me that I've just had about the saddest idea a human being can possibly have.

"What the hell's a psychophysicist?"

"Fuck it."

2

FRIDAY, OCTOBER 11, 1996 (CONT'D)

I drive west toward La Vieja. I haven't been this deep into the Valley for years. When my mother and I first moved to California, it was still the Los Angeles I recognized from books and movies. Now, it defines urban sprawl—strings of North Hollywoods, Burbanks, Sylmars, and Pacoimas spreading off in every direction from the ocean to the mountains and all the way up the sides of those mountains as far as they can get without falling back on top of themselves.

Following a Thomas Guide, I find Shoemaker Drive just below the foothills. The houses are a mongrel mix of brick, stucco, and wood. As I drive nearer to the mountains on the north, I see a road sign: *NO THRU TRAFFIC.* Shoemaker Drive seems to be ending. I drive around for a while trying to find a continuation.

Finally, I make my way back to a gas station/restaurant I passed a quarter mile earlier. It's a bleached clapboard structure with a couple of pumps out front. A sign hangs from a frayed wire cable. It reads *DICK'S GAS AND HOT FOOD.*

Inside, a middle-aged woman sits behind the cash register waxing hair off her legs. A Sally Hansen box lies open on the counter, spilling out a half dozen strips.

"Hi. Excuse me. Can you tell me what happened to Shoemaker Drive?"

She glances up at me but her concentration remains on her chore.

"Shoemaker's right out there." She nods in the direction I've come from.

"But it ends at fifteen hundred."

She chuckles. "Yeah. I know." She rips a strip of hair off her leg and winces. "Jesus, I hate that."

"Do you know where the rest of Shoemaker Drive is?"

"Can't say I do."

"Is anybody around who would? Is Dick around?"

"No, but I'm his wife. My name's Bernice."

I see. "Okay. Thanks anyway." As I start to leave, she heaves a sigh, as if she's telling me this against her better judgment.

"If you just drive down that road by the wash there and take a sharp left just before it dead-ends, I bet you'll run right into Shoemaker again."

"Thanks."

"Come again." She rips another strip of hair off her leg.

I find the rest of Shoemaker Drive; 1833 is at the head of another cul-de-sac.

It's a two-story Georgian home made of stone and brick with impressive, peaked dormer windows on the second floor and a portico over the front entrance that's supported by white fluted columns and looks as though it has been magically lifted from its natural setting somewhere in nineteenth-century New England and set down by way of some absentminded real estate developer's typographical error in the San Fernando Valley.

I park my Jaguar on the street at the end of a long flagstone driveway lined on either side by a density of blue agaves, walk to the front door and ring the bell. No one seems to be in any hurry to answer. I notice that two of the columns supporting the portico must have collapsed or almost collapsed once, judging by the white plaster patch job and some steel support struts. I hate being under heavy things that look like they could fall on me, so I move back to the front steps and gaze around at the neighborhood.

La Vieja, "the old lady," is unsurprisingly not a newly developed area of the Valley. The houses nearby are mainly single-story wooden structures barely substantial enough to keep out the Santa Anas, and very few of the lawns are well looked after. On a couple of them, old cars sit rusting, but there is a pleasing variety of trees: elms, oaks, Brazilian peppers, olives, silver maples, liquidambars, a full range of citruses, a half dozen varieties of palm, loquat, guava. Some of the trees have buckled the sidewalks they shade.

I ring the bell again and move back to the front steps. A little girl is pedaling a tricycle a few houses away. I wish Sophie and I hadn't put off having children.

Oh, God. That's all we need: another victim of a toxically ambitious actor.

Maybe this is turnaround day. Maybe today I'll put an end to the world of the terminally self-involved. I need to explore other places, other people; actually see the world through the eyes of the CHARACTER I hope to God is somewhere inside me. I look out at La Vieja again and feel in my guts that there are new and friendly universes somewhere out there, ripe for discovery. I've been so obsessed I've finally gotten to crisis point, my dried up humanity like a thirsty dog lying by his empty water bowl, hoping his master—or actually, any passerby would do—will spot his problem before it's too late.

"Good afternoon, Mr. Cade. Thanks so much for coming."

I swivel around. She's opened the door without a sound. A handsome woman, about thirty-five, with a way of looking deep into my eyes. She has an athletic, feminine figure and is dressed in tailored slacks and a matching silk blouse. She wears her auburn hair in an attractive blunt cut.

"Dr. Peacock?"

She corrects me. "Partridge."

"Oh, of course. I'm sorry. I think I remembered that name from the game Clue—Mrs. Peacock."

A whisper of a smile. "It's perfectly all right."

Inside, seeing the gray slate floor of the foyer, I look abruptly up toward the top of the stairway and the second floor.

A blade of ice stabs into my spine and slices out to every extremity. Even in the warm light of day and from this reverse angle, I recognize the scene of my nightmare.

She leads me through a low-ceilinged passageway, no more than six feet long into a spacious, once-elegant living room. I feel dizzy. I stare at several nicely made reproduction Victorian pieces—a moss green sofa with a pattern of pale yellow flowers, a rocking chair, a couple of small tables, and some imitation Tiffany lamps. On one of the walls, over a massive stone and carved mahogany fireplace, is an oil portrait of a lovely golden-haired woman. I don't know why—she isn't a lookalike—but she trips a memory of the picture of Marilyn Monroe in the window of Morgan's Gifts.

A modern television monitor is in the nearest corner next to a camcorder on a tripod.

Dr. Partridge gestures to a low-backed chair upholstered in faded velvet. "Would you like some coffee? I brought a thermos."

"No, thanks." I sit heavily.

"You're sure you're all right? You look pale."

"I'm fine. What is this place?"

She is charmingly embarrassed. "I'm sorry, love. You don't know anything about this, do you? This is a wonderful old white elephant of a house, leased to the county by the private party who owns it. It was built in the 1930s by an eccentric old man who loved this climate. He did it for his wife. But as it turned out, she didn't love this climate. She spent one night here and fled back to Boston. Now the county takes care of it. They run occasional tours through it, although as you can imagine, this part of the Valley doesn't draw many visitors. The owners would like to get rid of it, but they can't get their money out of it. So they've just been sitting on it for years. You're sure about the coffee?"

"Yes."

"And you don't know why I've asked you here. I'll get to the point." She sits across from me on a small settee. "You took part in a field experiment in hypnosis a couple of years ago with something called the Southern California Psychology Group through the Screen Actors Guild, right?"

"That's right. How would you—?"

"Would you mind telling me how you happened to get involved with that?"

"I don't mind. I was between jobs. Sometimes out-of-work actors get approached to do that kind of thing. They paid me basically carfare to be hypnotized and to answer a bunch of questions."

"What questions?"

"I don't know. I was hypnotized." I feel as if I should be angry, but I'm not. For some reason I feel giddy. "How did you know about that? Did you have some connection with it?"

"No. But audiocassettes were made. The project fell apart—insufficient funding—and the tapes were destroyed, but not before I came across some of them. Most were not very interesting, but yours were. If it makes you feel any better, I was told at the time that the participants had signed off on those tapes."

"How did you reach me?"

"Through your agent." She clears her throat.

Looking around the living room, I have the feeling I'm in it for some good reason that I simply haven't heard yet and that soon this game will be over and everything will be made clear to me.

"Then, listening to your tapes, I made a discovery. And I couldn't keep it to myself. This hasn't gone beyond me, and it won't." She gazes into my eyes without blinking. "Don't you want to know about my discovery?"

"Okay."

"How would you feel about my videotaping our conversation?" She points at the camera.

"I don't think I'd like it. Are you going to tell me why you asked me here?"

She takes a sip of coffee from a plastic mug and puts it down. "What do you know about string theory?"

"Pardon? Not much. Very little. Something to do with physics. Infinitesimal strings inside … what, quarks? Something like that?"

"That's right."

"Why do you ask?"

"I don't know much about it either," she says. "The best of us don't.

We're just pretty sure we're on the track of something that's up there in significance with the wheel, the printing press, and digital technology. Did you ever hear of someone called Richard Blake?"

"No."

"Your tapes from that experiment told me very little about you but a lot about a man named Richard Blake, who lived in this house during the fifties." She gets up and moves to the television. "I'd like to show you a piece of videotape." She turns on the monitor.

A tall middle-aged man with a high forehead, long but fleshy face, ears flat to his head, twinkling eyes and an open, cheerful smile appears on the screen. He is delivering a lecture that is intercut with shots of an attentive audience of college students. On a blackboard behind him is an equation: $R_{uv} - \frac{1}{2}\, g_{uv}R = 8\pi\, T_{uv}$. Beneath that is scrawled "Einstein's ten independent equations, condensed into one."

The man speaks enthusiastically in a croaky baritone. "Light travels at one foot per nanosecond. If you stand eight feet from a mirror, the image you see of yourself is sixteen nanoseconds younger than you are as you see it. If we had a mirror in a distant galaxy and looked at it through a more sophisticated telescope than now exists, it might show dinosaurs walking the earth. Einstein explained gravity by showing how mass causes space-time to curve— not to obey the rules of Euclidean geometry. A time traveler is someone whose timeline loops back and intersects with itself—as a helix does. This, despite the fact that from the time traveler's perspective, he has been traveling toward the future all the time."

The professor smiles at his mesmerized listeners, then continues, "According to quantum mechanics, you can make an object appear spontaneously. Physicist George Gamow demonstrated that years ago on a subatomic scale."

"Wait a minute."

Not taking her eyes off the screen, Dr. Partridge says, "Listen. Please."

"Time is the fourth dimension," says the lecturer. "If I am to meet my daughter in the city, we must agree on three space coordinates and another number signifying time. Aboriginal wisdom, however, tells of a second time:

dreamtime. If that existed, the universe would be five dimensional. Some theorists, myself among them, are saying that if there were two dimensions of time—time, and let's just call it dreamtime—I could meet not only my daughter, but also myself."

With conspicuous glee, he throws a hand over his head and sweeps it around in a large circle.

"We could loop around in the time/dreamtime plane and visit anywhere in time we wanted. If I'm an eligible subject, I can see myself off on the journey I just completed, simply by capitalizing on my presence in time/dreamtime. Superstring theory suggests that our universe actually has eleven dimensions. Some physicists have discussed the possibility that one of the curled-up dimensions connoted by superstring theory could be a time dimension—such as dreamtime. If it exists, then we can most certainly time travel. Now, then"—he rubs his hands together like he's about to serve barbecue—"we know that there are two subject requirements for movement through time: an absolute duplication of location and a person wholly susceptible to hypnosis."

"This man's insane."

Partridge hits the freeze-frame, leaving the professor with his mouth half open on the screen.

I'm woozy all over again. "Who *is* that?"

"This is a tape of a lecture delivered recently by a physicist named Robert Hinkle. And he's anything but insane. He's one of the leaders of a small group of physicists who have recently reopened dialogue on the possibilities of time travel."

"And you're showing it to me because …?"

An audible gulp of breath, then, "I think you're more than coincidentally tied to a man who once owned this house. I think you used to *be* …" She pauses and takes in another gulp of air. "I think you used to be someone called Richard Blake."

I find the presence of mind to close my mouth. When I open it again: "Is this a *joke?*"

"I want to try to send you back in time."

I look over my shoulder. "Am I on *Totally Hidden Video* or something?"

"This is very difficult." She seems hurt. "I believe absolutely in what I'm saying." Behind her, the professor is still frozen on the screen midlecture. "I'm trying to give you some context to help you understand my work and the reason I've asked you here ... Mr. Cade?"

"You want to send me back in ..." She opens her mouth to speak, but I find my voice again. "You're a *psychophysicist*?" This has come out of me piercingly, nearly at the top of my voice.

She blinks, startled. "Yes. I am. Actually, ours is a subspecies of the psychophysics that was coined by Gustav Fechner in the middle of the eighteenth century."

"What are you *talking* about?" I stare at her stupidly. "Have I been hypnotized again? Is this a follow-up to that ... to that earlier thing?"

She shakes her head, then blinks again. "Okay, yes, it is hypnosis in a way."

"What do you mean 'in a way'? I'm either under hypnosis or I'm not. Those people that other time apparently thought I was a good candidate for it."

She's watching me steadily. "All right, yes. You're hypnotized. You have no choice but to do what I tell you to."

I manage to stand up.

"That's what *you* think. I'm sorry for whatever's wrong with you, but I have to go now."

3

I stumble, then regain my footing and weave toward the passageway.

Either through stunning determination or exceptional agility, or both, Partridge stands between me and the way out.

"Dear God, hear me out, please. I beg you!"

There is such utter desperation on her face, it feels as if it would be the cruelest thing I've ever done if I don't hear the rest of what she has to say. I suppose I can put up with her psychosis for a few more minutes. I summon all my resolve, turn around, make it back to where I was, and sit again.

"I don't blame you for thinking … whatever you're thinking." She gathers herself, breathing deeply again. "We've been working on Einstein's theories for a relative nanosecond. The Kaluza-Klein theory unified the forces of gravity and electromagnetism, explaining both in terms of curved space-time, even though serious doubts were raised … You have a question?"

"If there's such a thing as time travel, why haven't I ever met a time traveler?"

"Good. You've nicely rephrased Stephen Hawking's question, 'Why haven't we been overrun by tourists from the future?' But who says we haven't? Maybe there's a reason we haven't. It's easy to postulate a dozen. For example, aren't we likely to think of those who tell us they've traveled to us from the future as psychotic?"

"But how can there be time travel if the … way to do it hasn't been discovered before now?"

"Wonderful question."

My God, she's sucking me in again.

"It's called a Cauchy horizon, named after a nineteenth-century French mathematician. The Cauchy horizon separates regions of time that are not available for time travel. Such regions are like the inside of an hourglass—there's no way to get to them." She holds up a hand. "But then, in 1976, a researcher named Frank Tipler studied Cauchy horizons under the theoretical conditions of zero mass energy density, suggesting that occurrences of Cauchy horizons might alter, depending on energy fields. Recent hypothetical experiments have connected that concept with dreamtime theory."

The words squirt out. "I'm no more hypnotized than you are."

She holds up a hand and seems to consider this. "It's all right for you to believe either way. All I'm saying is that if you hear the case I'm making for exactly what it is, you will understand more, and it'll work better."

"I'll tell you what I think will work better: I think this will all make more sense if we both agree that you're an escaped mental patient."

She smiles. SMILES!

As I think of getting up and heading for the door again, I remember the thought I had—not much over an hour ago—of going to sleep and never waking up. I don't move.

"Think about this," she says. "Max Planck, the father of quantum physics, said, 'Science cannot solve the ultimate mystery of nature, and that's because we ourselves are part of nature and therefore part of the mystery we are trying to solve.' But Planck's further inference was—given the nature and breadth of his own work—that we can realize incredible scientific achievements simply by believing we can."

"If you build it, they will come?"

She laughs. "Oh, yes. They'll come. Please listen." She seems so sure of herself. She points at the television set, takes another deep breath, and switches it on again.

Robert Hinkle continues where he left off. "The surprising but not surprising aspect of all this," he says, "is that no one has yet demonstrated publicly what has already been verified privately." There is a murmur from the audience. "Exactly. People don't elect politicians these days who vote for expensive avant-garde programs. As a result, some experimental projects are operated in a completely classified manner." He spreads his arms, his palms turned upward. "Which means nobody knows about them but the people involved."

Partridge turns off the VCR. "Assume for the moment that I am crazy. What have you got to lose?"

I realize I've been giggling. "No. I've changed my mind. I don't think you're crazy. I'm positive now; it's not you. It's me. I don't know exactly when it happened or what caused it, but for some reason I'm not computing properly. I seem to be in a dreamtime of my own."

"Which brings me back to why I contacted you."

"Am I dreaming you? Am I dreaming all this? The reason I ask is that I've been here before—in this house, in this room, in a nightmare. Do you know anything about that?"

"It's your unconscious confirming exactly what I'm telling you."

I get up, walk to the front window, and look out at my Jaguar in front of the house and the double row of blue agaves next to the driveway. The smell of sage has filtered into the room from the Valley outside, acrid like the pain of loneliness.

I turn back toward her. "Let me tell you some private thoughts I'm having. I don't know you, so I shouldn't care what you think of me." I realize my eyes haven't adjusted from looking out into the bright sunlight and I can't make out her face. I can't seem to remember it either, even though I'm still talking to her.

I cross back to her and feel a rush of relief that I recognize her. "I've just lived through the most bewildering twenty-four hours of my life. And now I'm out in the middle of the desert, listening to a perfectly reasonable-sounding woman suggest I do some time traveling like she was outlining an investment plan or something. I don't suppose you know why my wife has left me, do you?"

She frowns and looks at me with what seems to be genuine sympathy. "Sorry, love."

I extend my right hand to her. "Do you know how I came to have this ring?"

"I beg your pardon?" She looks at the alexandrite, obviously puzzled.

"Whoever orchestrated this little fantasy knows something about show business. You seem well cast." I look back at the television set. "You know, what that man said was all just … Greek to me. I'd have been more convinced if you'd told me you were going to shoot me back to a previous incarnation by magic."

"But I am—if everything goes right."

"Pardon?" I watch her lips move, but I'm not sure I'm hearing all her words.

"What is real magic but the bending of natural law past where we'd heretofore thought it could bend? Jesus walked on water. But maybe he just understood how to use the laws of a category of physics we haven't yet become aware of. We all have perceptual filters," she says. "It's a commonly ignored fact of life. Certain things we pay attention to; others, we have zero patience for. For example, if I were to ask you to fall to your knees and repent your original sin, you would probably get up and tell me you had an appointment right now, yes?"

"Yes."

"There are trigger words and phrases—trigger thoughts in our culture— that we tune out because we perceive that they're saying something crazy, or at least something that distinctly repels us." She claps her hands together, creating a pistol shot effect. "I'm saying the ramifications of becoming aware of that fact are earthshaking. My work is based on the premise that our perceptual filters shroud almost entirely an incalculable mass of what in plain speak we would otherwise call miracles."

I consider the possibility that a part of me may not be in this room with my body. I'm pretty sure she just used the word "miracle."

"If I were to take you to a 'psychic,' and if that someone were able to tell you things about your life that he had absolutely no way of knowing—and this sort of thing does happen, whatever the cynics may tell you—a rational reaction on your part might be, 'Well, that is indeed spooky.' And you'd tell the story of that experience for the rest of your life. But you probably wouldn't make any more out of it than that. Well, what I and some of my colleagues are saying is that there is a growing mass of real evidence by those who study time, space, and the human mind's 'extrasensory' potential, that clearly indicates we are not dealing in this regard with—as most of the world thinks of it—supernatural phenomena; that our theories are in fact not supernatural at all, but lie entirely within the confines of natural law. We just haven't been able to communicate it yet. And the reason we haven't is people—their limitations, their selective perceptual filters."

I feel myself grinning shark-faced at her, like Jack Nicholson having just heard a clever double entendre. "Well, okay. Cool. I'm hooked."

Partridge frowns.

"I don't have any plans today. So I'll just see if I can't suspend my perceptual filters for a teensy bit. Do you know why I *really* got fired from *Hamlet*?" I giggle again and scratch at my face like I'm on methamphetamines. "Never mind. What time in old Richard Blake's life would I go back to?"

She clears her throat. "It would be a time, we believe, when something memorable was taking place. A person remembers smelling a flower, receiving a raise at work, getting married. There's no way to predict."

I'm amazed at the matter-of-factness with which I react to all of this. I know now that I'm out of my mind, yet I'm listening to her time-travel prospectus (and her scientist on tape) for the most part politely. It's as if I've watched too many absurdist comedies in a row and my frame of reference has gotten bent around to the point that everything seems preposterous and nothing provokes surprise.

"What happens if I don't come back—can't find the right wormhole or whatever?"

"Don't worry, love. You'll come back."

"How do you know? I mean, couldn't I just get … stuck in Richard Blake's life?"

"No, that couldn't happen."

"Why not? It would save my wife the trouble of divorcing me."

She waves that off. "You have to live your own life. Jack Cade's life can't just end arbitrarily because of a psychogenic experiment. Everything that happened in the past and everything that will happen in the future is all happening right now. Your life has to continue as it would have."

"This does bring up another minor issue that I wouldn't ordinarily expect to be discussing with a physicist—not that I talk to that many physicists. Do physical scientists dabble in reincarnation these days? Because, unless I'm hallucinating, you did say you think I used to *be* this Richard Blake. Didn't you?"

"Yes, I did."

"So then …?"

"I told you, I'm a psychophysicist. And I do indeed dabble in … such things. Physics and metaphysics haven't traditionally mixed, but who says they shouldn't? They're not mutually exclusive. Great breakthroughs usually happen when someone realizes that two things thought to be incompatible turn out to be profoundly harmonious." She takes in the expression on my face. "Look, there was no scientific knowledge that recommended going out into a developing rainstorm, as Ben Franklin did, and flying a kite with a key at the end of the string." Seeing the expression on my face, she interrupts herself. "All right, maybe that story's apocryphal, but you take my point. A huge number of the most important scientific discoveries are generated outside normal scientific guidelines."

She studies me and steeples her fingers to her lips. "Maybe the way you're seeing it is useful." She spreads her arms. "Okay. You're temporarily deranged. I'm a master magician, and the only thing left is for you to put yourself completely in my hands and you'll be safe. Magician's ethics, okay?"

Feeling like a hunter stalking something that's actually over my shoulder, in the shadows, watching me, I show her what is no doubt a goofy smile. Then, abruptly, for no reason, I feel resigned to whatever awaits me. And again, I'm giggling.

"Well, what the hell. My wife's left me. I can't get a job. There's nothing else happening on the crumbling back roads of my life. When would we begin?"

"Anything wrong with now?"

"Yeah, sure. Why not? How long would it take?"

"Not long. Minutes, I think." She's telling me I'll be back from this acid trip, from this gig as a magician's subject, in time for my dinner date with my mother.

"I just have one question before we do this."

She nods.

"Who the hell is Richard Blake?"

"A gemologist," says Dr. Partridge.

"What?"

"A gemologist."

"I heard you." My voice sounds as if I'm underwater. "You're kidding."

"Why would I be?"

"You know as well as I do that this whole thing is someone's elaborate put-on." I try to recall how I could have accidentally taken that acid. I feel as if I'm being carried along like a cork in the white torrents above a waterfall. "Was Richard Blake married?"

"Yes."

"Aren't you going to give me the rest of this character's bio?"

"I don't know much more than that. But I'm not sure I should tell you, anyway."

"Why?"

"I don't want to send you back there with any preformed opinion from me."

"All right, I think you've laid it out clearly enough. So since I'm obviously already in 'dreamtime' and none of this is actually happening—at least the way it feels like it is—why don't you just go ahead? What do you do, wave a watch fob or a coin at me? I don't have to ingest anything, do I? I'll be honest, the part of me that thinks I'm really doing this is doing it despite the fact I don't think I should be making *any* decisions today." I hear Sophie's voice in my head: "Is this an emerald?" I stare into the probing eyes of Dr. Partridge. "The thing is, I sort of *have* to take any challenge that sets itself up for me now. If I don't, I'm just … *nothing*." I wipe at my cheek and am surprised to realize my hand is wet. "How do you plan to … get me back there?"

Without a word, she reaches into a leather Coach bag and pulls out a shiny ebony music box about seven or eight inches square. It looks like some mystical article stumbled on in the attic of a gypsy fortuneteller. Strains of a generic early rock and roll song—not tinny-sounding as I would have expected, but a gentle, haunting replication of rock and roll as if played by miniature guitars and basses—flow from it as she removes a front plate and reveals a tiny enamel painting of deep space, black with tiny white specks: stars.

"Perfect." Even though I know none of this is real, chills surge up and down my spine again. "And when does this thing you're going to do to me start to work?"

"It already is."

4

It's like being a missile in one of the early video games that goes off the right side of the screen and immediately reappears on the left.

I'm driving a big car through partially irrigated terrain. Or it seems as if I am. Chills come in waves now, down then up my spine and down again and up and across the top of my head. I'm rolling through what looks like the San Fernando Valley, except that there are citrus groves in every direction and the whole region looks more rural. My first emotion: desolation. The word "marooned" pops into my head, and I know what it's like to be alone in the world. These feelings hit me all at once, like snapping out of a daydream to realize you've wandered away from familiar paths onto a dark, forbidding landscape.

Only I'm still dreaming. I have to be. None of this is possible. My problem is that no matter how hard I concentrate on waking up, I can't do it.

I pull off the road at a Dairy Queen and, startled by the odd sound of my own voice, order a cone from a pretty brown-haired teenage girl dressed in a pink angora sweater and black skirt under a blue-checked apron.

She smiles brightly at me. "That'll be twelve cents, sir."

Behind her, on the wall, is a calendar. I can't make out the day or month but as I fish into the pockets of the baggy seersucker suit I'm wearing, I see that the year in this dream is 1956. I guess it's spring—according to the feel of it—although it's hard to tell in Southern California. If it is Southern California.

"Pardon me. Can you tell me the name of this area?"

Her smile remains bright. "Sure. The town right over there—well, kind of a town—is La Vieja." She points behind her.

I pull a quarter out of my pocket and hand it to her as she gives me my cone. "That's a lot of Dairy Queen for the money," I say.

She looks doubtful. "You think so? They raised the price last month from ten cents. My mother won't come here anymore."

I use a world-weary smile and join her on the other side of the issue. "Yeah, a buck doesn't go very far these days."

She serves up a little hum of agreement with my vanilla cone and thirteen cents change. "There you are, sir. Thank you. Come again."

It crosses my mind to grab her by the shoulders, shake her firmly and say, "What the hell kind of a dream is this?" But she is so young and sweet, and I don't want to alarm her.

I get back in the car, noticing it's a tan Oldsmobile 88, and drive on along the country desert road in the West San Fernando Valley. I don't know where I'm going. It's as if I'm not dreaming but am newly awakened to discover myself, not driving this car, but as a tongue-tied passenger in the back seat of a speeding limousine whose destination I don't know. There is nothing I can do about it and no way to get out. At the same time, I don't want to get out. It is simply my path for the moment and there's no point in fighting it. I remember going to Saturday matinees when I was a kid, peeking out between my fingers at Godzilla on the movie screen. It's like that, too. I'm scared to death, but I have to know what's going to happen next.

Glancing at the rearview mirror, I see the Valley and the Santa Monica Mountains to the south behind me.

I hit the brakes and pull to the side of the road. I turn off the engine and swivel the mirror to look at myself.

It is not Jack Cade.

But whoever it is, he is definitely wide awake.

I wish I'd stopped in at Carmine's Car Wash for the free psychiatric help. I've paid too little attention to such needs—probably why Sophie is leaving me. From the moment I got the pawn ticket, my life has been moving in slow motion. Now it has decelerated to a bare crawl. All my boundaries have become blurred. The boundaries between the boundaries have become blurred—between now and time past, between day and nighttime, between what I wish for and what I get, between who I am and who I think I am. And what I wish for now is that it could all be simple again, and that I could be in some warm, friendly restaurant with Sophie, sipping coffee and feeling … unafraid.

And now, *reductio ad absurdum,* what's left of my mind conjures the final image of my nightmare: someone sitting in a rocking chair, lit by a single lamp.

I look again at the image in the mirror. The notion that I might possibly be conscious and now no longer one but two people slowly begins to turn itself over in my mind like a loop of film in a projector without a light source, and I'm helpless to provide one. One thing I know: This is beyond doubt not a man in a typical state of twilight sleep.

I stare at the man in the rearview mirror for I can't imagine how long. No illuminating thought comes to me, except that we seem to be traveling together, this Richard Blake—if that's who he is—and me. We are, for the moment it seems, chauffeur and visitor. But it's as if there's a sign that says DON'T TALK TO THE DRIVER. And Richard, the driver, won't or can't talk to me.

I continue staring into the eyes the way Maggie Partridge stared into mine. She used the word "miracle," then dismissed it. She said miracles only appear to be miracles because of our selective perceptual filters. I examine the face of the man in the mirror.

What would I have expected if I could have imagined this? That Richard would look like Jack? The truth is, if my eyes are giving me accurate information, Richard is better looking; not exactly an Adonis, but a solid leading-man face and head attached to what appears to be a well-toned body. He has deep-set hazel eyes, a straight aquiline nose a little on the generous size, good cheekbones, utilitarian mouth and chin, and thick brown hair brushed back from his face. It occurs to me that I could have borrowed this guy's looks for a couple of movies I was up for in the early nineties. We're about the same age. I could have done worse. The only thing I might have tried to do something about was the lack of humor in his eyes.

But that's not so surprising. It doesn't take much imagination to figure out Richard may not be finding this to be an amusing experience.

Why doesn't he speak up? Are these my thoughts alone? Does this other … person have no say in his own life? If I am now myself, Jack Cade, sharing a body with this Richard Blake, is he letting me control him? In any case, he doesn't look like a miracle, he looks like a … guy … and for sure not a guy in a dream.

But between me and me, what does it matter? The business I've spent almost all my adult life in is, face it, escapism. I and whoever this is I'm being carried around in—this Richard, I guess—we are a study in escapism. We seem to be coming together to play one role for the moment. No! Two roles.

Driving again, feverish as Frankenstein's monster out on his own for the first time, I take a right turn off the road I've been on and head northwest. The San Gabriel Mountains rise from the desert floor ahead of me, richly mauve and purple, and more vivid than when I last noticed them on the way out to meet Maggie Partridge, only about three hours after my wife told me she thought we needed some time "away" from each other.

I make another turn, drive through scrub bush and scattered boulders for about fifty yards, then pull to a stop, partly in the shadow of a scrawny yucca tree. I reach into the back seat, grab a case of geologist's tools, open it, and find exactly what I somehow know I will: a couple of short-handled shovels, some hand hoes, several other small digging/scraping implements, and seven or eight variously configured files.

There is some quartz on the underside of a sandstone cluster at the bottom of a crevasse beyond the yucca tree. I work my way down and proceed to harvest as much as I can.

I am a gemologist scrambling around an arroyo, collecting a kind of quartz I've never heard of before—desert rose. It is gray-lavender, and the variety I've found is so granular that it's used mostly for decorative purposes and has little industrial value.

"It's got to be a dream," I say out loud, recognizing but not recognizing the voice.

I hold my right hand with my left to pinch it.

I feel a ring on the ring finger. I hold up my hand and stare at it. It looks like Jack Cade's alexandrite.

But that's impossible. I bring the ring closer to my eyes, squinting at it. "It's im-fucking-possible."

I turn, lose my footing, and lurch off to do what I know I have to do—travel with Richard Blake. He's alive in there; he's going to do at least some of what … he's going to do. But I have a say in his life.

Then again, I don't know. Right now, it's obvious Richard Blake is due somewhere, and I don't have any choice but to go along for the ride.

I pack up the quartz in small plastic canisters and drive off, still heading northwest in the Valley.

I pull into the driveway at 1833 Shoemaker Drive again.

It looks the same as it did when I got there after my stop at Dick's Gas and Hot Food, only now the trim needs painting and it seems as if the place is not being cared for as well as the county will be doing it forty years later. The driveway is now cement and the agaves have not yet been planted alongside it. The surrounding area is almost all brand new. Most of the houses have been built very recently, and there are several under construction. Off to the north, which will be developed all the way to the mountains by 1996, there is nothing but a vast sweep of orange groves.

As I walk around toward the back door, a sinewy, rodent-faced woman of about fifty-five peers over into my backyard. Her eyes are dark and purposeful, mean like a cartoon rat.

Our gazes meet for an instant, then she acts as if she hasn't seen me. She produces a pair of pruning shears and behaves as if her only purpose for being at the edge of her property is to trim a camellia bush.

I walk into the backyard.

Two women sit beneath a large mesquite tree. I wonder who they are and what I'll say to them, although I realize with fascination that part of me already knows.

The elder of the two, who is in her midthirties, is seated in a lawn chair with a cocktail in one hand and a book in the other. I (Richard) look at her again, and I (Jack), for the first time. I see that she is a striking woman. She has shining black hair pulled tightly back into a chignon and fastened with hairpins. I often find myself casting people I meet in roles they might play if they were actors. This woman would play headmistresses or mother superiors—ones who might be in danger of transgressing in dark and unnatural ways. Her name is Margaret Blake. She is Richard's wife.

The other woman, whose name is Lily St. Carnes, is her sister. If Margaret's arresting looks don't always register, it's because she is almost always with Lily, whose beauty commands attention. She has a satiny complexion and dark eyes like her sister's, but larger and deep. They are a bottomless cobalt blue. They watch people with an unashamed curiosity that invites intimacy and sometimes slides over into insolence or a childlike vulnerability.

Something else about her: she is the golden-haired woman in the oil painting that was hanging over the fireplace in the living room of 1833 Shoemaker Drive when I met Maggie Partridge. If I didn't know that Lily has been mentally troubled from birth, I'd cast her in a second as Helen of Troy or a blonde Cleopatra, or possibly—as I glance warily at her—Marilyn Monroe.

It strikes me that Marilyn is still alive, and at the peak of her career. She is probably, at this moment, only a few miles away on the other side of the Santa Monica Mountains. I wonder what she's doing. She's probably looking around at her peculiar surroundings like I am at mine, nervous as a cat set loose in a strange neighborhood.

Lily sits in a children's swing that hangs from the bottom limb of the mesquite tree. Her eyes glow and she beams an open, enchanting smile at me.

I kiss Margaret on the cheek. "Hello, dear. Good evening, Lily."

Margaret makes no effort to return the gesture, but Lily echoes the greeting in a happy, quavery voice. "Hello, Richard." She continues to swing.

"What is it, Richard?" says Margaret as I study my circumstances.

"Nothing." I study her. "I'm sorry I'm late. I found some desert rose quartz over on Hillshire. The University of Wisconsin wanted me to find them some, so I stopped to collect it."

"Do you remember we were planning to go out to eat tonight?"

"Of course I do." There is a combative edge to my voice.

There are no words to describe how startling it is to have such firsthand knowledge of another human being's … *being*. But again, although I sense Richard intimately, I don't think I sense him—at least yet—very deeply. I'm aware of one other thing: Richard seems to be *very* interested in Jack.

"I'm going to wear my elegant dress," says Lily.

"Are you?"

"Oh, yes. But Margaret hasn't pressed it yet. Margaret had better press my elegant dress."

Margaret makes a clicking sound with her mouth. "Would you like to hear me scream, Richard?"

"No, thank you."

"She can, too," says Lily. "Today she screamed at the radio. I don't like it when we're not nice." She smiles. "We're not always in our right senses out here."

Margaret makes her clicking sound again. "That about sums it up."

"You don't have to be alone. You can come with me."

"Rock hunting? It gets old, Richard. It gets old if it's not your passion."

"I have to earn a living." She doesn't respond. "You have books and radio … and the television."

"Have you looked at the television, Richard?"

"I know the reception isn't too good."

"Isn't too good? Like any other sensible thing, the TV signals don't want to come all the way out to this godforsaken nowhere."

"They're working on a cable system. Once it's perfected, they'll be able to send TV signals anywhere."

"That's nice. Only by then I'll be as batty as my sister." She looks at me with something both pleading and dismissing.

I hold my hand out, just as I did to Maggie Partridge—moments ago? An hour ago? I say supercasually, "Do you remember where I got this ring?"

Margaret studies me as if I'm the crazy man I'm sure I am. "I have no idea, Richard. You've always had it. Don't you know?"

"I forget. Isn't that odd?" I don't wait for a response; I grin foolishly and excuse myself.

Inside the house, I notice several not only nicely made, but I'm pretty sure the real deal, Georgian pieces of furniture. They must be worth a small fortune. Margaret and Lily inherited them. At a well-stocked bar, I pour myself a double Dewars over ice and move out onto the back porch, a large screened-in room furnished with rattan chairs and a glass-top rattan table.

I sit in a comfortable chair next to the backyard, sipping the drink. I can taste the Scotch. I feel hunger pangs and a soft breeze on my face, hands, and arms, and the relief of sitting in a comfortable chair. I also have the dismaying sensation of not knowing, if I had to sign my name right now, whose signature I'd use. It is not clear who's driving this Jack/Richard buggy. So far, the control seems to be very much mine. So far. This occupation of Richard's body feels as if it's the most challenging role of a lifetime.

From where I am, I can hear and see Lily and Margaret, but they couldn't see me unless they were to get up close to the porch and peer in. Neither of them shows any indication of having heard me.

Lily is humming. Margaret sits as before, her book in her lap, sipping her drink.

Now Lily sings in time with her swinging:

Two old maids in a folding bed—
One turned over to the other and said—

She segues into:

I'll get by as long as I have you—

She stops, looks over at Margaret, and says in a pouty voice, "You always laugh when I sing that." When Margaret doesn't reply, Lily tells her, "That's a radio song."

Margaret looks up listlessly at her. "I know."

Lily winds the swing up as tight as she can with a series of little steps around and around in a small circle, then lifts her feet, leans back, and lets herself spin until she and the swing have come to a near rest. "That makes me dizzy every time I do it." She leans her head back and stares up at the sky. "Read to me from the story."

"But you don't know what's happened in the last three chapters."

"That's all right. I still like it when you read the mysteries to me."

Margaret sighs, then reads aloud:

"'Marianne felt as if she were slipping now, slipping through all the years of her youth—afloat in a whirlpool of all the times, places, and people she'd ever known. But always, always aware of the eyes, the eyes of the man who was watching her now—'"

Lily has started to hum "I'll Get By" softly, widening her eyes then closing them, over and over, as she listens to her sister.

When Margaret trails off in disgust, Lily looks up. "Why did you stop?"

"You're humming. I won't read to you if you hum."

"But I like to hum."

I was once arrested. I was a child, sitting in a roomful of comic books, reading. A friend and I had gone in through a window that somebody else had already broken in an abandoned house, and we'd found someone's Golden Age comic book collection of vintage Atlas and National titles. We sat among these four-color treasures, poring through them—until a routine check of the neighborhood and this abandoned house by the local police yielded up a pair of villainous comic book aficionados. The other kid was cool about it. I froze, as if I'd been caught strolling into the Department of the Treasury with a sawed-off shotgun. It was the pressure of the moment. It was real life that was the problem. Once I get to know the situation, I'm okay. It's just these extemporaneous moments in unfamiliar circumstances that give me difficulty, occasions like this whole thing, for example—being under posthypnotic suggestion in some strange house at the far end of the San Fernando Valley and a raw-boned female physicist suggests that I spend a little time in a previous incarnation, and I immediately respond as if she's asked me to pass the salt or something—that I find myself in trouble. I'm a good actor when I can slip into the flow of things, but a lousy auditioner. I don't or can't apply cold, detached logic to a problem—except at moments when I'm not trying, or at least not trying too hard.

Only now I have no choice but to bear down and think this out rationally. Even if it doesn't work, I have to try to apply some common sense to this one.

I don't know where to begin. I've always hoped my unconscious has its own kind of intelligence, to guide my hapless conscious—if it can ever get through to it. I'm convinced that if I've ever had an important thought it has come from deep in some vault I have no wakeful access to.

But now I have two vaults to try to crack and one of them appears to be sealed as tight as a pharaoh's tomb. The only thing I know for sure at the moment is that this Richard Blake has some strange and shadowy forces at work inside of him. Talk about the ghost in the machine.

Looking out a living room window, I notice a newspaper on the front porch. I bolt outside, pick it up and read the headline: *DE GAULLE OUT OF RETIREMENT.*

I look at the date:

Tuesday, April 10, 1956

"Jesus." I repeat myself, whispering it slowly: "JE-SUS!"

In the bright sunshine, I look at the alexandrite ring I clearly recognize and wonder how it will find its way from bright green on Richard Blake's hand in 1956 to murky purple on Jack Cade's in the dusky gloom of Morgan's Gifts in 1996.

I close the front door behind me, go into the living room and stare at the picture of Lily above the fireplace. I'm amazed at how accurately the painter has captured her vulnerability, the detail of her, her overall beauty, her essence, her touching fragments of hope.

I climb the stairs. At the top, I stop and look back down at the foyer and the passageway beyond it.

I unlock the door to my room with a key. I know it's the only interior door in the house with a key lock. I feel as if I ought to know why, but I don't know a lot of things yet—including whether I ever will, and Richard is volunteering nothing. I go into the room—a large, all-white chamber with a vaulted ceiling and two dormer windows, plus a spacious bathroom with art deco porcelain fixtures.

I turn the key from the inside and lock the deadbolt. Although Margaret and Richard are married, they don't spend their nights in the same bedroom.

Richard is scrupulous about his privacy.

I lie down on his single bed, which has a very soft mattress, and try to feel what it's like physically to be Richard Blake. I stretch out my arms and legs, and after a few moments experience the odd sensation of being comfortable living in someone else's body.

I get up from the bed, take off my jacket, shirt, and tie and look at myself in the mirror above a mahogany dresser. Richard Blake takes care of himself. Except for Jack's judo practice and a little weekend tennis, I've never been able to find the discipline for regular physical exercise. Now it's been done for me. Richard is very fit, with good definition to the muscles of his arms and chest. I suppose it's all that running around the countryside digging up mineral specimens.

I feel a little embarrassed about what I do next, but there is no question of not doing it. I take off my shoes, socks, pants, and underwear and have another good look at myself.

"Du-ude."

5

I'm driving the Oldsmobile. Margaret sits next to me. She has a silver French flask with a filigreed overlay in her purse from which she takes a sip every once in a while. Lily is in the back seat. The night is clear and starry, the moon full with only an occasional wispy cloud drifting in front of it.

"If we got pulled over by the police and they found that, we'd be in trouble," I say.

"We aren't going to get pulled over, Richard. You never drive over the speed limit." She stares out at the passing countryside. "Who'd have dreamt my heart would one day go pitty-pat from the thrill of getting out to a scrubland suburb for a not even mediocre dinner."

"We could go into the city," I suggest.

"You know we can't do that. You know it excites her too much." She glances over her shoulder at Lily, who is gazing out the side window. Margaret takes another sip from her flask. "My father took me on a business trip once when I was a child. And he always wrote me when he was away. He always called me his 'best beloved. Do you see?' See, after he called me his 'best beloved,' he would always add 'Do you see?'" She giggles. "Do you see?"

"I'm sorry, Margaret," I say. "I'm sorry."

"For what?"

In the back, Lily chants, "I'm sorry. Do you see? I'm sorry. Do you see?" Abruptly, she informs us, "Mr. Eisenhower played golf today."

"Did he?"

"Oh, yes. He played golf all right."

"Well, that's nice." My reactions are getting automatic.

"Oh, yes. I heard it on the radio."

"Did you?"

"Um-hmm. But he didn't break eighty. He's always wanted to break eighty."

"Well, someday perhaps."

There's a short pause.

"Eighty what?" She doesn't wait for an answer. She is looking out the window again. "Ooooh. The lights. Look at the lights."

We've come to the center of a village on the road to Ojai.

Margaret says, "Can't we just skip the restaurant, Richard?"

"But you haven't had dinner."

"I'm not hungry, and Lily's not going to be able to eat. She's too excited. Let's go in here." She points to a big square building with a neon sign that announces *THE RAT HOLE*. A few people who look like stunt doubles for Marlon Brando, Audrey Hepburn, Frank Sinatra and so on stand around in front of the place. The steady thrum of rock and roll can be heard from a jukebox inside.

"We don't want to take her in there," I say.

"She might just enjoy herself," says Margaret. "She might like to have the experience."

I feel like I've had a dozen cups of coffee. I pull the car off the side of the road and we get out.

Inside, the Rat Hole is a homey kind of dive. There are eighteen or twenty linoleum-topped tables with fake candles on them. The windows are decorated with red chintz curtains, and the two waitresses and both bartenders wear white cotton shirts with humorous red and black rat logos. There is a dance floor that can accommodate about two dozen couples, and on one side of the room, a long bar with imitation oak veneer on the front of it. Opposite it, surprisingly, against a pale green cinderblock wall, is a state-of-the-art Wurlitzer jukebox.

We take seats at a table off to the side as "Mr. Wonderful," sung by

Sammy Davis Jr., plays. A lean, laconic waitress who stands with all of her weight resting on one leg, which clearly says she has better things she could be doing, takes our order. Margaret asks for a gin and tonic. I order a beer for myself and a Coke for Lily.

Lily is pouting. "No. I want a grown-up drink."

The waitress, chewing gum, stares at her, and Margaret says, "Let's let her have a drink tonight. It's an occasion."

"It's not a good idea."

Margaret ignores me and tells the waitress to bring Lily a Tom Collins.

"Yes, ma'am," says the waitress, glancing at Lily and cracking her gum.

Margaret and Lily survey the room, and I watch them.

Margaret looks at the people around us as if she's trying to remember something she's lost, as if the disappointments of her life might still be reversed and—with a little luck, if she concentrates hard enough—this could be the night and the place.

Lily thinks the Rat Hole is a wondrous discovery. Everything she sees and hears fascinates her—the people, the atmosphere, Nervous Norvus singing the novelty hit "Transfusion" on the jukebox. Her only frustration might be that she can't take it all in at once.

She watches with great interest as a beefy young man approaches our table. He has a pack of cigarettes rolled up in a sleeve of his T-shirt and sports a carefully tended duck's ass haircut.

He stops in front of Lily. "May I say that you are a mighty, mighty fine-lookin' dish? My name is Daryl. You're not with him, are you?" He points at me.

"He's with me," says Margaret.

Daryl is still looking at Lily. "May I have the pleasure of this dance?"

Lily shows him a shy, almost flirtatious smile, then she looks at the floor. Richard's knowledge of her tells me she is always bashful when spoken to by strangers. Daryl stands in front of her, waiting.

Richard churns up enough courage to say, "Sorry, but she can't. She's … just not able to."

"I saw her walk in here, studly."

"She can't dance with anyone," says Margaret. "Richard?"

"Look, really," I say to Daryl. "She doesn't dance."

Daryl swings his gaze toward me and raises his upper lip on one side, the way Elvis could, exposing—in Daryl's case—one yellow incisor. He blinks several times, slowly, dead-eyed, like an iguana. Then he looks back at Lily, opens his mouth and rolls his eyes a little, indicating what an amorous guy he can be. He turns around and swaggers back to the bar.

"I want to leave," I say. Both women ignore me.

Margaret, already pretty buzzed from her tippling as we drove here, accepts her gin and tonic, then when the waitress has gone away, says to no one in particular, "My daddy called me his best beloved. That comes from Rudyard Kipling. He would say to his reader, 'In those high and far-off times, there was a painted jaguar. And so that was all right, Best Beloved. Do you see?' After 'best beloved,' he would add, 'Do you see?'" She looks at me. "Do you see?"

"Yes, I see."

She looks away again.

I think of the concept I learned in acting school called "cognitive dissonance." Tonight, I feel as if it belongs to me alone (well … and Richard, too, now). The idea is that people believe in what they find themselves doing—that it creates a new and complete reality. A girl is walking home at night from the corner store. She thinks she hears footsteps across the street. She looks over and sees no one. She walks faster, only now the footsteps seem to be directly behind her. Whoever it is is catching up to her. The girl begins to run, but she's waited too long. She still hears the footsteps—except now they're the pounding footfalls of something huge, not human—subhuman, brutal, a monster with blood in his eye who means to snuff out her life, and this thing is running now, too, and he's almost on top of her, and he *will kill her*. In the grip of terror, her entire organism is frozen by feelings so primitive reason can't penetrate them. She stops—so terrified she can't run, or turn around, or even breathe.

I look at Lily, still scanning the room, bright-eyed. I want more than ever to get out of here, but something is stopping me from mentioning it again.

"Richard, I want to dance," says Margaret. From the jukebox, Pat Boone sings "April Love."

I frown and nod toward Lily, but Margaret gets her attention. "We're going to dance now, Lily. Lily? Do you mind?" It makes me nervous, Margaret asking her that, but Lily smiles distractedly and says she doesn't mind; she'll be fine by herself.

Margaret's feet aren't steady beneath her, so I hold her firmly. She smells like musky roses—Tabu perfume and gin. I feel a tingle in my groin. It's awkward, being close to her, foreign, but familiar. I like it, but more than ever, I don't want to be here.

"April Love" ends, and Elvis begins to sing "I Want You, I Need You, I Love You." Margaret looks up at me. "See how nice it can be?"

"I used to love dancing with you."

She sighs, puts her head on my chest, and holds onto me tightly.

On the jukebox, Elvis is replaced by the Cheers featuring Bert Convy singing "Black Denim Trousers and Motorcycle Boots." We don't know how to dance to that and give up.

As we start back to the table, we both see Lily at the same moment. She is on the other side of the dance floor, swaying back and forth from one leg to the other. Daryl is holding her close to him. His hands are on her hips, and his head is crooked in over her shoulder, his cheek crowded up against her neck.

I send Margaret back to the table, walk over to them, take Lily's arm and tell her it's time to go.

Daryl whacks my hand away. "I'm dancing with the lady."

"I told you she can't. We've got to go. I'm her brother-in-law." There is a claw of fear in my belly. "She's not well. I've got to take her home."

"She looks real healthy to me. What do you say, sugar?"

"Excuse us." I step quickly between them, grab her by a shoulder and walk her as fast as I can back to our table, where Margaret is waiting. I push both of them ahead of me and, without looking back, out the front door.

Outside, we hurry along the gravel sidewalk toward the car, which is parked on the same side of the road as the Rat Hole, just past a side street. As we get to the intersection, Daryl, flanked by two unclever-looking country boys, appears in front of us, blocking our path.

Daryl has his thumbs in the front belt loops of his Levi's. He makes a loud sucking noise with his tongue and teeth. "It don't pay to be a gentleman anymore."

Lily and Margaret look at me.

I concentrate on not swallowing. "We're going home now."

"A lady wants to go home," says Daryl, "I say the gentlemanly thing is to let her." He looks from Lily back to me. "But the thing is, you see, I didn't hear the lady say she wants to go home." His eyes return to Lily. "Do you want to go home, puss? Or do you want to stay here with me?" He smiles obscenely.

Lily looks up at me and says softly, "I want to go home."

Daryl draws back his upper lip, exposing his teeth again. Neither of his companions makes any move to get out of the way.

"Listen, we made a mistake to come here," I tell them. "Would you please just let us pass?"

Daryl emits a low, mirthless rattle—his laugh. "Would I pul-eeze just let you pass? Well, pul-eeze just pardon me all to fuckin' hell." He does his version of a court bow to Margaret and Lily. "Go ahead, ladies. I guess you'll want to be on your way then."

He moves off to one side, and the two rednecks back off to the other. Margaret hurries between them. Lily follows, but when she passes Daryl, he reaches out with one meaty hand and grabs her around the waist. He pulls and lifts her to him, forces an open-mouth kiss on her, then sets her back on her feet again. "That's the kind of lovin' you ain't gonna be gettin' none of tonight."

Richard's voice is high and thin. "She's been haunted by people like you her whole life."

"Wha-aat?"

"I mean it's easy to be a bully when you have your friends with you."

"Friends?" He thrusts his face to within inches of mine. "Well, I'll tell you, *Richard,* the truth is, I can be a motherfucker of a bully all by myself." The cast of his eyes pirouettes into a fair impression of psychosis. "But I always make a point of being a gentleman whenever it's possible."

He slowly smiles and starts to move away. Then, after a flawless pause, he turns around and takes a step back. "Of course, the way some people are, it ain't always possible."

He gut-punches me five times, rhythmically, as if a metronome is timing him, until Richard and Jack feel themselves drop in slow motion to the gravel below.

We look up to see Daryl standing directly over us.

"Good evening then, *Richard.*"

Listening to the retreating footsteps, I review the circumstances, skipping the immediate predicament of being on my back in the gravel with aching innards.

I know for sure that Jack can't talk to Richard, and Richard can't talk to Jack. If there *is* a Richard (if there is even a Jack, for God's sake), they don't conflict. But they don't communicate, either—except, now that I think about it further, maybe we are starting to. It feels to Jack as if Richard is an innocent bystander in his life, but it also seems obvious that we are changing and becoming a not-quite-so-naive amalgam of both of us. Jack thinks this because he is aware that he is acquiring at least some embryonic access to Richard's knowledge and experience, and he assumes it works both ways.

The thing that puzzles me most is the distinct feeling that I've known Richard all my life. The only possibly good thing about that is that I am now able to put a tentative name to the alien within me.

The downside is that it feels as if I am in jeopardy of completely losing myself to it and to this trance I appear to be permanently stuck in. Then again, maybe it's the upside. I once did what I considered, while I was doing it, an extremely wacky, "spiritual" sort of play.

I wish I could do it again. I'd do it with a greater sense of … uncertainty. In that play, I recited a line by mystic and philosopher Omraam Mikhael Aivanhov:

Turn back to the higher planes and plunge into the cosmic ocean once again … People think that it is in the details that they will find the light, the precision, they are looking for, but this is an illusion. You will find far more light in what is vague and indistinct … The human soul needs immensity; only in immensity can it be happy and feel free to breathe.

Sophie once told me the idea of immensity scared her. It's big and unknown and space junk could hit you, and you're hopelessly lost if you're out there in the immense cosmos.

But what if the immensity is inside you, and you have all that room to wander, and it's not scary, it's safe? It's a different kind of immensity, a peaceful lostness. This immensity is your home, it's your garden, and it's welcoming and altogether friendly.

I could be just fine in an immensity like that.

Margaret has sobered up fast and drives us home.

I sit in the passenger seat.

At one point, Lily says, very brightly, "The man kissed me. Maybe he loves me."

I turn on the radio as Margaret looks at me out of the corners of her eyes. "What did you mean about Lily being haunted?"

"Nothing. He's just the kind of man who does that to girls like Lily."

She frowns.

A country vocalist sings about trouble. There is a burst of static, then silence, and I remember the radio has been failing lately. Now, it seems, it's completely gone.

When we get home, Lily kisses both Margaret and me on the cheek and goes up to bed. Margaret brings me a cup of tea and one of those old-fashioned ice packs that look like a deflated chef's hat for me to hold against my gut. She sits down next to me.

"It was my fault," she says. "I drink too much. But do you understand?"

"I'm sorry."

She flares. "For what?"

"I'm sorry that life is … hard for you."

"You've never objected to Lily living with us." She shakes her head minutely. "The alternative is just too awful. I could never do that to her." She looks at me, then away again. "You could get another teaching job—back east. You could get a job in New York. We could sell this house and move back east."

"I don't seem to do well teaching, do I?"

"You're afraid of people. That's your problem. You're terrified of people."

"It's not only me. It's you too. You could get out more. You could get a part-time job or take a class. You use Lily as an excuse."

She looks away.

"I feel badly that you have to stay with her all the time, but you have to do something about it for yourself. She's not going to burn the house down. She can be on her own for a few hours at a time."

"You don't know her."

"Yes, I do. I know her. Very well."

She swings her gaze back to me. "What is it you want, Richard?"

I feel as if Richard's response might be that it would take several years to answer the question. "I'd like to have … a little freedom sometimes."

"And sometimes not, right? Because freedom means responsibility?"

"I'm only suggesting you might be a little happier, and maybe so would I, if you could get away from Lily once in a while."

She doesn't say anything, but watches me for a longer moment than I ever noticed before, and it's making me edgy, like I'm about to be found out. I'm afraid she might cry out "Trespasser" and call the police or the FBI or … whoever.

"Maybe what you say about me is true," she says. "Maybe we found each other for a reason. I'd like to go back in time and change a few things, but I think it's too late for that. I think we've waited too many years."

"Things will change, Margaret. Things will change."

"Yes, they will, Richard. I'm sure of it."

It crosses my mind to wonder if that's a threat.

My nightmare wakes me up at four A.M. I put on my robe, unlock the door, go out into the hall and move cautiously to the top of the staircase. I look down at the foyer.

It's exactly the same as in the nightmare I'd been having before I ever saw this place, except that now there is no light coming through the passageway from the living room.

A feeling of dread passes through me, compounded by the overtones of the dream I'm now living. I feel like a hostage, manacled and gagged—the ghost in somebody else's machine. As I stand, looking down, wanting to descend the stairs but afraid to, I wish I could wake up.

But I'm already awake.

6

WEDNESDAY, APRIL 11, 1956

When I open my eyes, it's nine in the morning. I shower, shave, and brush my teeth with a brush I've evidently used many times. I get out a clean shirt and start to put on the seersucker suit from the day before, then stop myself and decide instead on a pair of khakis and a short-sleeved blue-green madras shirt.

When I get downstairs, Lily is working on a jigsaw puzzle at the dining room table. It's a surprisingly difficult-looking puzzle.

Margaret says, "Your eggs are almost ready." She always starts Richard's breakfast when she hears the water from the shower being turned off.

I eat toast, bacon, and two poached eggs. I have cholesterol misgivings but think, Why not? I'm only subletting.

The rodent-faced neighbor from next door comes by after breakfast to collect on a pledge Margaret has made to Easter Seals.

Her name is Amy Jaekel. Richard doesn't like her. Yesterday wasn't the first time he's caught her in the act of what looks to him like spying.

A Richard memory kicks in of Amy Jaekel peeking at him through a window. When he looked up and saw her eyeing him, she immediately rapped on the window and told him she'd knocked at the door but nobody had answered.

I answer it now. "Good morning, Mrs. Jaekel."

"Hello, Richard," she says with a toothy smile. "Isn't it a lovely day?" She speaks with an Irish lilt that sounds like it's out of a bad road-company production of something by Sean O'Casey.

"Yes, very nice."

"I'm collectin' for the Easter Seals. Your lovely Margaret made a pledge for two dollars, but she said I'd have to collect it from you. So here I am just as brazen as you please to ask you to fork it right over." She pronounces fork "farrrk," with a trilled "r."

I reach into my back pocket for my wallet.

"Oh, I wouldn't be keepin' my wallet there if I were you, Richard, the world being so full of deceitful people. I read that a man should never carry his wallet on his hip for fear of pickpockets."

"Well, mine's still here after a lot of years."

I "farrrk" over the two dollars and put the wallet back in my hip pocket.

"I know I'm right, young sir. Thank you for this." She puts the money in an Easter Seals envelope, then cocks her head like an attentive golden retriever. "How's poor Lily doin'?" She always calls her "poor Lily."

"Just fine, Mrs. Jaekel. Lily's doing very well, thank you." I hope I sound testy.

"Well, if there's ever anything I can be doin' farr you, you let me know, won't you?"

"I will. Thanks for coming by." I put my hand on the door to close it.

"You won't be farrrgettin'?"

"No, I won't be farrrgettin.'"

"Bye-bye, then." She turns and strides down the front steps and back toward her house.

I watch her until she's disappeared into her own yard, remembering the dirty look she gave me the day before. Under my breath, I say, "I hope you trip and break your neck." Then, also under my breath, "That was unnecessary."

"What are you doing, Richard?"

I turn and see Margaret watching me, giving me the same look medical doctors give you when you tell them about the Chinese herbs you're taking.

"I was just … getting ready to go look for the obsidian I need."

"I see. All right, Richard. You go on then. You go right ahead."

She gives me a grocery list, and I go out to an old-fashioned market called Harry's Stockroom. I buy milk in a bottle and Bab-O sink cleanser and a bar of Lava soap and a sack full of Mary Jane and Necco candies that are one of Lily's weaknesses and a lot of other products that, except for the packaging, are the same things I always buy. I think about buying a pack of cigarettes that promise "Smooth smoking, mild tobacco pleasure." Another brand's advertising features a genial-looking Ronald-Reagan type saying, "We're tobacco men, not medicine men."

Oh, what the hell? Even though I've given up smoking, this has to qualify as an occasion. Who knows what a surgeon general is in 1956, anyway?

I stop by Dean's Drugstore on the way home. I'm not sure if they sell drugs. They have everything else: cosmetics, gifts, various grocery and hardware items, greeting cards, stationery, school supplies, and almost every kind of candy there is. It's like a tiny Walmart but with charm, and there is no doubt that the smiles I get from Mr. and Mrs. Dean are genuine and not company-authorized policy.

I sit at a soda fountain with a beautiful old green marble counter. Two teenagers, a boy and a girl, sit at it too, separately sipping their drinks. The girl, who is only one stool away from me—a skinny, pimply fourteen-year-old with suspiciously large, rigid breasts and too much makeup—is reading a dog-eared EC horror comic, on the cover of which is a frightened-looking woman peering into a mirror. You can see the woman's reflection in the mirror. It's a skeleton.

As I wait for Mr. Dean to come take my order, I see that the voice bubble coming out of the mouth of the skeleton in the mirror is saying, "This is the way you REALLY are and will eventually look—unless you ..." The girl studies the story, knitting her brow in uneasy concentration, trying, I assume, to come up with a tactic to avoid ending up like the woman on the cover.

There is a paperback book rack near my end of the soda fountain. Some of the titles are *Peyton Place, Kiss Me Deadly, The Power of Positive Thinking,* and *'Twixt Twelve and Twenty* by Pat Boone. Among the publications displayed on the magazine stand are twenty-five or thirty comic books, several newspapers, *TV Guide, US News & World Report, Time,* and *Newsweek,* as well as *McCall's, Look, True, Life, Collier's, Boys' Life,* and *Confidential.* On the cover of that is a picture of a smiling Marilyn Monroe and the playwright Arthur Miller, who is gazing fondly at her.

Being so close to her in time, I feel a confusing jealousy. I imagine her in Beverly Hills on the other side of the Santa Monicas, relaxing in a bubble bath, looking dreamily off into space.

Disgusted with myself, I pick up that day's *Los Angeles Times* and am sitting back down on my stool when Mr. Dean appears to take my order.

He is small, with dyed-brown hair, and smells of bad cigars and Listerine. "What can I do you for, Dick?"

"Oh, just the usual, I guess, Phil. How's the missus?"

"Pretty much the same, thanks. We're both just grateful to be alert and vertical."

"I know what you mean."

Phil Dean goes off to get me the usual, leaving me to wonder what that might be.

It's a cup of the best coffee I've ever had. The one I had with breakfast wasn't much. I imagine doing a commercial for Phil's rich brew: "Brisk. Old-fashioned. Delightfully un-Starbucks-y."

I fire up a cigarette and look at the *Los Angeles Times.*

I shake my head, staring bug-eyed, then look around to see if anyone has seen me. I look at the date again—April 11, 1956. My eyes are no doubt wobbling with disbelief despite having seen yesterday's paper. I'm humming under my breath, "Happy birthday-hmmm-hmmm. Happy birthday-hmmm-hmmm."

The next day, the twelfth of April, is Jack Cade's birthday, my actual birth *day,* as in the natal kind, not an anniversary. I blink my eyes, again feeling marooned. If anything could, something as unhinged as this ought to have snapped me out of this dream.

In the newspaper, Ike has had a scare with heart disease but is still going to run for a second term. France is being severely tested in Algeria, and there is discussion as to what de Gaulle should do about it. There are rumors that Britain is going to try to land troops along with the French on the Suez Canal, but President Nasser says, "Egypt has always been a grave for invaders." Martin Luther King is lobbying for the first federal civil rights legislation since the Civil War. The Cold War is hot, and according to an Orange County mayor, "The red menace has not diminished, is in fact growing, and there are still communists lurking in every corner of hometown America."

James Dean has been sighted in a public place, even though he was killed in a car accident last October. The Giants are still playing at the Polo Grounds. The Dodgers are still "Dem Bums" from Brooklyn. The baseball season is just starting, and Ted Williams and Stan Musial are expected to have good seasons—which they do.

Richard Blake disagrees with Madison Avenue about "smooth smoking" and "tobacco pleasure." After a coughing fit, I stub out the cigarette.

At one point, the teenage boy gets up from the counter and leaves. As he does, he brushes against the girl reading the comic book and says "Sorry" in a way that has nothing to do with apology. The girl says, "Gah-aieee" in a sliding nasal tone of disdain, then looks wistfully after him as he saunters away.

Richard needs to gather some fine-grain obsidian and knows of a field near the Mount Wilson Observatory where he can find it. (My knowledge of Richard's day-to-day life seems to wax and wane. I don't know why—it continues to feel as if he's more interested in what I know than what he does. I feel him listen with fascination as my mind jumps around.) James Dean filmed *Rebel Without a Cause* at the observatory the previous year, a few months before he took off in his new Porsche 550 Spyder on his way to

Central California's Cholame Valley and a head-on collision with a Plymouth—and destiny.

I take the groceries home, promise Margaret I'll be back by six, then drive south and east toward Pasadena.

On Riverside Drive in Studio City (the Hollywood Freeway has not yet been constructed to that point), I burst out of my manacles.

We'll find the obsidian tomorrow. I'm too excited. I guess it's okey-doke with Richard; he's letting me do this. I don't think this guy has a lot in his life he really cares about.

I turn onto Laurel Canyon and set off south over the Santa Monica Mountains. When I get to Sunset, a few blocks past Hollywood Boulevard on the other side, I take a quick jog to the left and park on the street, east of Schwab's Pharmacy.

I sit at the counter, order a cup of coffee I don't want, and eavesdrop on two longtime character actors, Charles Lane and Phil Leeds, talking together at a nearby table. Charlie is in the middle of a decades-long career playing judges, accountants, the IRS man in *It's a Wonderful Life,* and various other functionaries. Phil has played a fascinating collection of Peter Lorre kinds of characters, including Dr. Shand in *Rosemary's Baby* about thirteen years from now.

Charlie is saying, "If you keep your left arm stiff as a board, I mean you don't bend it even the tiniest bit, and you keep your right elbow tight into your waist, then you'll never hook a drive."

Phil looks at him from under his hooded eyelids and says dryly, "But Charlie, I don't play golf."

With his characteristic bark, Charlie says, "There. I rest my case."

I remember a moment in my past (actually, forty years into the future), realizing—despite the fact that I'd never wanted it in the first place—how much I'd absorbed my mother's love of show business: *Life with the dull parts left out.* And for a short time when I was still a kid, I thought I might become one of the lucky few and had the exhilarating sensation of the whole world belonging to me—no, revolving around me.

Sophie apparently thinks I still feel that way.

Not today.

I once did *A Man for All Seasons* in Buffalo. The man staying in the room next to me at the Lafayette Hotel was a fat character actor named Ralph Groaman. He played Cardinal Wolsey in the show. I once asked him, "When do you get over being in love with yourself as an actor?" Ralph glowered at me—not meanly—and said, "As soon as you grow up, kiddo." I cherished him like a grandfather. I hung onto an image I'd conjured of Ralph riding the elevator to the eighth floor late Saturday night after a performance, turning on the radio in his room, undressing, pouring himself a large Scotch, hoisting himself into a hot bath and sitting there listening to Guy Lombardo, his drink held loosely in the fleshy hand that hung over the edge of the tub, a weary nobody to most of the world who an hour earlier had been Cardinal Wolsey.

My dilemma is that if I let go of my character, Jack Cade, even though, in a sense, he is now fictional too, I might slip down into the water and drown.

I go up to the newsstand, buy a copy of *Daily Variety,* and sit back down to read it.

The King and I is in preproduction. Deborah Kerr is to headline, and "hot young newcomer" Yul Brynner will repeat his Broadway role. *The Threepenny Opera,* which opened last season Off-Broadway, is planning a second national tour. The Platters have two songs at the top of the charts: "My Prayer" and "The Great Pretender." Edward R. Murrow is in trouble at CBS once again for expressing his social conscience, but board chairman William J. Paley is standing behind him. *Life Begins at Eighty* has been picked up for another season. The studios are shuffling executives as always, but not to the same degree they will after Harry Cohn of Columbia dies in 1958.

A stocky young man with crew-cut sandy hair sits down on the stool next to me, asks the waitress for a cup of coffee, and opens a copy of the *Hollywood Reporter.*

After a minute or so, he looks over and asks, "Did you do a *Dragnet* a few months ago?"

"No. I've never done a *Dragnet.*"

"I could have sworn we've worked together. My name's Jesse. Jesse Littman. What have you done?"

Like most actors in that circumstance, I don't miss a beat. "I'm Richard Blake. I haven't done any film yet. Only stage." To give myself some credibility, I add, "I understudied Gooper in *Cat on a Hot Tin Roof* on Broadway last season."

"Did you get to go on?"

"Yeah, a couple of times. How's it going for you?" I have a moment of panic trying to remember if *Cat on a Hot Tin Roof* was on Broadway last season.

"Not bad. I've done a *Schlitz Playhouse* and a *December Bride* and a couple of industrials this year." Then he tells one of my favorite actor jokes: "An actor comes home," he says, "and finds his best friend, Wally—also an actor—in bed with his wife and says, 'Wally! What are you doing?' And Wally says, 'Well, I just finished an *Alfred Hitchcock,* and next week I'm starting a *Gunsmoke.*'"

We both laugh and Jesse says, "Are you up for *Bus Stop?*"

I have to think for a second. 1956. They're shooting *Bus Stop,* with Marilyn Monroe. I didn't see anything about it in *Variety.*

"Who's directing?" I say, although I'm pretty sure I know.

"Josh Logan."

"Oh, yeah? No, I'm not up for it. There's nothing in it for me."

"Yes, there is. There's a role that wasn't in the play. They wrote in a scene between Cherie and an East Coast urban guy to provide some conflict before she ends up with the cowboy. It's the role of Lawrence. You should get your agent to send you up for it."

"I haven't got an agent ... yet."

"That's too bad. You're perfect." He looks me over appraisingly. "'Cat on a Hot Tin Roof,' huh?" His thoughtful frown reconfigures itself into the beginnings of a smile. "You know, when I first came out here, somebody gave me a tip that ended up getting me a job." He taps three fingers on the countertop. "You reap what you plant, right?" He gets up from his seat. "Hmmm. 'Cat on a Hot Tin Roof.' Tell you what. Hang on a couple minutes."

Less than five minutes later he returns, sits down again, writes out a name and address on a piece of paper, and hands it to me. "Here. Jerry Kennents. He's my agent. He's down on Doheny. I told him about you. I told him you were perfect for Lawrence in *Bus Stop.*"

"How am I perfect?" I can't imagine why I would ask such a dumb question.

"You give off the feeling of being kind of urban, a little wry, but ... pleasant, sincere ... straightforward. You're the right age. Right look." He shrugs. "Fuck it, you seem like this guy ought to be."

My eyebrows are locked in the up position. "That's really ... really nice of you."

"Don't mention it. What goes around comes around. I told him you'd be right over."

"I don't have any pictures and résumés with me."

"Well, shit. You should always keep some in your car. Where do you live?"

"In the Valley."

"Well, shit. I told him you'd be right over." Jesse deliberates for a couple of seconds. "Listen, go give it a shot anyway. You can get him your stuff tomorrow if he's interested."

I grin at him. "Listen, I ..." I reach into my pocket for change. "How much is the coffee?" As I ask, I realize I already know.

Jesse looks at me oddly. "A dime."

I turn away and look at the coins in my hand. I have two dimes, three quarters, a nickel, and a few pennies. I check the dates, thinking I don't want to leave any coins from the nineties. But of course, Richard's coins are all from 1956 or before.

I put the nickel and one of the quarters on the counter to cover our coffees, plus a ten-cent tip. Jesse wishes me luck, tells me he's usually in Schwab's on weekday mornings, and that I should stop in and tell him how it went.

I would have liked to stay longer. I would have liked to speak to some of the actors here in their younger years, but I don't want to hurt Jesse Littman's feelings.

I know there's no such character as Lawrence in the movie of *Bus Stop*. When I was twenty-two, I tried out for the role of the cowboy, Bo, for a summer stock production. I didn't get cast, but I worked hard on the audition and got to know the play pretty well. I remember the movie. There is no Lawrence to "provide conflict" before Cherie (Marilyn Monroe) ends up with Bo (Don Murray). But if there had been, Richard would have been perfect. Jesse said so. Damn it!

I get into the Olds, look up at the Chateau Marmont hotel and wonder if Harriet Brown is staying there now, then give some thought to how much fun it might have been if Jesse Littman had been able to give me a real lead.

I drive west on Sunset Boulevard. It doesn't look a whole lot different. Some of the names have changed—the Saint James Club is back to being the Sunset Towers Apartments, the Comedy Store is Ciro's again, the Rainbow Bar and Grill is the Villa Nova once more. A few of the high-rise office buildings are yet to be built, but to Jack's eye, things look very much the same. I pass the Garden of Allah, due to close its doors for the last time in August 1959, Scandia, and the Cock and Bull, which will survive until the late eighties, and the Roxy will still be there on the day I meet Dr. Partridge. But the Trocadero, Mocambo, and the Sunset Strip of the rowdy early Hollywood days are all long gone in 1956.

As I pass the Cock and Bull, I pull convulsively into the left lane and, fighting a fit of giggles, turn onto Doheny and roll down to the address Jesse Littman gave me.

Jerry Kennents' office is on the second floor of a modest white adobe house. The office door is on the side at the top of a flight of white wooden stairs that could use a paint job. A mousy-haired young woman with braces and wire-frame glasses sits at a dull yellow Formica-topped table that serves as a reception desk just inside the screen door. She is reading a copy of *Photoplay*. Mitzi Gaynor smiles out from the cover.

I rap on the door. "Hey. How are ya? I'm Richard Blake."

She thwacks her *Photoplay* down on the desk and smiles nervously up at me. "Hi there." Then, recovering, "Do you have an appointment?"

"Jesse Littman told Mr. Kennents about me. I'm expected."

"Oh. Okay then." She picks up the phone and after a moment, says, "Mr. Kennents? Richard Blake's here to see you … All right." She hangs up, giving me a friendly smile along with a tiny shrug that says she isn't really part of this world, just an unintentional witness to it. "You can go right in."

Jerry Kennents looks about fifty years old but, because he carries excess weight, could be younger. He looks up from some papers on his desk.

"Whaddayasay, Dick. Jesse tells me you're a helluvan actor."

"Thanks."

"So let me see your picture and résumé."

"I'm sorry. I don't have one."

"You're kidding?"

"No. I'm sorry. All my things were shipped out from New York, and they haven't arrived yet."

"I see. You're from New York." That interests him. "Broadway?" he says hopefully.

"I understudied Gooper in *Cat on a Hot Tin Roof.*"

"Did you ever play it?"

"Oh, yeah. Thirty … forty times."

Kennents' lips and eyebrows arch up, a sign of grudging respect that makes him look like Mussolini. "Uh-huh. What else? What other shows you done?"

Jack, not to mention Richard, is drawing a blank on pre-1956 plays. "Shakespeare. I've done a lot of Shakespeare … *Hamlet.* I played Hamlet."

"Where?"

"At the … Hayes Theatre Festival."

"Helen?"

"Beg pardon?"

"Helen Hayes?"

"Yes. It's in Connecticut—her festival."

"Never heard of it."

"It just started up a couple of years ago."

Kennents narrows his eyes. "How did you come to the business so late? Were you in the service?"

"Yeah." I nod. "That's right."

"Where were you? I was in the Pacific. Navy."

"I was in Europe. Army. Just after Normandy."

Kennents looks out the window, remembering. "It was hell, huh?"

"Hell," I say. I look out the window too.

The agent tells me a few stories about his time in the Pacific. A tear comes to his eye as he remembers friends who were killed at Guadalcanal.

I try to remember any of my father's stories from the war as they were passed on to me by my mother, but my father had never really gotten close to any action. I say, "I remember crawling toward a German bunker during the Battle of the Bulge. We'd been driven almost back to the Meuse River. It was Christmas Eve, 1944. I couldn't feel my feet it was so cold. Then the sergeant raised his hand and all that was left of our company began to charge the bunker. I hadn't taken two steps when I felt something hit me in the gut, and I fell. I remember lying there with my face in the snow and mud, wondering if my mom was thinking about me on Christmas Eve and whether we'd win the war or not."

"My God," said Kennents. "What happened?"

I'd done the piece as well as I had for the acting class I'd learned it for in the late eighties. Now, I begin to improvise, encouraged. "I was flown back stateside. By the time I was fully recovered, the war was over." Concentrating as hard as I can, I manage to come up with an actor's tear. Or maybe the tear comes from Richard, who's never heard that story before. "I lost a lot of my buddies too," I say.

Kennents nods and wipes at his cheek again.

Now I remember the names of a few plays. I tell him I was in Tennessee Williams' *Glass Menagerie* and *All My Sons* by Arthur Miller, and *Beyond the Horizon,* the first Pulitzer Prize winner by Eugene O'Neill.

Kennents smiles warmly, then seems to take me in all over again. "You know, Jesse's right. You're perfect for that role." He picks up the phone and dials. "Hey, Peggy. Jerry Kennents. Let me talk to Joyce, will ya? Yeah, I'll hang on." He covers the mouthpiece. "The secret of Hollywood is not being too proud to wait on the line while somebody plays their furshlugginer power game with you."

He speaks into the receiver again. "Hi, Joyce. Yeah. I know. I know. Brutal. You're right … Yeah, vermin, all of them. Listen, I've got an actor here with fantastic New York experience who's right on the money for the role of Lawrence … Dick Blake … Oh Christ, he was in *Cat on a Hot Tin Roof* on Broadway last season. Incredible reviews … Well, if you've got to make a decision today, you'd better see him today …" He grins appealingly. "Perfect … Fan-damn-tabulous. He's on his way over."

He hangs up the phone. "You're going to Twentieth. Do you know how to get there?"

"Yeah."

"You're going directly to the *Bus Stop* production office. Ask for Joyce Faberman. Don't waste any time. They're casting this role today."

I stare dumbly at him.

He grins at me and winks. "We gotta look out for each other." He gets up and puts his arm around his potential new client's shoulder. "I just hope to hell you can act."

The lot at Twentieth Century Fox is buzzing with activity, the television and movie industries working side by side, although I know movie veterans still view television with no more enthusiasm than reluctant cattlemen beholding the sorry reality of sheep.

The first thing I notice about it on this April 11th is the penetrating, fusty smells of the place, like the ones I remember from when I was a child and first visited movie studios with my mother. (She would say to me "Break a leg, baby" as we entered each one. Rita is more than averagely superstitious and she imagined such things might one day influence the fates into making her little boy a star.) Now I'm reminded of old Hollywood—the way it must have been when it was bristling new, before all the crazy myth-making and the celebrity mania became so totally deranged.

But old Hollywood still does exist in 1956. Bogart is still here, Edward G. Robinson, Gable, Cooper, Rita Hayworth. Paul Newman is just a kid from Broadway. Brad Pitt won't be born until the mid sixties.

Feeling scared but excited, like a ten-year-old set loose in Disneyland without his mommy, I walk toward the *Bus Stop* production office.

7

Joyce Faberman, the casting director, tells me she's agreed to meet me because she likes Jerry Kennents and because Mr. Logan is having trouble making up his mind on who to go with for the role. She says Logan is a lovely man, "and a perfectionist," and she knows he won't mind seeing one more actor before he makes up his mind.

She gives me the scene and tells me to look it over as quickly as I can, that Mr. Logan is in his office at the moment, but that he has a meeting with the movie's screenwriter, George Axelrod, in less than half an hour.

I am going to meet Joshua Logan, one of the biggest names in American theatre and film. By the end of his career, Logan will have directed or cowritten *Knickerbocker Holiday, Charley's Aunt, Sayonara, Middle of the Night* by Paddy Chayefsky, *Camelot, South Pacific, Annie Get Your Gun, Happy Birthday* by Anita Loos, *Mister Roberts,* and *Picnic.* It's an awe-inspiring list that goes on and on. For any actor, just a meeting with Josh Logan is something he will never forget.

To calm myself, I think back to my actor's anthology of mind-control techniques. Unfortunately, that slim volume has been out of circulation for a while. Anyway, by now, it's no more than a muddled compilation of superstitions and the mixed-bag wisdom of old actors who teach and write about what they—most of them—would give a kidney to still be hired to do.

I try to lose myself in the task at hand.

It's a three-page scene. Lawrence works for the Department of the Interior. He's been at a weather station about a mile away from the bus stop where the passengers have gotten snowed in when the blizzard hits. I am to walk over shortly before the final scene between Cherie and Bo to see if everybody is all right. In his scene with Cherie, she tells him her troubles and starts to get a crush on him.

I go out onto a balcony that overlooks several soundstages and a big chunk of Los Angeles—borderless suburb masquerading as a city. I look toward the east, the vista limited only by the haze of millions of cars and trucks and by industry and the inversion layer that pushes the whole repugnant miasma down to the level where everybody is driving around, or God forbid walking, trying to grab enough lungfuls of air to sustain life.

At first, the scene looks easy. I read it over a couple of times to get the feel of it, then go back to Lawrence's longest speech and work on that.

Cherie: "You're a real good listener."

Lawrence: "You're nice to listen to, miss. I've been out here for quite a while now, and I've felt all alone every minute of that time. But, in about two minutes, you've made me feel like we're kindred souls. I think it's your eyes. You have more love and kindness in your eyes than I've found in this whole damned state."

Then she is to start to kiss him, and he says, "I wish I wasn't married."

It occurs to me why—if the scene was shot at all—it ended up on the cutting room floor.

I have other problems. My timing feels off, and along with that I can't seem to judge how much emphasis to give each word. Whatever Jack Cade has as an actor doesn't want to come out of Richard Blake.

"Mr. Logan will see you now."

As Joyce and I come into his office, Joshua Logan is seated behind his desk, taking a bite from a sandwich. He puts it into his left hand, brushes the right one off on a crumpled napkin, shakes the actor's hand and says, "Excuse me." He indicates his lunch, then points to a leather Queen Anne chair in front of his desk. I sit down where I'm directed to and Joyce sits nearby while Logan finishes chewing his mouthful of food. He looks like a frazzled elder out of something by F. Scott Fitzgerald, his hairline on its way from high to receding, his intelligent eyes seemingly gazing in several directions at once, apparently distracted by competing directorial dilemmas.

Finally, he looks up and scrutinizes me. "What do you think of the movie business so far?"

"It looks pretty hectic."

Logan smiles. "It makes the biggest Broadway production look like a stroll in the park. Joyce tells me you're from New York."

"That's right." I pray I won't be asked anything specific.

"I love stage actors," he says. "People tell you that stage acting and film acting are very different things. They're not. The big difference is that for film, you don't have to worry about anyone beyond the first row."

I grin earnestly, trying to think of a cool response to that, then find myself blaming Richard as he falters, "Uh-huh, right, yes. Oh yes, right, that's, that's, that's … for … absolutely."

"Umm-hmm. Okay," says Logan, his pensive smile dissolving into fey puzzlement. "Shall we have a crack at it?"

"Yeah, sure. Yes. Okay." I look at the first page of the scene. The words swim on the paper. "Can I have a … just a second?"

"Of course."

I stand up, walk to the window, and take a long, silent breath, trying to remember something an acting teacher once told me about playing this kind of scene, but I can't. I can't remember the acting teacher's name. I can't remember my name. Names.

I move stiffly back to my chair, sit down, and try to focus on Joyce.

It's impossible to make her Cherie in my mind. In the corner of my field of vision, Logan sits behind his desk, impassive, waiting.

The words come out of my mouth like leaden things. When I get to my big speech and say, "I think it's your eyes. You have more love and kindness in your eyes than I've found in this whole damned state," it flashes through my mind what a crummy thing I'm doing, destroying the good relationship Jerry Kennents has with this casting director. She'll never see any of his clients again.

It's over.

I put my script down and force myself to look at the director. Logan doesn't say a word. He blinks two or three times, seems to sniff the air around him, puts an index finger to both sides of his mustache, looks at Joyce, then back at me and says, "That is the most splendid audition I have heard in longer than I can remember."

I stare at him.

"That is the truest, most honest, unactorish reading I've heard in a long, long time. You made me believe this was a man who'd never stepped foot on a stage. Who did you study with?"

"Herbert Berghof." My throat is completely dry.

"I'm not always Herbert's biggest fan, but you made that scene come to life. You weren't afraid to show me a lost, awkward ... ambiguous soul. If it were up to me, I'd offer you the part right now ..." He shrugs. "But Marilyn has final approval ... I wouldn't worry, though. She'll go along with what I want. Can you come in tomorrow morning and meet her?"

"Yes ... Yes ... I ... I can."

"I was hoping she'd be here today, but ..." He turns his palms up, as if to say you may as well tell the winds to turn around and blow the other way. "Why don't we say ten o'clock then, all right? You probably won't be seeing her much before noon. She has a little ... tardiness problem. But you'd better be here at ten, just in case."

"All right."

"And be prepared to start rehearsals right afterwards. Is *that* all right?"

I nod stupidly. Logan smiles at me. Joyce gets up, and I follow her out of the office.

After I've floated out of the production offices, I find the nearest public telephone, call Jerry Kennents' office and leave Richard Blake's home phone number with Virginia, his secretary. She tells me Kennents is on another line but that Joyce Faberman has called to confirm my meeting at ten o'clock the next morning with Joshua Logan and (as Jack shouts in a hoarse whisper after Richard has hung up) "Marilyn fucking Monroe!"

8

I drive over Beverly Glen Canyon into the Valley and travel almost a mile east on Ventura Boulevard before I remember that Jack Cade doesn't currently live in North Hollywood, and that I'm not even going to be born until early the next day. I think briefly about trying to forget Richard Blake and driving to Kingman, Arizona, where Jack Cade will be coming into the world.

But that would mean I'd miss out on meeting Marilyn. My heart is hammering.

I turn around and head out to the West Valley and 1833 Shoemaker Drive. I grip the steering wheel of the Oldsmobile with all the strength in my hands, then relax. Then I squeeze it again until Richard's hands ache.

I'm halfway to La Vieja when I realize I'm going to be home early. It's only midafternoon, and I have no obsidian to show for my time. Richard knows Margaret won't care about what mineral specimens he brings home, but she might wonder at him having none.

Lily is in the library, watching television. The channel she has on isn't currently broadcasting. There's only snow on the screen.

"What are you watching?"

"The television."

"There's no program."

"Isn't there?"

"No. You don't want to waste your life staring at an empty screen."

"There's no talking, but I like the fuzzy silence. Sometimes I watch this program for hours."

"How about working on your puzzle?"

"I finished that."

There doesn't seem to be any point in continuing this conversation. "Where's Margaret?"

"Margaret," she repeats. "Margaret went back to bed."

I stare at her, absorbed in the fuzzy silence, and try to figure out something about her that's niggling at the back of my composite mind, but nothing occurs to me, so I leave, put my tools away, and start up to Margaret's room.

At the top of the stairs, I stop and look back down the way I've come. I wonder if I've carried Richard Blake's memories in my deepest unconscious all my life—and if I have, how many more people are in there? And have I ever been who I've thought I was? Or have I always been the distillation of a long, not necessarily genetic line of my forebears? And where would such seemingly random associations stop? I'm thinking the ghost in my machine may be way more complex than I ever dreamed. The notion of the many-worlds interpretation of quantum physics runs through my mind, then I jerk my head back and forth vehemently, which hurts my neck, and I feel as if I've brought on a headache.

Margaret is sitting up in bed. In her lap is a small mahogany box. She closes it when she sees me and puts it on her bedside table. "Hello, Richard." She looks tired.

"How're you feeling?" I kiss her on the forehead and sit down on the edge of the bed.

"I have a headache."

"Me too."

She frowns. "Did you find what you were looking for?" She looks away.

"No, I didn't. But I'll try again later."

"Tomorrow?"

"Yes."

"You got a phone call. You got two phone calls." She makes the clicking sound with her mouth. "Both from a man named Jerry."

I feel my heart jump. I should have told the agent's secretary I'd call when I got home. "Kennents?"

"That's it. Who is he?"

I'm tempted to ask who she thinks he is, to see if Kennents has said anything about *Bus Stop,* but she makes it easy for me.

"I asked him the second time if I could take a message, but he said he wanted to talk to you. Who is he?"

"It's just about work."

"He said he'd like you to sign agency contracts. Is that about work too?"

"Yes." I look her straight in the eye, but her gaze wanders away again. "I'd better call him back."

"I spoke to somebody else on the phone today." It's her most maddening tone of voice. "But I suppose you wouldn't care to know who."

"Whatever you say. I'm going to return that call." I aim a feeble smile in her direction. She looks away, and I seize the opportunity to leave.

Kennents says he wants me as a client. We leave it that I will go by the office during my lunch hour the next day to sign agency contracts. Kennents' advice to me for my meeting with Marilyn Monroe is to "just be yourself."

I don't ask which one.

I go to my bedroom, lie down, fall immediately asleep, and become a visitor in my host's dream. I am flying, slowly, in a heroic Supermanish pose, with Margaret and Lily over an immense, motionless landscape, surrounded by sand and brush flats and creosote bushes and the bones of sheep in a limitless sweep of total erosion. It is dead silent, without even the screech of a hawk to break it.

I look at Margaret's and Lily's faces and now, it's no longer Richard's dream. It's Jack's, or at least partly, because the faces have become the faces of everyone I have ever known, all in a tumble, and seemingly it all happens at once, as if I'm seeing every face I've ever stopped to focus on.

And now I'm sitting in a small room. In a straight-back chair, right next to me, is the little girl I gave the perfume to in the seventh grade. Her back is to me.

She turns, and I see that she's matured and is now a beautiful young woman. But I can't make out for sure who she is.

She smiles to put me at ease. "It's okay," she says. "Don't be afraid. There is nothing in this world to be afraid of."

"But who are you?"

"Oh, nothing so unusual. Perfection, they tell me." She shrugs and smiles. "The answer to all your hopes and dreams—nothing more than what you deserve."

And she's gone.

I hear the voice of Mr. Parsons of Jewels By Jaxon say, "Plato believed that precious stones were living beings. And this is an alexandrite. This could be your friend." The voice becomes the scream of a hawk, and Lily and Margaret, once again on both sides of me, peel off like jets at an air show, and I realize it's only me now. I am traveling by myself.

Then I realize the scream I've heard was not a hawk, it was me, and that I'm standing in the dark at the top of the stairway at 1833 Shoemaker Drive.

I wake up.

Lily is knocking at the door. "It's time for dinner, Richard."

I've slept for over two hours. "Thanks, I'll be right down."

"Are you all right, Richard?"

"Yes, I just had a little nightmare."

I hear her move away from the door.

As I rub at my eyes, trying to wake up, I feel the alexandrite on my right ring finger and think about Marilyn. She was born on June first. Her birthstone is alexandrite.

I didn't know that the day before yesterday.

The Blakes don't eat very well, although Richard seems to think everything is all right.

We have overcooked canned string beans, Spam with salt and pepper, and some kind of packaged macaroni product that tastes like it's been laced with Limburger cheese.

After dinner, I do the dishes, then join Margaret and Lily in the library where they're watching a special news program about a platoon sergeant who's been found guilty of negligence in the drowning of six marines at Paris Island in South Carolina several weeks ago. There are interviews with the families of the men. The mother of one says, "We just hope nothing like this could ever happen to anybody else."

The TV is a Zenith console model, boxy and solid-looking, in an oak cabinet. The picture is black and white, of course. I keep starting to reach for the remote. Fleetingly, I think of taping the show and watching it later, then chuckle to myself, which produces an odd look from Margaret.

There is a piece about preparations for the marriage next week in Monaco between Prince Rainier and Grace Kelly. I think about the three children she will have, and how she will be America's princess until the car crash that kills her in 1982.

"It makes me sad."

"Why?" says Margaret.

"I don't know. They're just so goddamn frail. Like everyone else."

Lily barks, "I'm watching the show!"

Margaret watches me for a long time. I can feel it as I look at the television. Finally, she says, "Would you get me another gin and tonic, Richard?"

I get up, fix her drink, and pour myself a double Dewars. It's my third one of the evening. Richard Blake is thirsty. He's thinking maybe he'll tell Margaret about his acting job and how he's no longer the same man he was two days ago. I try to convince him that's a bad idea, but I don't think he's heard me.

We watch *Dragnet* (Jack Webb looks too young to be Joe Friday) then *Four Star Playhouse*. Ida Lupino is a woman stranded on an island in a lighthouse with a crazy man while a ship that has no people on it floats into the island, and rats from that ship eat through the door of the lighthouse and then slowly corner Ida Lupino and the crazy man on the top level. Finally, Ida Lupino goes crazy too.

Margaret watches with split focus between the television and me, and Lily laughs maniacally at the scary parts.

When the late news is over, Margaret gets up to go to bed. "Were you going to say something to me, Richard?"

"I was thinking about it."

"What were you going to say?"

"I wanted to tell you …" I stop myself from saying I'm sorry. "… Maybe we should … unh … talk about it later, when things are more … settled."

She studies me, then looks away. "More settled. Yes. When things are more settled. Good night, Richard." She turns and walks toward the front stairs.

Watching her leave, I have a craving for another drink. I pour just a splash. I need to be sharp tomorrow.

I sit down in my chair in front of the television.

Lily is watching snow again. I look at it with her.

After a few minutes, she says, "You're drinking whiskey." She looks at the television, then back at me, then at the television again. "Frisky whiskey." She chants it: "Frisky whiskey. Frisky whiskey. Frisky whiskey. Frisky whiskey."

"Lily, do you know that I'm afraid? I don't show it, do I?" It doesn't seem to register on her at all. "I might as well be alone."

"*I'm* here, Richard."

I get up and make another drink. Jack thinks we should quit for the night, but Richard will not accept no for an answer.

I sit down again and Lily repeats, "I'm here, Richard."

"I know you are. I know you are." I stare at her. "But who are you, Lily?"

Lily smiles, again chanting, "Frisky whiskey …"

She gets up and goes upstairs.

I turn off the television and the lights, check the doors to be sure they are locked, and go upstairs to my bedroom.

I brush my teeth, get undressed, put on my pajamas and robe, and turn off the bedroom light.

I walk quietly to Lily's room and let myself in.

Lily gets to her knees on the bed. She's naked. Even though I can only make her out by the glow of a half moon through the window, there is no way I could take my eyes off her. She stretches her arms out toward me.

"Richard? Come to me, Richard. Come to me."

9

THURSDAY, APRIL 12, 1956

My eyelids are heavy, but Richard never allows himself to go to sleep in Lily's room.

He lifts his legs off the side of the bed, bends over for his pajama bottoms and slips them on. Lily is turned away from me, snoring lightly. I am putting on the top, buttoning it, when I hear Margaret.

"Richard? Richard?"

I want to hide but can't imagine where.

Lily is not waking up.

Margaret calls again. "Richard …?"

I put on the robe and slip out of the room.

I take a step toward the top of the stairs, then stop and contemplate going the other way. I could get into my own bed and pretend I haven't heard Margaret's call. I look toward my room.

The door is open. I know I locked it.

It hits me in the pit of my stomach: *Margaret has a key.*

My pulse is pounding. I look back toward the top of the stairs and, with an almost physical revulsion, feel myself drawn to it. I move carefully, as if approaching the precipice of the highest, sheerest cliff, and at the bottom, it's exactly as in the dream. The light from the living room shines through the passageway like a beacon repelling, beckoning, and I clench my fists. I descend the stairs toward it and continue through the foyer, into the passageway, and I am cold, and I am drenched with sweat, and I walk into the light.

Margaret sits waiting for me in the rocking chair that is most often used by Lily.

I speak first, in the most natural tone I can manage, "What are you doing here? Why aren't you in bed?"

"I couldn't sleep."

"I'm sorry." I move closer and notice the eight-day mariner clock on the mantle behind her. It is exactly three in the morning.

"You're perspiring, Richard. Do you have a fever?" She says it flatly without any note of commiseration.

"No, I'm … I'm fine. I'm sorry you can't sleep."

"You're always sorry, Richard. More and more lately, you're apologetic. Why?" She looks away.

I see that the mahogany box from her room is in her lap. Her hands are loosely clasped together, resting on it.

She looks at me again, then drifts away as if I'm not there. "When my father was away, he would write me wonderful, gentle letters. He would begin them 'To my Best Beloved—do you see?'"

I'm still waiting, heart thumping. "It's late. You should go up to bed."

Her eyes meet mine again, and this time they remain focused on me. She makes her clicking sound, but softly. "Knowing her, did you think she wouldn't tell me? Knowing my sister, what did you *think*? Did you think there was any way in the world she would *not* tell me?"

Her hands touch the mahogany box. I'm fascinated.

Margaret takes a small revolver out of the box. Richard has never seen it before.

She aims it at me.

"Goodbye, best beloved."

She pulls the trigger.

"Do you see?"

10

I see Mr. Parsons from the jewelry store leaning very close to me, speaking in his high-alto voice: "The changes in hue are due to the delicate balance maintained in the absorption color; a change in the color of the light transmitted is all it takes to produce a change in the color of the stone."

Now, the old jeweler says, "If I were you, I'd try to figure out where it came from."

I know what I have to do. I have to get up and drive down to Morgan's Gifts.

"Open your eyes, love."

FRIDAY, OCTOBER 11, 1996

Maggie Partridge is bent over, her hands on her knees, looking directly at me.

"Jack, are you all right?"

"What time is it?"

"Three forty-five."

"What day?"

"It's Friday. It's still Friday."

I stand up, feeling surprisingly steady on my feet.

I move to the front window and look across the large, well-cared-for lawn at my Jaguar out on the street. I turn back to Maggie Partridge, still standing by the flowered sofa. "I don't remember lying down there." My eyes find the portrait of the golden-haired woman on the wall. I point to it, but now have trouble finding my voice. Finally, I groan in primal tones that seem to rumble out of me like Othello over Desdemona's body: "She's back there. Her name is—" I see the alexandrite on my right ring finger. "Look at that."

"What?"

"Nothing. Her name is Lily."

Maggie Partridge frowns and moves directly to me, reaches up and squeezes the back of my neck. Very quietly, but with commanding intensity, she says, "We *did* it. You became Richard Blake. You *are* Richard Blake. *And* Jack Cade." She takes her hand from the nape of my neck and looks even deeper into my eyes. "What happened?"

I walk, now not steady at all, to the passageway into the foyer. I turn back and look at the spot where Margaret sat in the wooden rocker. I hear my words once again coming from someone else's mouth: "I was murdered … I …"

"I know. Tell me."

"I came down the stairs from …" I point toward the foyer. "I came down the stairs …" I stare at her. "You know?" I replay what she just said. "How do you know?"

She looks down.

"*How* do you know?" My words come out hoarsely. I'm trembling.

"Old newspapers, microfilm, the library," she says quietly. "Why did she kill you?"

"I don't know."

I remember the sound of Margaret's gun being fired, a searing pain in my chest. "I'd been alive. I touched things. I saw, I smelled. It hurt when I was shot."

Maggie Partridge runs to me, takes my hand and leads me to the sofa. She sits beside me and speaks quietly. She holds my hand in both of hers. "It's okay. It's okay."

"What happened to Margaret?" I say.

She gently withdraws her hands, avoiding my look. "She killed herself."

"And Lily?"

"She died in a mental home."

"You knew I'd be killed, didn't you?"

"You might not have gone back if I'd told you."

"How could you do that?" I get up, livid, but my legs dissolve under me, and I buckle to the carpet.

"Jack?"

"I'm okay." I brace myself against the sofa with one hand and get to my feet. "I'm only a little … lightheaded."

She stands, facing me. I take her in as if I've never seen her before. I try to clear my head. "I'm going home now." I bolt, weaving, toward the front door.

She calls after me, "Please give me five more minutes."

As I enter the foyer, I glance up at the top of the stairs to the second floor. I can see the victim coming down the preordained path to his murder.

I turn back toward the living room. She's right behind me, waiting to hear whatever I have to say.

"I need something to eat."

We sit near the window against the back wall, at the table farthest from the front entrance in Dick's Gas and Hot Food. I'm having a piece of cherry pie and Maggie Partridge is sipping coffee.

After I've gulped down most of the pie, ravenous, Maggie says, "You still think you're dreaming, don't you?"

"I came out here because you asked me to." I finish the pie, nauseous, draw breath. "Why? What are you doing? What do you want?" I know she won't answer me. "Of course I was dreaming … but in the last part of that dream, I was … sleeping with Lily. We were having an affair. I'm not sure for how long. I think Richard Blake was ashamed of it."

"Why was he ashamed?"

"Why? *Why?* Well, for one thing, she was mentally impaired—or some kind of … I don't know. She's a lot smarter than you would think. I saw her putting together a very intricate picture puzzle."

I look out the window at a white wood-frame house with a flat gravel roof. A big sign next to the front door advertises CHIROPRACTOR & BEAUTICIAN. An elderly woman walks slowly up the steps to see one or the other or both. My gaze wanders to Maggie's long, athletic arms and the line of her breasts beneath her blouse.

She looks away, obviously deep in thought. "You could go back and not get killed," she says. "You understand that, don't you?"

I laugh like the village idiot—a cliché of a madman. "And you understand you're insane. Or some kind of witch."

She doesn't react, just goes on watching me.

It feels as if I'm losing any tiniest grip on sanity I might possibly still have. I know that I'm committable and believe this woman is too. I wonder if it's too late in life to go into full-time psychoanalysis. The pills I take obviously don't work. "Are you saying to stay out of her sister's bed? Is that what you're telling me to do?"

"No. Absolutely not. I can't do that. I'm not your moral judge. I'm not telling you what to do, other than to be careful and not get yourself killed next time."

"Next time? What are you talking about?"

"I'm suggesting that you go back and behave more cautiously this time. But it's not my place to tell you how to live your life."

"*My* life?"

"You know what I mean."

"Actually, I fucking well don't." I'm staring at her with an intensity that must match hers. There is a long silence before I finally say, "Would I go back to the same time?"

"I think so."

"If Richard Blake goes on living, does Jack Cade get …? Does he get born?"

"Yes."

"Are you saying I'd split in two? I'd be back there with Richard Blake, but I'd also be Jack Cade as a … an infant—at the same time?"

"I don't know."

"Well, I'd sincerely love to hear anything you do know, and please don't quote Dr. Hinkle or Albert Einstein."

"How about T.S. Eliot? And the end and the beginning were always there, before the beginning and after the end. And all is always now."

"Well, that's all just peachy fucking perfect, but all is not always *me*. Are you saying I'd be in two places at one time?"

"I couldn't possibly answer that."

I poke at the crumbs of my pie with my fork and ask her about ramifications.

She reaches out as if to touch my face, then seems to think better of it. "There's a theory that if it were possible to change an event in our past— even if it were, say, something as insignificant as the alteration of the lives of three average people in the San Fernando Valley—there is a theory that such a change could drastically alter the history that follows, that two different paths of reality would be created." She looks at something over my shoulder. "I don't believe that."

"Going back wouldn't set up a chain of events that would change the world you and I are living in?"

"You're only one person. It would be insignificant."

"The amoral side of me doesn't really care." I'm thinking about Marilyn, wondering if I could meet her. It's still … possible, if I'm determined. "Why aren't you more … surprised—that it worked?"

"I am and I'm not," she says. "I've known for years it could be done."

I snap out of my daydream about Marilyn. "I have a theory why you're not. I think you know as well as I do that none of this is happening."

She looks deep into my eyes.

11

I drive back to North Hollywood on surface streets, avoiding freeway traffic. On this Friday evening in October, the smog isn't too bad in the West Valley, but the sun shining from low in the sky behind me illuminates brown, smudgy pictures of Van Nuys, Studio City, North Hollywood, Burbank, and eastward. I'm to meet Maggie Partridge at noon on Monday at 1833 Shoemaker Drive.

I roll up to my mother's house, park behind her white Cadillac with the personalized license plate *LKY RITA,* and wander up the walkway, feeling a heightened awareness of each breath I take, of every sensation in my body. It's as if I'm feeling the miracle of all of my muscle groups working in perfect synchronicity, of my blood coursing, exactly as my organism requires, through every part of it.

Rita opens the door, talking: "Did you hear about Paramount?" She's dressed in jogging shorts and a tight pastel sweatshirt with a blue and gold paisley silk scarf around her neck.

"Why aren't you ready for dinner?"

"They fired everybody, top to bottom."

"I thought we were going to Santa Monica for dinner."

"That last crew seemed to be doing fairly well," she says. "But they did three sequels last year. You and I and Zippy the chimp could produce three sequels."

"Are we going to dinner or not?"

"I've got to walk first."

"Mom?"

"Come with me, and we'll grab a bite afterwards."

We face a wall of mirrors at the New Hollywood Health Spa, walking into ourselves on adjacent treadmills in a bank of eight.

After Rita's personal perspective of the news in *Variety*, I ask her if she knows where I can find a videotape of *Bus Stop*.

"Eddie Brandt's should have it. Why?"

"I'd just like to take a look at it."

"It's not much of a movie. They cut out the story about the alcoholic teacher and the young waitress. Don't you remember seeing it?"

"Yeah, but I'm not sure when. It's been a while."

"We saw it together right after she died. They had a retrospective in Chicago. I took you to it. You were about six. We saw maybe eight Marilyn Monroe movies. You seemed to enjoy them."

I almost lose my footing on the treadmill. "I don't remember them." I recover my balance and realize that for some odd reason, I'm thinking of Sophie, almost smelling her perfume. I wish I knew where she was right now.

"Well, you seemed to enjoy them. Watch your step."

I'm staring at her image as we walk. I had no idea my relationship with Marilyn went back that far.

"You could play the cowboy's pal, the part Arthur O'Connell played. Who's doing it? ... Darling? What is it, dinner theatre? I really don't think you should go out of town, Jack—not in the middle of television season. I'm sure Sophie would disapprove."

Rita has always used Sophie as a tool to leverage whatever she's currently promoting. "I'm not talking about the play. I'm just curious about the movie."

"It's not much of a movie." She flicks a wrist, a disdainful Ping-Pong backhand.

"If I did go out of town to do a play or if I was away on location for a long time, how would you do?"

"What do you mean?"

"Would you be okay by yourself?"

"I'm not by myself. I've got the Friends of the North Hollywood Library and the Hollywood Sign Preservation Committee and all the screenings I go to." Then, as if she must say it to be polite, "And of course, I'd spend whatever time I could with Sophie."

It's not that she's ever disliked Sophie; it's just that she hasn't shown much interest in her one way or the other. It's not her fault, and it's not Sophie's; Sophie has always tried to be nice to her. It's simply that Rita sometimes thinks of me more as … her own project than as an actual … son with a personal life.

"I just wondered what you'd do if I was away for a while," I say.

"Are you planning to go somewhere? What about Sophie?"

"Oh, she'll be okay." I see Rita's eyes on me in the mirror. "Actually, we're not doing so well right now." Her expression doesn't change. "I was just thinking, what if I did … go away?"

She shrugs, still watching me. "Don't worry about me. I'm a survivor."

"Are you ever."

"Don't be smart."

We're both doing about four miles an hour on our treadmills. I'm starting to get winded and slow down to cool-off speed.

"What time of day was I born?"

"You were born at night."

"I thought you told me it was morning."

"Nope. Night." Still walking, she purses her lips and closes her eyes, remembering. "Your father and I were on our way from Jackson to Los Angeles for a vacation, and just outside of Kingman, Arizona, I felt a labor pain. We'd just had a dubious restaurant dinner of fish cakes and some noodley thing. Never order fish in this country if you're more than fifty miles from a major body of water." She veers back to her subject. "So I was going into labor almost a month and a half early. That's why you're so artistic. You were premature and, consequently, awfully sensitive."

"Mom, children and girls and … poets are sensitive, not your son into his forties."

She makes a foxy little smile. "See what I mean?"

"What time did you get to the hospital?"

"A little after midnight."

"On April twelfth?"

"Of course."

"And what time was I born?"

"It was 3:07, mountain time. I remember because it's a good number."

The mariner clock on the mantle in the living room at 1833 Shoemaker Drive had read three o'clock Pacific time when Richard Blake last looked at it on April 12, 1956. Jack Cade was born in Arizona seven minutes later.

"Why is 3:07 a good number?"

"Have you got a couple of hours?"

"No, Mom, I don't think I do. Not tonight. What's the difference between mountain time and Pacific time?"

"No difference at all—in April. Not in Arizona. Most parts of Arizona ignore Daylight Savings Time."

When I get home, Sophie's not there. There's a note pinned to the bulletin board in the pantry off the kitchen:

I'll be staying with Jean for a while, until you and I can sort out what we're going to do. Please don't call me. There's nothing to talk about right now. I wish there was, but there simply isn't anything either of us can say that will change the way I feel. I love you, but there's no point in pursuing "us" right now.
—Sophie

"Right now." She's left the door open.

SATURDAY, OCTOBER 12, 1996

In the morning I call the *LA Times* Public Information Service, and I say I want to find out if a Richard Blake was shot to death in the West Valley on April 12, 1956. The young man I speak to tells me he'll look it up and get back to me in the afternoon.

I go to Eddie Brandt's video rental store and bring home a copy of *Bus Stop*. Don Murray has just walked into the bar near the end of the film when the guy from the *Times* calls back.

"Yes," he says, "Richard Blake was shot and killed on April twelfth, by his wife, Margaret."

There was no mention of her killing herself. I decide she must have done that later. There is also no mention of Lily. The reporter who covered the story said, "There was no apparent motive." He left it at that. The murder was not a headline. The research guy looked through the next seven days' papers. There was no follow-up.

I telephone Morgan's Gifts several times, but no one answers. I call Jewels By Jaxon in Beverly Hills. I want to ask Mr. Parsons a couple of questions, but he isn't in on Saturdays.

Even though she's asked me not to, I try calling Sophie on her Motorola flip phone. All I hear is static. I hate technology. I ring her at her friend Jean's. All I get is Jean's message: "You know what to do," she says.

"Actually, Jean, I don't." I hang up and try Morgan's Gifts again.

On the off chance, I drive to Morgan's Gifts, thinking they might be in, but not answering their phone.

They're closed.

I knock on the door for a long time in case somebody is in the back, but I get no response. I peer in through the window gates.

From her haunt on the wall, Marilyn stares lopsidedly back at me, her Mona Lisa smile not as intriguing as usual, trapped in such a bad rendering, and nowhere near the magic it is on film. Still, I have the familiar feeling that she's speaking to me alone.

I decide that everybody feels that way, that that was, and continues to be, the essence of Marilyn's appeal. One of her publicists, Roy Craft, said, "Marilyn had such magnetism that if fifteen men were in a room with her, each man would be convinced he was the one she'd be waiting for after the others left."

I watch *Bus Stop* again, not knowing what else I expect to see. I stop the movie several times to study Marilyn's face, quivering in freeze-frame. Once again, I try to figure out what that something is behind her eyes and her mournful smile. I have no success, and it crosses my mind that I have spent most of my adult life looking at things, not into them. Until recently, I've avoided thinking about what goes on in other people's psyches. It makes me feel uncomfortable—like a peeping Tom, like if I can see them, maybe they'll be able to see me. Now I wish I'd paid more attention to such things.

I remembered playing opposite Susan Strasberg in a television show and talking with her about Marilyn. She told me, "All those still photos of Marilyn? That wasn't Marilyn."

"How did you know her so well?" I asked her. Susan was still several years away from writing *Marilyn and Me: Sisters, Rivals, Friends.*

"Oh, God." She smiled and shook her head. "I knew her—as well as anyone could. She was like the adopted third child in our family." In 1954, Lee Strasberg and his wife, Paula, took Marilyn in, and she did effectively become the third child in their family, along with Susan and her brother John. "We loved each other; we hated each other. I was insanely jealous of her. She was even jealous of me. She used to say she'd give anything to be like me, that people respected me. She never believed she was as good as she was."

I didn't question Susan further, but I remember her looking off into middle distance, as if that moment and her memory of Marilyn were separated by no more than a heartbeat. "She had more sides than a diamond," she said.

Watching *Bus Stop,* I see several of those sides: the troubled, sad, lost, the half-formed.

Everyone is multifaceted.

Everyone does not live in a glass cage.

I watch her act. Damn, she's good. She knew what she was doing by the time she made *Bus Stop.* When Joshua Logan was told she would be playing the role, he originally said, "Oh, no. She can't act." After filming was complete, he'd changed his mind: "I could gargle with salt and vinegar even now [for saying that] because I found her to be one of the greatest talents of all time." Later, he said, "She is an artist beyond artistry. She is the most completely realized and authentic film actress since Garbo. She has that same unfathomable mysteriousness. She is pure cinema."

The next day, before I return the tape, I watch it again. I look at the parts with Marilyn in them and fast-forward through the rest.

When I've turned the videotape off, a commercial on regular television shows a woman who claims she doesn't believe one size fits all. A moment later she's standing on top of a mountain, raising a bicycle over her head, telling me she wants to howl at the moon.

SUNDAY, OCTOBER 13, 1996

I reach Sophie on her flip phone. She asks me if I've learned anything about the ring.

"Not yet. I'm thinking of selling it. It's a lot of money." I hear her exhale sharply.

"I think you should keep it for a while," she says in her patient voice. "At least until you can figure out how it came to you in the first place."

"What if I never do?"

"At least you will have tried."

"Anyway, I can't keep running around with fifty thousand dollars on my hand. What if I got in a stickup?"

After a long silence, she says, "If they demand your ring, you'd better insist they shoot you."

"Can we get together and talk?"

"I'm with the old boy from one to eight."

"I can come over and meet you after you get off. We could have dinner."

"We can't afford it."

"Why are you so mean?"

"Because you're such a cement salesman."

"No, I'm not. Sometimes I can be an adventurous guy. Just day before yesterday, I time-traveled to 1956 and got murdered."

"Pardon?"

"Nothing. It's a joke." I don't mention that I came within a day of meeting Marilyn Monroe.

"Jack, did you hear what I said Friday?"

"Yeah."

"I wasn't kidding. You're not … you anymore. We get what we ask for."

"Please spare me the Oprah."

Her voice goes cold. "Did you check the computer?"

"What for?"

"I sent you an email."

"You did?"

"From Jean's computer."

"Oh. No, I haven't looked at it. What did you say?"

"Why don't you read it."

That feels so … I am chilled in a way that only the thought of the possibility of losing Sophie can chill me. Her voice sounds so … sad. I can't seem to find any words. Finally, I tell her I will. I will read her message.

"I don't think you want me very much," she says.

"Yes, I do."

But that doesn't sound convincing even to me. Why am I always not saying what I want to say to her? Why didn't I just say, "You are what I'm asking for? I want to live forever under your wing"?

But everything is too complicated. I couldn't possibly explain anything until I've begun to explain it to myself—which would probably involve more years of psychiatric help than I have years of life ahead of me.

Which is a crazy thing to say. I'm no longer sure that lives are measured in years.

I sit down at the door-sized, plain wooden desk we had made at an unfinished furniture shop on Magnolia Boulevard, and turn on our computer. Almost immediately the chirpy little bastard from AOL tells me I've got mail.

I feel a shot of adrenalin, find her message, and start to read it.

Jack, it's me, Sophie.

This is awkward. But this is not how I pictured my life. You don't seem to want to … or to be able to control your drinking. Maybe you can get it under control and we can try it again. But I have to go before I start hating you. I deserve better than this. So do you. It's funny, I want to go stay with my best friend. Nothing against Jean, but you're my best friend.

GOD! I'm so sick of Hollywood! Show business! Acting! Watching you bang your head against that wall. I remember you testing for that pilot. I think it was five times over about two months, and you got it, and the day before you were supposed to start shooting, they cut your damned part out of the show. Why would you want to go on living that way? And that kind of thing happens over and over.

I feel like we're falling down a hole and there's no way out. I'm scared. I'm afraid I can't make it on my own—thanks, Mom and Dad. But you seem so helpless and I'm not strong enough to save the both of us. Sometimes I think I'm still young enough and pretty enough to attract another man but that scares the shit out of me even more.

I don't want much. I just want to pay the bills and go out to dinner once in awhile—maybe a weekend in Palm Springs. Oh golly, Jack, I remember one time going swimming in a motel pool, then making love, lying in bed with you a whole afternoon and evening, our hair all snarled and tangled, and we still smelled of chlorine when we went out for dinner at ten o'clock that night. And it was just an ordinary motel, but who cares? We were alive and feeling … joy and blissful just being together.

But now we're always, always scrabbling for a living. Our cars are held together with duct tape. I actually fantasize being with one of those weekend roadie cyclist guys who wears one of those dopey hats, but I wouldn't mind, because at least he can afford his dopey hat and his bike and all that snazzy spandex. That scares me. I've had some wine.

We don't have children. That's my fault, I know. You told me in the beginning that we could but I was even terrified of getting married. We don't even have a dog or a cat or a fucking goldfish. I'm amazed we have a few plants. I'm missing out on life, it's going fast and so far I haven't done what I ought to do, or what I wanted to. You're not the only fuck-up here.

Oh, never mind, Jack. I can't say anymore now. Maybe I've said too much already. I don't even know if I should send it. I love you, but, apparently, that's not enough.

I'll talk to you later.

I turn off the computer.

I try to imagine how I might turn my life around. Now. Right this second. And then I'd send an email back to Jean's computer and tell Jean that I've got a message for Sophie. I try to think what that message might say. I could tell her that I want to hold her. And God, I do. I want to make all the sadness in her go away. Forever. I want to make everything all right again, the way it used to be. I want to laugh with her again.

I need to make some new plans. I need to make it okay for "us" again.

How? What do I tell her? Why would she believe whatever I say? She wouldn't. Not now. I've been telling her the same lies for … a long, long time. And she's not going to believe anything I say to her until some kind of change comes over me that I can believe in myself, before I can have any hope in hell of expecting her to believe anything I tell her.

I organize my life, pay my bills, and clean the refrigerator.

I pile every old newspaper and magazine in our house, plus the 1995 *World Almanac,* onto our bed and pore through them voraciously, with an uncharacteristic curiosity for politics and world events.

Before I go to bed, I look for a long time at the alexandrite, deep red under the lamp by my bedside. It is blue and murky purple as I carry it to the bathroom, and a pale shade of green under the fluorescent lights. It's extraordinary—like having my own personal aurora borealis.

I try not to think about Sophie.

MONDAY, OCTOBER 14, 1996

We sit opposite each other in the living room again.

"This means a lot to you. What's at stake? For you?"

"I'm not sure I can tell you," she says.

"I wish to hell you'd tell me something." I stare back at her. "It feels to me like you have a kind of desperation about this."

Partridge frowns. "Of course I do. Almost everybody has something they want very much to do." She looks past me, over my shoulder. "And it's different for each one of us." She locks eyes with me. "I've been thinking about you scolding me for not warning you last time—about what might happen. Remember Dr. Hinkle?"

"Your scientist on tape."

"Right. Remember when he talked about running into yourself?"

"Right. What about running into, oh say, Marilyn Monroe?"

Her eyes widen. "Well, I suppose if you can run into yourself, you can just as easily run into … Why do you mention her?"

"No reason. She just crossed my mind."

"Uh-huh. Well, what I'm telling you," she says, "is that anything is possible—just so you know. You can run into Marilyn Monroe, or Alexander the Great, I suppose. This is all theoretical, of course—or it has been. In one analysis, it falls under the heading of the many-worlds theory of quantum mechanics."

"Parallel universes?"

"If you like."

"And how is that useful to me?"

"I can't predict." She shrugs helplessly. "I only work in this field. I don't understand it; I can't tell you what it is, any more than Edison could have told you what electricity is." For a nanosecond, she gazes away, looking small and lost, like some terrified child in an institution, staring off into the scattered shards of her memory. She blinks. "I'm simply trying to do the right thing, love. I'm sorry I can't help you with … everything that's on your mind. But you will solve whatever it is. I'm sure of it."

She takes one of my hands in hers and squeezes it. "I want nothing more than for this to work out, not just for me—but for all of us."

She squeezes my hand once more, looks deep into my eyes, then reaches for her ebony case.

"Why? Why do you want this so much? I'd really like to know!"

"I am"—she shakes her head—"for reasons I hope you'll understand eventually, unable to tell you." She sighs. "I'm afraid I have to ask you to trust me."

I review my other choices. It doesn't take long. There aren't any.

12

TUESDAY, APRIL 10, 1956

I steer around the wash onto Shoemaker Drive again. I look at his hands on the wheel, aware for the first time that Richard Blake has more hair on the back of his hands and wrists than Jack Cade and that he wears a gold Bulova wristwatch.

And the alexandrite ring.

My heart flip-flops when I walk around to the back of the house and Margaret and Lily aren't in their places beneath the mesquite tree. I hurry into the kitchen, open up Richard's workbox, then realize I haven't stopped to get a Dairy Queen or to harvest the quartz, or to spend however long looking at myself in the mirror, and am home earlier than I was the last time.

"Richard?" It's Margaret.

As I close my workbox, I glance out the window. Amy Jaekel is lying on a chaise lounge on a redwood deck in her yard. She might look as if the only thing on her mind is a suntan, if she weren't gazing, cold-eyed, directly at me.

Margaret calls my name again. I concede the staring contest to the spooky next-door neighbor and follow the sound of Margaret's voice into the library.

Lily is in front of the television, watching cowboys chasing each other across the Republic back lot. Margaret sits at a small cherrywood table beneath a high bookcase crammed with gemology books. She is working on a gin and tonic. Her checkbook is open. She is paying bills. She holds herself stiffly as I kiss her on the cheek.

"There's not enough money," she says.

"I know."

"There's never enough money."

"I know. I'm going to do something about that."

"Maybe we should sell some of the furniture."

"I'm going to take care of our money problems," I say.

"How?"

"I've got some coming in the first of the month."

"From where?" There is ridicule in the question.

I lie. "Some back payments that are due me."

Richard remembers the previous New Year's Eve at the home of his recent boss, Dr. H.P. Tandler, the head of the UCLA geology department. Richard poured a tumbler of Scotch and disappeared from the party in the middle of the evening. Margaret found him an hour later watching television in the Tandlers' library. He'd already been in trouble with Dr. Tandler. Since he began the affair with Lily, his conduct at school had been erratic. But he hadn't made his fatal mistake until he'd returned to the celebration at the New Year's Eve party.

At midnight, when Dr. Tandler's wife lifted her face to him for the ritual kiss, he considered it briefly, then said, "Thanks, but I think I'll pass."

He didn't have tenure and was fired the following week.

Margaret is watching me, waiting for an explanation.

On the television, a young woman is singing, showing the world her soft and manageable hair.

Halo, everybody, Halo.
Halo is the shampoo that glorifies your hair.
So Halo, everybody, Halo.
Halo Shampoo, Halo.

One day, her granddaughter will believe in standing on mountains and howling at the moon. And she will reject that one size fits all. But she will also try to keep her "whistle-clean hair." And it won't be easy.

"I'm really going to try to make things work."

There is a flicker of hope in her eyes. "Are you?"

Upstairs, I take off my jacket and quickly make an entry in Richard's notebook about rose quartz.

I go out into the hall and check the top of the stairs to make sure Margaret isn't on her way up, then walk back down the hall, past Lily's room and Richard's, to Margaret's.

I open the door, go inside, move directly to her bedside table and open the mahogany box. Inside is a Smith & Wesson .22-caliber, five-chamber revolver. I check the safety, then, taking the gun with me, get out of the room and back to Richard's as quickly as I can.

I put the revolver in the back of Richard's underwear drawer and sit down on the bed. I hear a thunk from the hall, but realize it's only a house-settling sound. It reminds me that I have to change the lock on my bedroom door.

I hear voices from below. I get up, move to one of the dormer windows, and see Margaret and Lily under the mesquite tree exactly as I remember them from my first trip back, only from a higher angle now. Margaret is in her lawn chair, Lily in the swing.

I am moving out of synch through a replay of the day I originally arrived.

I can't hear what they're saying, so I go downstairs to the screened-in porch, where I eavesdropped on them the last time, and do it again.

Lily is spinning in the swing again, singing:

Two old maids in a folding bed—

One turned over to the other and said—

And then, as before, she segues into:

I'll get by, as long as I have you—

But now the dialogue changes. Lily doesn't chide her sister for not laughing, because Margaret does laugh—a little. Then Lily giggles, and then Margaret really laughs.

With obvious warmth in her voice, she says, "Would you like me to read to you from the mystery, dear?"

"No, thank you, Margaret." She stops spinning and puts her feet on the ground. "If I'm very careful, may I press my elegant dress by myself?"

"All right. If you're very careful, and you tell me when you're finished."

"Sometimes Richard helps me. Richard's very kind to me."

Margaret weighs that. "I suppose he is, isn't he?"

"Oh, yes. Richard's very good to me. I love Richard."

Margaret can't keep herself from sounding off a dry response to that. "Yes, I know that."

Lily throws her feet out and sets the swing into motion. "I love Richard because Richard is kind. And he helps me do things that are hard for me, and he's ... kind."

Margaret is silent for a long time, then says, "I guess he tries in his way, doesn't he?"

Lily is swinging and softly humming to herself and doesn't answer.

13

There aren't many restaurants near La Vieja, and Margaret doesn't feel easy going too far from home, so we dine at Milt's Fine Cuisine, once again on the road up to Ojai. Richard has two crusty lamb chops slathered with mint jelly. Margaret and Lily order the Tuesday Night Special, an inoffensive-looking chicken dish.

Lily watches the other customers and practices her best table manners, as Margaret has told her she always must when they eat out. Richard and Margaret talk about music, books, and politics. There is a lot of discussion in the air about rebellion, and Margaret doesn't understand it. Richard doesn't either, but he's decided that he should try. Margaret finds Marlon Brando, Brigitte Bardot, Mickey Spillane, and Allen Ginsberg offensive, even though she's never seen or read them. They agree that all of that rebellion probably has a lot to do with rock and roll, although Richard secretly suspects Margaret of liking it, and he himself admits he sort of "likes the beat."

Margaret talks about Adlai Stevenson, who she hopes will be the Democratic Party's presidential candidate again. Richard is glad Ike has finally spoken out about McCarthyism, calling it "McCarthy*wasm*." Jack has known actors, writers, and directors whose careers had been ruined by McCarthy and the House Un-American Activities Committee, but he prevents Richard from going entirely out of character and saying "self-righteous pricks."

Toward the end of dinner, we have a lively conversation about whether UFOs really are vehicles from outer space or not. Margaret and I agree that nothing as crazy as that is possible.

But Lily stubbornly takes the other point of view. Her eyes grow large and she insists, "There are aliens all around us."

Driving home, I realize with fascinated horror that I'm slowing down. I cringe as Margaret, animated by the wine she's had with dinner, says, "Richard, can we go inside that place and take a look? I'd like to see it. I'd like to have a dance."

I stop the car as if hypnotized; magnetized by the Rat Hole like a murderer returning to the scene of the crime. I whisper under my breath, barely moving my lips, "Oh my God. We want revenge."

"Revenge for what?" says Margaret.

"I was just thinking about … Dr. Tandler. I guess I still feel a little bitter about that."

"Well, it's too late now."

"I know. I know." What I am actually thinking about is who is inside the Rat Hole with his mean little eyes and thrashing hormones. I stare out the window, thinking *I'd like to kick the son of a bitch from here to …*

The women are staring at me.

Jack and Richard have come to know each other a little, like a dog owner knows his dog and vice versa—although who is the owner and who is the dog, neither of us could say. And now, neither is absolutely sure which one of us has most been nursing the itch to even a score. Each curses the other's testosterone, although to be honest, most (but not all) conclusions that Jack draws about Richard come from some unspecified lobe of he's not sure whose brain.

"We'd have fun," says Margaret.

Lily agrees. "Oh, yes. Let's go in, Richard. Let's go in the dance hall."

I tell myself that maybe the timing is different, that Daryl may have moved on by now.

He hasn't.

I take Margaret's arm and Lily's and steer them to a table up against the pale green cement-block wall. It's as far away as I can get us from the table where Daryl is seated, talking to a plain but large-breasted strawberry blonde.

Gogi Grant is singing "The Wayward Wind" on the Wurlitzer. When Margaret asks me why we can't sit closer to the dance floor, I tell her it makes me nervous sitting in a crowd of people, and she believes me.

We're served by a different waitress, an older woman with dyed-red hair, thick mascara, and a resentful expression augmented by full lips painted barn red. Margaret has her usual, I have a beer again, and Lily accepts a 7 Up.

Again, I dance with Margaret. When we get back to the table, she suggests with no apparent malice that I dance with Lily too.

With a laid-back smile, I say, "I really don't think that's a great idea, hon."

"Why not?"

Lily rocks from one foot to the other and looks brightly around the room as we dance to Nelson Riddle and His Orchestra's "Lisbon Antigua."

She looks up at me, smiling sweetly.

Perspiring, I smile back.

I think of Chris Isaak's "Baby Did a Bad Bad Thing." Jack has a new feeling in common with Richard as he holds Lily, dancing. The feeling is remorse. Not that that changes anything. *"Hey listen, I feel BAD that I raped you—my wife's mentally challenged sister."*

All we can try to do now is dig up enough beginner's humanity not to do it again.

And … yet—being close to her like this—I feel like the obsessed, spinning, mad James Stewart in *Vertigo,* unable to control his feelings, or even to make out for sure who this woman is. It feels as if I'm barely able to keep myself from sweeping her into my arms and spiriting her out of this place.

The music changes, calling for us to tango, which is out of the question.

"I think that's enough for now, dear."

"But I *like* dancing. I like dancing with you, Richard."

As I lead Lily back to the table, I see Daryl across the room at the far end of the bar, talking to a tall brunette.

We finish our drinks and I suggest we leave, but Margaret hears the opening strains of "Moonglow" and insists we dance to it.

Toward the end of the song, Margaret puts both arms around me with her hands on the back of my neck. I lean my cheek against her forehead and am unclear if Richard has any desire to pick up with her where he left off when they were first together and in love and if he could, and did, and lived past 3:07 mountain time in Kingman, Arizona, (and Pacific time as well) the morning after next, would Jack's particular collection of memories within Richard Blake cease to exist?

Would he vanish?

"Moonglow" is still playing when I open my eyes and look over toward our table.

Daryl is seated next to Lily, leaning over, his face almost touching hers.

I move off the dance floor, followed by Margaret.

When I get to the table, I say, "Excuse me."

Daryl looks dully up at me. "Yeah?"

"These are our seats."

"Is that right?" He rises slowly from the chair and, without any earnestness, says, "I beg your pardon." He turns back to Lily. "Would you like to dance, sweet cheeks?"

"I'm sorry. She can't."

"You her father?"

"That's right."

As quickly and decisively as I can, I pull Lily up by the arm and escort both women out of the Rat Hole.

Daryl stands in front of us once more, along with his friends, the two rednecks, blocking the path back to the Oldsmobile. He's making the same sucking sound with his mouth and slowly drawing up one side of his upper lip like a junkyard dog.

Margaret and Lily look at the man in their lives. I've come back to this place on purpose. I wish I hadn't but it doesn't matter now, it's too late. I have to face this—I can't suppress a smile as it occurs to me what it is— *pattern of harassment.*

"Whatcha grinning at?" says Daryl.

"Nothing. Please get out of our way."

"You didn't pay me any courtesy in there."

"Can't we try to avoid this?"

"Avoid what, studly?"

I take Margaret's arm, then Lily's, and try to move around them again.

Daryl pokes his finger into my chest. "I was feeling like a gentleman when I came here tonight." He leers at Lily, "Then I saw this fine little dish of custard. Guess I'm just a gentleman who prefers blondes."

Lily makes a whimpering sound, and Margaret puts an arm around her.

"Listen, why don't you let us pass?" I say, blinking.

"Why don't I let you pass? How about because I don't fuckin' well feel like it?" The rednecks chortle appreciatively.

"We just want to go home. We don't need to have any trouble."

Daryl looks at the two rednecks and grins. "This guy says, 'We don't need to have any trouble.'" They share another laugh. Daryl turns back to me. "There's something about you just pisses the shit out of me. And to be real honest, I *like* trouble."

"Please, just step aside." I put a hand on Daryl's shoulder and start to push him back.

Daryl knocks my hand away. "You don't *ever* fucking touch me, ass-face. I'll rip your nuts off and feed 'em to you."

Without warning, his knee comes up hard into my groin.

I pitch toward the gravel sidewalk and have barely hit the ground when I sense a foot kicking out toward my head.

Richard and Jack misjudged their mutual muscle memory the last time. This time, we don't stop to deliberate at all because by now we are extremely upset with this guy's lousy personality, not to mention his lethal-looking boot that's coming toward us on a trajectory calculated to remove several of our teeth.

I twist my head to the left and bring up my right hand, catching Daryl under the back of the calf and throwing him off his aim and his balance at the same time.

Daryl is suddenly seated next to me, a startled look on his face.

I get to my feet, still reeling from the crushing, sick pain in my groin.

When Daryl realizes he isn't hurt, he gets up again, his lip curling back in its Evil Elvis way.

He unleashes a fist at my face.

I take a quick step back, twist my hips, and grab Daryl's right wrist with my right hand while thrusting up with my left forearm into his locked elbow.

I can't see his face as I hear his arm break, but I see it immediately after he's landed. The leverage I've used to propel him flat onto his back has snapped it like a twig. Daryl kicks his legs and flails his remaining workable arm, trying to get his lungs to fill up with air again. He looks like a man who's undergone a sudden shift in priorities. The most important thing to him now is to breathe again. He doesn't look angry or chastised—only as if he has other things on his mind.

I turn my attention from the injured man to the rednecks, who, seeing what's happened to Daryl, fall all over each other clearing a path to the Oldsmobile.

Margaret and Lily stand dead still, neither of them saying a word, just staring at me with the look of mingled adoration and awe that I associate with Lois Lane right after Superman has pulled her ass out of the fire again.

The first part of the drive home passes in silence.

"If you could be that vigorous about your career," Margaret says finally, "then perhaps we could make some plans and improve our lives."

I remember the other reason Richard turned to Lily.

That night I have one of those sexy dreams that feels so real you can smell it. I'm dreaming of Lily, or Marilyn … I'm not sure. It's every teenage boy's fantasy come true. It's that thing that owns him, conscious and unconscious, day and night. It's all his animal longings—fulfilled, and nothing else in the world matters.

It's gratification so perfect he could never experience it outside of a dream, but so real, it couldn't have been a dream.

Unless it was someone else's.

14

WEDNESDAY, APRIL 11, 1956

I arrived at Schwab's Pharmacy at eleven in the morning the last time. Today, in my nervousness about missing my moment, I get there shortly after ten. I notice now that a table has been drawn up to one of the booths at the side of the store and a group of eleven or twelve actors, all men except for one girl, about twenty years old, are sitting around drinking coffee and talking. I didn't notice this party the last time, but decide I just didn't look in their direction or that they had already moved on.

I recognize three of the men. One of them is an actor named Frank Stafford, around thirty years old. We did a *Bionic Woman* episode together in the late seventies, when I was still a young leading man. The story was about people who turn into ghouls on an Arctic island and only Jaime Sommers (Lindsay Wagner) can do anything about it because she hears a certain bacterially-induced tone with her bionic hearing, a tone nobody else can hear and that triggers all the trouble. Frank played a navy flier who turned into a monster just before I did and just before Jamie found a way to reverse all of the zombifying effects and save everybody.

I saw Frank on an old kinescope of a *Schlitz Playhouse* recently. In it, he was just a little younger than the age I look to be now. He will be into his sixties when I work with him years from now. Today, he is a young man again.

I go over to the soda fountain, get a chocolate Coke, then go back and sit in a recently vacated chair next to Frank.

After a while, Frank's attention seems to wander from the conversation around him.

"Nice work on the *Schlitz*."

He looks at me oddly. "How did you know?"

"Beg pardon?"

"How did you know I was up for that?"

Shit. They haven't shot the damned thing yet.

As I try to think of a way to wiggle out of it, Frank frowns. "My agent says they may go younger."

"Don't worry. You'll get it."

"What makes you think so?"

"I'm sure you're exactly what they're looking for."

"You think?" He looks away, scratching some itch behind his ear.

I nod and turn my attention back to the actors' conversation.

I find all the stories, the inside Hollywood scoop, fascinating. Richard—the title-holder to the body I'm living in—feels as if gypsies have kidnapped him. But he's intrigued—bewildered. If he were from the future, he might be thinking "WTF?"

At five after eleven, Jesse Littman walks into Schwab's. I excuse myself, give Frank a wink, and tell him, "Good luck with the show," leaving him looking perplexed.

I hurry to the soda fountain, past Charlie Lane talking to Phil Leeds about Phil's (nonexistent) golf game. I arrive at my place at the counter just ahead of Jesse Littman. As I'm about to sit down, I involuntarily work my right shoulder, sore from its run-in with the gravel sidewalk the night before.

A passing waitress takes a step out of the way so as not to bump into me, and Jesse Littman, on his way to the same stool as before, pauses so he won't run into the waitress.

I hear a female voice call out, "Hey, Jesse."

Jesse turns so that he's facing the table where Charlie and Phil are talking.

He walks past them and most of the way across the restaurant to a young couple sitting at another table. After a moment, Jesse sits down with them.

I've missed my connection.

I order another chocolate Coke.

A half an hour later, Jesse Littman is still talking with the young couple.

I walk across the restaurant to them. "Excuse me," I say to Jesse, "Didn't we do a *Dragnet* together?"

The young couple watch as Jesse looks up at me. "I don't think so. Your face sorta rings a bell but …" He shakes his head and turns up his hands in polite regret.

"It just seemed that maybe we'd worked together."

Jesse doesn't want to encourage me. "Unh-hunh. Well, maybe."

"I'm *sure* we've worked together."

His smile evaporates.

I shrug and grin. "I guess I'm a little upset. My agent was supposed to send me in for *Bus Stop* today. But he … got … got sick and I can't reach him." There's a dreadful pause. "He died. My agent died. Got clunked on the head and drowned in his swimming pool." I suck in a mixture of saliva and air. "Shit."

The three of them stare at me somber-eyed.

Coughing, Richard produces a pathetic smile, turns, and rushes out of Schwab's.

I drive to Jerry Kennents' office. The secretary, Virginia, is pleasant to me again, but I don't have an appointment, and she can't help me. I ask her if she'll tell her boss that I'm an actor Joshua Logan has previously thought about for the role of Lawrence in *Bus Stop* and could I please go in and see Kennents now, but she tells me she'd lose her job if she did that, and after some fruitless wheedling, I leave.

I drive directly to Twentieth Century Fox, park down the street on Motor

Avenue, and walk toward the gate. Up against a storm fence are several sacks of cement. I heft one onto my good shoulder and walk undetected past the gate guard as a laborer.

I drop the cement around the corner of the first side street, take a second to catch my breath, then make my way past the gilt and teak exterior of the Royal Palace for *The King and I.*

When I ask for Joyce Faberman, it's later than it was the first time. The production secretary tells me she isn't there.

"Do you know where I can find her?"

"The role is cast."

"I'm not an actor, and Mr. Logan's expecting me." It comes out in a burst, with windfall confidence, born of desperation.

"Really? May I ask what it's about?"

"It's about … geology!" I keep myself from stammering. "I mean gems. It's about gems."

"Are you a … jewelry salesman?"

"No, I'm a gemologist."

"What's your name?"

"Richard Blake."

Looking very unsure, she dials two numbers on her phone, and a moment later says, "Sorry to bother you, Mr. Logan, but there's a Richard Blake here to see you … He says he's a gemologist." After a moment, she repeats herself: "A gemologist." She listens, nods, and puts the receiver back in its cradle. "I'm sorry to have kept you waiting, but I have to be very careful." She smiles conspiratorially. "Actors. They'll do anything, absolutely *anything.* If I were to tell you some of the tricks that have been pulled on this lot by actors looking for work, you'd be amazed." She shrugs apologetically. "You can go right in. He's through that door." She points toward Joshua Logan's temporary office.

I thank her and, nibbling on the inside of my lip, move to Mr. Logan's office, wipe my palms off on my shirt, and open the door.

Logan sits in the same chair. He's already finished his lunch. He has his elbows on his desk with his chin resting on his hands so that when he looks at Richard, it's like a little boy peering up at an adult. His look changes from dour to bemused.

"A gemologist?"

"That's right."

"You're actually a gemologist?"

"That's right. Um … I'm sorry to bother you at lunch time."

"Never mind that." He sits up straight and smoothes his mustache with the index fingers of both hands. It's about a half hour later than it was the last time. Logan looks pale. The blood seems to have been drained from his face. "I've just gotten off the phone with Miss Monroe … Did you know that I've been doing *Bus Stop* with Marilyn Monroe?"

I nod.

Logan looks out the window, distracted, ruminating out loud. "She's been the soul of professionalism and cooperation on this film—until five minutes ago."

"Really?"

Logan looks back, scowling. "She just put a condition on doing the additional shooting I think we simply must do to make this film work. We have to come up with a 'more exotic' profession for the character we have showing up now toward the end, at the bus station, and I was just wondering …" Blinking, Logan studies me, as if he's trying to read nearly illegible hieroglyphics on my face. "Miss Monroe doesn't want this character, Lawrence, to work for the Department of the Interior. She feels, or rather no doubt Arthur Miller feels … I'm sorry; I shouldn't have said that. He feels that this character doesn't serve his purpose if he's a bureaucrat. The problem is that we really need to shoot the scene tomorrow. It's the only day we can possibly do it."

"I see." I'm fascinated, baffled.

Logan presses the tips of two fingers against his forehead and drums the fingers of his other hand on the desk. "I was just wondering—"

The phone rings and he picks it up. "Yes?" An anxious frown forms on his face. He gets up and walks to the window, holding the rotary base in one hand and the receiver in the other. "No, love," he says. "No, love, I don't think so. No, love." He listens again, his frown deepening.

"Mr. Blake?" It's the production secretary, standing behind me, whispering. "Mr. Blake?"

Logan looks over his shoulder at us as he continues listening to the difficulty on the other end of the line. Shaking his head, he points at me and makes a flicking-away motion.

The secretary gestures for me to get up and follow her.

We go out into the reception area. The secretary says, "I'm sorry, Mr. Blake. This is an emergency. Why don't you telephone us next week? Mr. Logan may have some time for you then."

There isn't a thing I can do. I try to comfort myself that it wouldn't have worked out anyway, that I wouldn't have been cast, that you don't hire a gemologist to play a speaking role in your major Hollywood motion picture. At least I'd been able to meet Joshua Logan again. I think of friends I might tell about it—but most of them haven't been born yet or are out in their backyards or in school yards, playing on swing sets. Anyway, it would be small recompense.

I walk toward the commissary, wondering how I might find out where Marilyn's dressing room is and what unbalanced words might come out of my mouth if I should happen to run into her. Would I show her the alexandrite and explain to her that what it means is that we may both be— her and me, whom she doesn't know—teetering on the brink of a vast abyss?

"Excuse me?" A man on a stone bench beneath a Chinese elm tree, evidently reading a script, is pointing. It's Wendell Corey, the tall, stern-faced character actor. He is indicating something over my shoulder, behind me.

"That man wants you," he says.

I turn around and see Joshua Logan still standing at the window in his office on the third floor, beckoning for me to come back.

I thank Wendell Corey and rush back toward the *Bus Stop* offices.

Rita's voice echoes in the back of my brain as I run: "So tell me, Wendell, did you have any idea what a classic *Rear Window* would turn out to be? And what was it like, working with Hitchcock and Grace Kelly *and* Jimmy Stewart? You know who *I* love? I just love Thelma Ritter. I'll bet she was a trouper, right? You could always count on Thelma Ritter for a solid piece of work. What a great picture. I'll bet I've seen it ten times."

But Rita is anxious to hear what Josh Logan will say too, and manages to contain herself.

Logan cocks his head and speaks to me from his window on the third floor. "I just wanted you to wait outside while I tried to talk to …" He frowns and strokes his mustache with a thumb and forefinger. "This character I'm dealing with … This character could be a … gemologist, couldn't he?"

"Sure. Why not?"

"Could he be on a dig or something in Utah, looking for some kind of gemstone?"

"Sure," I say, my head bobbing up and down.

"Well, come on back up."

"Isn't it winter?" I say, in the director's office again.

"Maybe it hasn't been snowing all the time." Logan is thinking out loud, the pallor gone from his face. "We don't know exactly when the blizzard started." He studies me. "A gemologist could conceivably be caught out in the boondocks doing his work, couldn't he?"

"Absolutely."

"I've been racking my brain trying to think what kind of exotic thing this guy could be. Of course, we've eliminated artists and writers."

"Of course." I'm standing in front of Logan's desk again.

"What kind of a gemstone could he be looking for?"

"They mine sapphires in Montana."

"How about Utah? Do they mine any gems in Utah?"

At the moment he asks me that, I'm twisting the ring on my right ring finger with the thumb of the same hand, around and around. "Alexandrite. They found alexandrite in south Utah about 1950."

Logan chooses his words carefully. "Would it be possible … Would it be *reasonable* for a gemologist to be coincidentally near the bus station in this story, looking for alexandrite?"

"You would normally choose the summer, but yes, of course. If a company had reason to try to determine if there is alexandrite on a tract of land … Sure, a gemologist could very well be there looking for it."

Logan starts to smile, then the smile slowly becomes a grin. "If Miss Monroe will go along with it, you may have solved our problem." He smoothes his mustache again, but now it comes with an expression of relief. "I didn't think to ask why you came to see me. How may I help you?"

The phone rings, and he picks up the receiver. "Yes? … Thank you, Dottie." Logan hangs up the phone.

I'm still standing in front of his desk.

Logan smiles again. "Have you ever met Marilyn Monroe?"

"No."

"You're about to."

I hear the door open and feel her behind me. I turn around and, framed in the doorway, there she is.

15

She stops momentarily when she sees me standing between her and Logan. Then she moves quickly around me to Logan's side behind the desk and leans over him with one hand on the desk, the other on his shoulder.

"I want to do this scene. And I think you're right. We need it. I spoke with Arthur just now, and he agrees with me. He feels Lawrence could be a writer after all."

Logan looks pained. He speaks patiently. "I just don't think so, dear heart. Audiences are suspicious of writers. And this character doesn't have enough screen time to win them over. He's got to be a bit of an eccentric, but there can't be anything calculated. And there's nothing more calculated, no offense intended, than a writer."

"So what do we do?"

"I was thinking about a gemologist."

"What's a … gemologist?"

"Well"—he points at me—"this is one."

She looks up. "Who is he?"

"A gemologist," says Logan.

"What does he do?"

Logan smiles again. "Why don't you tell her, Mr. Blake?"

She is dressed in blue jeans and a man's white shirt, the tails of which are tied in front, at her waist. She wears light makeup, skillfully applied, her pale skin glowing. Her hair is drawn behind her head in a low, loose ponytail held by a pink elastic band. She is not exactly beautiful, but lovely in the way of a young girl who's just come of age and hasn't yet fully realized how pretty she is. She has a warm, clean smell of freshly laundered clothes and Ivory soap.

My mouth opens, but no sound comes out.

"I'm sorry," says Logan. "Marilyn, this is Richard Blake. Richard, Marilyn Monroe."

I extend my right hand over the desk.

She gazes at it, obviously fascinated by the alexandrite, then she looks up at me. A smile slowly forms. She takes my hand and gives it a squeeze. "How do you do?"

I find my voice. "Fine … Thank you … I'm both a gemologist and a geologist. My specialty is the … indexing of the wide range of North"—my mouth is totally dehydrated—"American gemstones."

"Lawrence could be a gemologist," says Logan. "It's perfect. We save the problems of his being a writer or an artist, but we also elevate him above the commonplace of being a bureaucrat. He'll have been nearby looking for alexandrites. That's a kind of … gemstone … er, right?" he asks.

"Right."

"Maybe," says Marilyn. "Maybe that would be okay."

My moment is over. I'm about to be dismissed. I've served my purpose. I've given them an identity for Lawrence.

I blurt out, "I'm an *actor*, too."

Logan's head retracts into his neck.

"I was on Broadway in *Cat on a Hot Tin Roof.* I understudied Gooper. I went on several times. Could I read for you? I heard you hadn't decided on your Lawrence."

"How did you hear that?"

"Actors' grapevine."

Logan shakes his head. "You're a curious man."

Marilyn is staring at me. "Maybe we could read the scene together," she says.

She turns to Logan, who looks at me as if for the first time, appraising my possibilities as Lawrence. He turns back to Marilyn and shrugs. "We've got to cast it today. I guess it couldn't hurt. Actors have gotten roles in crazier ways." He looks off with a faraway smile. He had enormous success last year with the film version of *Picnic.* One of his accomplishments was to use real-people locals in peripheral roles. This original play, *Bus Stop,* was written by the same playwright as *Picnic*—William Inge. Marilyn is already giving Cherie a natural, unactorish performance. Logan smiles impishly. "It would be sort of poetic if he could act."

Although it's still unfamiliar terrain, channeling through Richard, I try out our most ingratiating charm on them. "I understand you'll do what you think is best for the film."

Even though I'm nervous, Marilyn and I seem to connect. This Richard can be kind of sweet when he tries. Or maybe Marilyn feels sympathy for his obvious unease. Or perhaps it's because she and I have always had a connection. I have the familiar feeling of being subsumed into that chaotic, spiraling part of my brain I have no choice but to give in to. It's the way I feel during jet takeoffs, a benign state of shock—an ocean of life, but inside me somehow. It's *Marilyn Monroe.* It's *immensity.* I wouldn't fight it if I could; it wouldn't be safe. I haven't a prayer of controlling it. I relax, cradled like a baby, into Richard's lack of acting craft.

Logan tells me I've brought an "open vulnerability" to the character, and for a second time he thinks I'm unactorish.

Logan looks at Marilyn, then turns back to me. "The part's yours. Who's your agent?"

"Jerry Kennents," I say, my heart pounding out fancy jazz riffs.

"All right. Fine. Have you had your lunch yet?"

"I don't eat lunch."

Logan laughs, smiles, and looks at Marilyn again. "How'd you sleep last night, sweetheart?"

"Not bad. Not bad-*ly.* Not badly at all."

"Me too. Go figure." He beams at her with fatherly affection. Apparently, they both suffer from insomnia, and each of them feels compassion for the other's problem with it.

"Well, if you're available right now," says Logan, glancing at the dumbfounded gemologist, "and if it's okay with you, dear, I'd like to get started rehearsing as soon as possible—although I think it's going to be an easy scene to do."

"I'm ready," I say.

In my excitement, it hasn't even crossed my mind to remember that there is no Lawrence in the movie *Bus Stop*.

16

Joyce Faberman, the casting director, is out to lunch when I'm cast. I call Virginia at Jerry Kennents' office. She tells me Kennents isn't in. I tell her they'll be getting a call from Joyce and that I want Kennents to negotiate my deal. "I expect he'll have to settle for what he can get because I'm already at work." Virginia sounds flustered.

We rehearse in Marilyn's apartment on the lot.

After an hour, Logan says, "You kids stick with it. It's going to be splendid." Then he excuses himself, saying he'll see me on the set at eight o'clock tomorrow morning. As he leaves, he says, "Will that be all right with you, dear?"

Marilyn smiles. "I don't know why, Josh, but there are a few things temporarily under my … well, sort of under my control."

"I've gotten a reputation for being late," she says after Logan has gone, settling into a plain, overstuffed chair. "Late for work, late for engagements." She hides for a moment behind a shy smile, raising her eyebrows, signifying there's truth in the rumors.

I'm sitting at the end of a reproduction Danish Modern sofa, three feet away from her. "How old are you?" I can't believe I said that. "I'm sorry. I have no idea why I … I'm really sorry."

She giggles. "That's okay. I'm twenty-nine. I'll be thirty on the first of June."

"What will you do when filming is over?" I'm not a lot more pleased with that one, but there doesn't seem to be any way to edit my careening thoughts.

"Who *are* you?" she says.

"Just somebody else who's looking."

"For what?"

"I don't know … Any kind of purpose."

She smiles. "It's a Barnum and Bailey world." She runs the fingertips of one hand lightly along the line of her chin bone. "Sometimes I think if I only knew the right questions to ask, I'd be able to learn a few things and maybe that would be enough." She looks at me as if I may have brought some answers with me. "Everyone wants to know me. Why is that?"

"Because if they can get to understand your story, it'll make theirs … clearer."

"Why me? … You mean the movie-star thing?"

"Yeah, but mostly the acting thing—that you do. Sometimes you reveal things to us about ourselves. We're human and hungry for ways to cope, and we want to know more."

"How do I reveal myself?" As I try to think how to answer that without accidentally hurting her feelings, she answers it herself: "I mean I'm trying in this movie to reveal this … girl. But that's a really different thing that doesn't help me be … what I want to be … Maybe that's what I'm revealing about Cherie—a girl so open and woundable she doesn't recognize the answers even when they're staring her in the face. I mean, Cherie doesn't seem to be the brightest coin in the collection—but she's a long way from being dumb, and some serious things are beginning to dawn on her."

"Yes, and she's gaining incredible spirit, the way you play her." Shit.

"How would you know *that?*"

"I can … I can just tell."

"I don't see how."

"By the way you were when I auditioned and the way you … are … now—your sense of serenity, your dignity."

"Really?" She smiles again but seems vastly unsure of her dignity. "Maybe it's the 'energy and excitement' thing Josh talks about. He's always trying to find ways to make me look on the positive side—you know, the side of me that feels that good things are bound to come my way if I just believe it? And along with that comes poise. He says that should be starting to bloom in me." She stares up at the canopy of a sycamore tree shadowing the manicured lawn outside the window, remembering. Now, she looks back at me. "Anyway, Josh said if he hadn't been the way he was—like me, he meant, I could tell— he would have missed 'the sharpest, the rarest, the sweetest moments of his existence.'"

She seems to hold her breath. She's watching me, seeing what I may have to say to that. But I'm tongue-tied, unable to do any more than smile at her.

She continues to hold my gaze. "This wonderful, poised man—Josh— said, 'Marilyn'—he spoke my name in such a … kind way. He said, 'Darling, your sweetest moments are still ahead of you.' I mean he's really smart and dear, and if he can say a thing like that—" She sees something in the look on my face.

"And that made you feel better?"

She hesitates, still trying to read a thought I'm glad she can't read. "More than that, it made me feel hopeful. I mean real hope. Now, if I can only keep it here—the hope." She taps herself on the forehead. "I know what he said will come true." She looks at her lap and emits a slow, soundless whistle. "My problem is, the better the advice is, the quicker I do the opposite."

She shrugs, gazes at me, then stretches both fists up in the air. It's meant to indicate triumph, but her moment of jubilation is gone now and her "positive side" no longer rings true. "Lately, I really do feel optimistic." She sighs. "Well, sometimes. But that is who I want to be all the time. Someday, I'd like to be a person who looks at life—at the whole world that way, you know? I just want to feel the hell with all these demons and ghosts and stop having to try to figure out the reason for every little emotional itch. I just want to *live*. You know?"

"Yes, I do."

"It's the way I want to feel *every minute*."

"Me too. I want to be alive."

She smiles a sad, longing smile. "But we *are*, aren't we. We are alive."

"Sure."

Her look darkens. "But in a few weeks I'm not going to have Josh, and ..." She shakes her head and looks out the window. "Well, I guess people can't feel that way all the time." She leans an elbow against the chair and, resting her chin on her hand, lifts a shoulder in resignation. It reminds me of the French actress Jeanne Moreau acknowledging that life comes without guarantees. "I started out wanting the world to know me," she says. "Like Cherie, singing at the Dragon Nightclub down by the stock yard. And now people do know me ..." She thinks about that. "Photography is so scary. I just go on and on living in pictures, but really I'm like all those people wondering who that girl is." She shivers. "And that's not the worst thing ..."

"What is?"

She looks down at her hands. "'The wings of insanity.' Somebody wrote that." 'The wings of insanity over my head.' Isn't that a terrible thing to say?"

"Yes, it is."

She frowns. "What will I do when filming is over?" She shakes her head. "The press is always asking me what I'm going to do next—like they want to know where to go hang out until I get there. And I can't tell them the real truth—that they might as well save themselves the trouble; that it's all over now. I'm never going to be better than I am in this movie. And it'll all be over soon, and they'll put me wherever they put used sex symbols ... Over a year in New York, in and out of therapy and the Actors Studio, and failing in love, and I have new friends and old ones, who are gone now out of my life, and I don't know—if I'm really honest—why the new ones are any better than the old ones. It's not enough to have people know you. What you need is for someone to know you're *alive*. The only one who knows I'm alive is ... oh well." She smiles, but it's half-hearted.

"I've made you unhappy."

She stares at me. "You haven't made me unhappy at all. Everybody's always interrupting me to give me advice and to tell me what to do." She looks at me for a long time, then out the window. She laughs, self-conscious. "This is me happy."

She turns back and looks into my eyes, as if trying to decipher an inscrutable code. "I think I'm having one of my instant crushes on you. I have to watch those, or I get into awful trouble." She frowns and looks away. "Which did you do first, gemology or acting?"

"Gemology."

"That's nice. It's good not to make the acting too important. I did a scene from *Anna Christie* … you know? Eugene O'Neill …? It was a few months ago at the Actors Studio, and I was so nervous, the next morning I woke up with laryngitis. I felt like I'd been strangled. It's not worth it." She looks at me for what feels like a long time. "Do you want to run the scene again?"

"Yeah, okay."

She sits next to me shyly, looking at me with the same puzzled expression, then slowly begins to tell me about Cherie's childhood in the Ozarks, hanging out with her sister Nan at Liggett's Drugstore in River Gulch. Finally, Cherie tells Lawrence he's a good listener, and he says she's nice to listen to.

She stops, just before the end of the scene, looks at me for a long time and says again, "Who *are* you?"

It's dark when I get home. Margaret is sitting in her usual chair in the living room. Lily is in the wooden rocker.

"I'm sorry I'm late."

"Where've you been?" Margaret is doing her best to cover her anger.

"There was a lot of traffic."

"Would you like to know how many times you've told me that?"

"No, thanks. Did anybody call me?"

"Yes. Jerry somebody. He said you'd know what it's about. The number is by the phone in the library. You didn't answer my question. Where've you been?"

"I did some work for a movie company today. They need some technical help for a film at Twentieth Century Fox. One of the characters is a gemologist. I'll be working on it tomorrow, too."

She weighs this. "Will they pay you decently?"

"Yes, very decently. That's what the phone call is about."

I wait for her to respond to that, but she turns away. "If you want your supper, you'll have to reheat it."

"I'm not really hungry."

"We had roast beef," says Lily, rocking.

"Did you?"

"Yes. It was overcooked. Margaret overcooked it."

"I'll bet it was good anyway."

"No, it wasn't. It was overcooked. It was burnt."

Margaret gets up and moves toward another drink.

I return Jerry Kennents' call and introduce myself. Kennents is mystified but was happy to negotiate my contract for me. He got me double-scale for the day's shooting. He says he'd like to have a meeting and discuss representing me on a permanent basis. I tell him I'll drop by his office Monday afternoon.

I climb the stairs to my room, unlock it, go in, turn the key in the lock from the inside, undress, and take a shower. It's the evening of April eleventh. I have to survive past three A.M. tomorrow morning.

I dry off, go back into my bedroom, and open my underwear drawer. The revolver is where I left it. I give a little thought to getting into the Olds, driving to a motel, checking in, locking the door and staying there until dawn, but I'm afraid I might not find time to sleep at all if I did that. Anyway, she no longer has a gun.

Downstairs again, I serve myself a plate of roast beef and take it into the living room.

"It's burnt, isn't it?" says Lily.

"It's a bit well done, but it's delicious."

"You're shameless." Margaret doesn't look up. "How did you happen to get a job with a film company?"

"They heard about me, I guess, and called to see if I was available."

"Why didn't you mention it when you first came in?"

"Didn't I?"

She stares at me with glacial eyes. Then, apparently looking for anything to hang onto, her features patch themselves into something like hopefulness. "Might there be future jobs with film companies?"

"Maybe."

"It would be nice to have a little security."

"I feel confident that our financial fortunes are looking up." I'm thinking about some information I remember from the *World Almanac.* I know that a horse called Needles, ridden by D. Erb, is due to win the Kentucky Derby on the first Saturday in May. The National League can be counted on to take the All-Star Game seven to three, and at the beginning of October, the Yankees will beat Brooklyn in seven to win the World Series. Don Larsen will capture the Series MVP by pitching in game five the only perfect game in World Series history.

We watch the TV show about the marines who drowned at Paris Island and Grace Kelly's upcoming marriage. I decide not to stay for *Dragnet* and Ida Lupino going nuts in the lighthouse from the rats. I tell Margaret and Lily I have work to do.

Looking puzzled, Margaret starts to speak, but I tell her as firmly as I can, "I've got to get this work done tonight, right now."

I go up to my room and lock the door.

I lie down on the bed and try to concentrate on the script. "You have more love and kindness in your eyes," Lawrence says, "than I've found in this whole damned state."

"Gag me with a spoon." Richard doesn't understand why Jack said that, but by now, almost nothing he says surprises him.

I think of my favorite theatre story: A young actor has been waiting for his big break. He writes in a journal, "Dear Diary, tomorrow I'm going to be a star. I have a great role in the best play of the season. I have a wonderful, moving soliloquy that I've worked on as diligently as I've ever worked on anything. I'm on stage all by myself, except for the character actor who has no lines and simply sits upstage at an old desk, writing a letter. There is no possibility I won't be brilliant. I will have the audience in the palm of my hand. Tomorrow, I am a star."

The entry in the next day's journal read, "Dear Diary, he drank the ink."

I freeze.

Someone is tapping on the door.

It's 11:30. There is a pause. The only light in the room comes from my bedside lamp. The tapping is repeated, not loud, but insistent.

I hear footsteps moving away from the door.

At least ten minutes after that, I move silently to the bureau and slide open the underwear drawer. The gun is exactly where I put it.

Leaving it there, I close the drawer, tiptoe to the bathroom, and rinse my face with cold water. My adrenaline will keep me awake until I safely pass three in the morning, the hour of Richard's previous departure.

I get into my bed again, sit upright with my back against the headboard, and turn my attention to the script.

THURSDAY, APRIL 12, 1956

I wake up confused and angry with myself for nodding off. I wonder if there's some other convoluted self in there with a death wish. I hear Santa Ana winds. They're buffeting the house over and over, striking, then waiting for a few seconds, then gathering force and pounding at the windows and shutters again.

Richard's Bulova is on the bedside table.

It is 3:30. I'm perspiring. In dreams I was flying into dark clouds, and again found myself at the top of the stairs.

I look at my hands. For a moment, groggy, I don't know whose they are. I move to the mirror in the bathroom and turn on the light.

It's Richard Blake.

It's also 3:30 in Kingman, Arizona. Jack Cade is squalling in the nursery of Saint Mary's Hospital. I imagine my father, whom I barely remember except from pictures, standing in the waiting room, elated but nervous as hell, looking through the window at his brand-new son.

I picture Rita, holding her baby boy, studying his little feet.

I did not die at the predesignated time. The changes I've made—both those that I know about and those that I don't—have caused other changes that have caused …

There is noise in the hall. It sounds like somebody with a broom. I unlock the door and cautiously peer out.

At the end of the hall, the glow from the lamp in the foyer below illuminates the top of the stairs.

I put on my robe, go out into the hall, close and relock the door, and move quietly toward the stairs. There's no light coming through the passageway from the living room. The sound of the sweeping broom gets louder.

I realize what it is. I go downstairs to take a look anyway. Several limbs of the pepper tree outside the living room are whipping up against the cornice above one of the front windows.

I'm ravenous. The burnt roast beef and cold potatoes and green beans from dinner are all I've eaten since breakfast. I go into the kitchen and open the refrigerator. Cold meat and cheese, white bread, no mustard, only mayonnaise. I fix myself an unsatisfactory sandwich and devour it by the light of the refrigerator.

"Richard?"

"Shi-iit!"

I'm sitting on a stool next to the serving table, facing the refrigerator, still eating my sandwich. I whirl around on the stool to find Lily standing in the doorway to the kitchen. She's barefoot, wearing only a thin white nightgown.

I whisper fiercely at her, "You scared me to death."

"I'm not sleeping, Richard."

"What are you doing up?"

"I'm not sleeping. I got up. I was awake."

I take a deep breath. "Did you tap on my door earlier?"

She shakes her head no, and I know it's the truth. It was Margaret. I'm surprised she didn't just use the key she's had made and walk right in.

I take my robe off and help Lily into it. She sits down on another stool.

"Why are we awake, Richard?"

"I was hungry. You'd better whisper. We don't want to wake anybody." In the light from the refrigerator, I see her eyes roll to the side as she looks toward the kitchen door. "Would you like something to eat?"

"Is it breakfast?"

"No, I'm just having a snack."

"A snack," she echoes. "I'm not hungry." She stares at me. "You didn't come to my room. You didn't want to dance with me, and then tonight you didn't come to my room."

There's nothing I can say.

"You didn't come to my room."

"I know. I mustn't come to your room anymore."

Her eyes widen. "Why?"

"Because I shouldn't. It's a bad secret. I don't want you to have to keep that secret anymore."

She puts a forefinger to her lips. "It's a secret."

"You don't have to keep the secret anymore. But I mustn't come to your room."

"You think Lily is stupid, don't you?"

"No, I don't think you're stupid at all."

"I think you do."

"No, I don't. I'll tell you why I can't come to your room anymore. Because it's not fair to you, and it's not fair to Margaret."

"You think I'm stupid."

"No, I don't, Lily. Come on."

I close the refrigerator door. I take her up to her room, then return to mine, shut the door behind me, and turn the key in the lock.

I'm exhausted after this day and evening, but I also have a bad case of nerves. I have three shots of Scotch and go to bed.

Jack remembers watching Sophie asleep next to him in what used to be their bed, when Leonard Cohen's line, "Your hair upon the pillow like a sleepy golden storm," ran through his mind. But Sophie's hair is not golden, it's a dark chestnut brown—almost black.

I dream of Sophie this night. She's at her sexiest. And that is sexy.

To my padded-cell mind, it's very strange timing for this dream.

And again it seems … too real …

Oh, Jesus!

I sit bolt upright in bed.

The door to my room is open.

Horrified, sweating, spent, I stare at the clock. It's 5:15.

With all the strength of will I have, I force my mind back to the scene I'm going to be doing today. After a while, I shower and shave.

18

Downstairs, I make a pot of coffee and drink two cups. I don't feel like eating.

At 6:30, I put my script back in my work case and let myself out the back door.

As I'm unlocking the Oldsmobile, Margaret whispers harshly at me from her window on the second floor, "Richard, when will you be back?"

"Not till this evening."

"We need to talk."

"We should have talked last night."

"I tried to say something to you last night, but you had to work."

"But why didn't you … Never mind. We'll talk tonight."

I get into the car and drive off.

I feel good—safe, a moving target. I'm not so easy to kill. I've learned a few things. I'm flying through spring like a hawk, lifting from the earth. As I travel to Twentieth Century Fox Studios, countless mica chips in the surface of the Los Angeles streets glitter like diamonds in the morning sunlight.

We're on stage seven. The gate guard directs me to it.

When I walk into "Grace's Diner," the crew is already busy at work, preparing the set where Cheri and Lawrence will play their scene.

Logan takes Marilyn's stand-in and me through it a couple of times for the cinematographer, the camera operator, and the lighting and sound guys, then I go out to my trailer to wait for the call to go to work. It's eight o'clock.

Just short of 8:30, the second assistant director knocks on my door. "We're ready, Mr. Blake."

Marilyn is only twenty-five minutes late.

By 4:30 in the afternoon, we've gotten the scene. Logan tells us it's perfect.

Marilyn is wrapped for the day. She gives Logan a kiss and goes to her trailer. I thank him profusely for the job and go to mine.

There's a knock at the door. It's Marilyn.

"Hi." I'm pleased but not completely surprised. Some oddity of my brain briefly causes me—as I look at this young woman—to picture her as Sophie out there, waiting at my dressing room door. They don't look anything alike. Well, maybe a little—something behind the eyes.

"May I come in?"

"Of course."

She's in jeans and a loose white shirt again. She sits down on my couch and looks around at my cracker box of a dressing room. "It's not much, is it?"

"I don't mind," I say.

She continues gazing around the small space, at the shabbiness, remembering. "I never did either. Now I'm not satisfied with a palace. Did you know I might have been Princess Marilyn of Monaco?"

"No, I didn't," I lie.

"Prince Rainier made inquiries about me. But I think they decided I was too crazy. They were right. But I could have left this whole thing, especially now that I've gotten to such a"—she struggles for the right word—"a crossroads, I guess."

I sit down in the chair that, because of the tiny quarters, is right next to her.

She looks at me unsteadily. "I'm not on the call sheet for tomorrow." She looks off with her faraway smile. "I've got an early day on Monday." She takes a deep breath. "But if you'd like to, we could be together until then."

I hold her hands.

"What do you want to do?" she says.

"I want to go to Arizona. Let's go to Arizona."

The phone rings eight times before Margaret picks it up. I can tell by the careful way she pronounces each word that she's drinking gin.

"I have to go on a field trip," I tell her.

"Where?"

"Arizona. I'm going to Kingman, Arizona. I'll be back Sunday night."

"Aren't you coming home first?"

"It wouldn't make sense to drive all the way out to the Valley just to turn around and have to come back south on my way to Kingman."

She doesn't say anything.

"Margaret?"

"Yes."

"Can you hear me?"

"Yes, Richard, I hear you. Do you know what I wish?"

"No." I don't want to hear it. "What do you wish?"

"I wish I was dead."

"Don't do that to me."

"I'm not doing it to you. You're doing it to me."

It comes out gutturally, as if from deep in a cave, "This is not me, Margaret."

"Drive carefully." She hangs up.

It takes us a little over five and a half hours of hard driving to get to Kingman. It crosses my mind to tell Marilyn the whole story from the beginning because she, more than anyone I can imagine, might listen, and maybe even believe me, but our time together is short, and I have no idea how to begin.

We roll through the nighttime flatlands of inland Southern California along Route 66 into Arizona and then up to Kingman. Sometimes we talk, other times she leans her head on my shoulder as the vast desert terrain slides by us, ghostly silent.

East of the Mojave Desert and Needles, after we've crossed into Arizona, I look out at the bulk of a huge saguaro cactus, then beyond it to an endless desert wilderness dotted with moon-frosted creosote bushes, prickly pear cactus, Joshua trees, and patches of night-blooming cereus. A mountain range rises darkly from the desert floor in the distance like an immense notched roller coaster, and part of me remembers being here before. I hear my young mother's voice as we drive in the opposite direction I'm traveling now. She's telling me that everything will be okay, that everybody has to die someday, and that it was my father's "time."

From the city limits of Kingman, it's only five minutes to Saint Mary's Hospital.

It's still Thursday the twelfth.

11:15 p.m.

I think about finding out what motel my father is staying in but then decide that he will undoubtedly be at the hospital in the morning and I'll see him then. I have to get to the hospital now.

Marilyn hasn't even asked me why I want to stop at the hospital. I say, "Aren't you curious?" She smiles and shrugs very slightly. I tell myself I'll come up with some kind of explanation later.

The moment for that never happens.

Not this time.

She stays in the downstairs waiting room. She has no makeup on. She wears jeans, an oversized sweater, and dark glasses. It's her usual camouflage, the one she wears to walk around New York City. No one gives her a second glance, even though she is now at the peak of her career. She has a practiced way of withdrawing into herself to reduce the frequency of those awkward moments when she doesn't want them. Susan Strasberg called her "a consummate disguise artist."

Marilyn holds her head down and might be a patient's anxious wife or sister or daughter.

I go to the elevators, push the button, and am surprised, when the doors open, to see an elevator operator, a short sixtyish man with steel-gray slicked-back hair. He looks ninety percent asleep.

"Obstetrics ward, please."

He doesn't look at me, just closes the doors with a sudden and surprisingly muscular motion and sets the elevator creaking and whirring up to the third floor.

There is a painstakingly hand-painted sign over the controls that reads: *The way up and the way down are the same.—Heraclitus.* Elevator humor.

On the third floor, the doors chunk closed behind me. I find a sign that says *OB* and follow the arrow down a corridor with green-and-white-speckled wallpaper and an old, cracking, but highly polished linoleum tile floor. There is a pair of green double doors at the end. I push through them and walk into the obstetrics waiting room.

There are seven babies in the nursery. I stare dumbly for a while, trying to comprehend that one of the infants I'm staring at is *me.*

After a minute or so, a nurse who has completely white hair but can't be over forty-five appears on the babies' side of the window. Approaching me, she says, "Is there some way I can help you?"

"I wondered if I could see the Cade baby. Jack … John Cade? I'm his uncle. I know it's way past visiting hours, but I've come a long way."

"All right." She starts toward the babies then turns back. "John who?"

"Cade. C-A-D-E."

She looks puzzled. "We have a four-day-old named John Harrington … I'm sorry, we don't …" Her face darkens. "I'll have to ask you to leave, sir. There is no baby here named Cade."

"Oh no, I'm sure you're wrong. I *know* that John and Rita Cade checked

in here about twenty-four hours ago." I hear myself become shrill. "Jack …
John Cade Jr. was born in this hospital at three A.M. this morning."

"I'm sorry, sir. That's not true." She seems so certain of it.

"Could they have checked out this fast?"

She's upset. "No, they could not have. There is no Cade baby here."

I redesign my technique. "Would you please do me a favor and look
again?" I go for a disarming smile. "I don't mean to cause trouble, but I *think*
you've made a mistake. One of those babies has to be John Cade."

"I'm sorry, sir, but you're wrong." Her eyes are blinking rapidly. "One of
those babies is John Harrington, and that baby"—she points to the nearest
crib—"hasn't been given a Christian name, but his last name is Moreno. The
other five infants are all girls."

"You're sure?"

"I *know* the difference."

I go downstairs, tell Marilyn I'll be just a couple more minutes, then cross
the lobby to the information desk. As the man on duty comes up from the
back, I glance at yesterday's copy of the *Kingman Daily Miner* lying on the
counter. Nat King Cole was attacked by a group of white segregationists the
night before last, the tenth, onstage in Birmingham, Alabama.

I shake my head and the man on duty, reaching the desk, says, "Anything
wrong, sir?"

"Well, quite a bit actually. I just found out that I don't exist and now
this." I point at the article about Nat King Cole.

The man stares at me. He has an unhealthy pallor and a nicotine stain
around his right nostril and just below it, on one side of his upper lip. He
cranes his head warily around, takes in the headline and shrugs. "Yeah, well
he probably had it coming."

"Pardon me?"

The man behind the desk—who, other than his views on attacking people
who are singing love songs, seems benign enough—says, "Well, people don't
just turn violent for no reason at all." As I gape at him, the man begins to

frown. "So what can I do you for, sir?"

I find my voice. "You could tell me if you've got a Rita Cade registered here?" He is now regarding me with undisguised hostility. "She's my mother," I explain.

"Oh … Okay." He checks the patient files. "Sorry, sir. There's no one here by that name."

After a long awkward moment, I mumble a phony thank you, nod, go to a phone booth, and call the police. They can't help me either.

I call information in Jackson, Michigan. They give me the number for John Cade. My father exists. But no one answers when I call. But they wouldn't. They're on vacation. They're in Kingman, Arizona.

Only they're not.

We check into a motel.

I'm sitting on the edge of one of the twin beds, my head down. Marilyn comes out of the bathroom.

"What is it?"

I search for some half-sane answer. "I don't know."

She sits next to me. I reach out and touch her hand, then I hold it tightly. I realize I'm at the edge of weeping and turn my head away. I can be kind of a drama queen at the best of times, and this moment, which may not fall under a best-or-worst heading, at least falls under the umbrella of way fucking odd.

She draws me to her, pressing her cheek against the top of my head.

I'm breathing in the sweet, sexy, and, at this second, comforting smell of her.

She touches my damp cheek and strokes my face and hair and says, "I don't want you to be unhappy. Please don't be unhappy."

FRIDAY, APRIL 13, 1956

I buy a pair of jeans and a couple of fresh shirts at a nearby shop, and we check out of the motel before noon. We stop at a coffee shop called Crow's for breakfast. A sign outside says *PHILLIP LINCOLN CROW, PROPRIETOR*.

I'm still nervous that someone will recognize Marilyn, but no one does. Most people picture her in tight dresses, platinum blonde hair, and considerable makeup. Now, on this airy, sunshiny morning, she's wearing simple clothes and no makeup. She's still got the sunglasses on, but otherwise she looks like a normal, pretty, fresh-faced young woman.

After the waitress takes our order, she starts back to the kitchen and Marilyn says, sounding very much like herself, "Could I please have some ketchup, honey?" Neither the waitress nor anyone else seems to notice. They never imagined Marilyn Monroe would be in John Crow's place, asking for ketchup.

It's the day after Jack's birthday. I have no idea who I am.

But it's springtime in Arizona, a long weekend stretches out ahead, and Marilyn Monroe is sitting across the table from me, smiling.

I think of Psalm 139:7, which I learned in Sunday school in Jackson, Michigan: "Whither shall I go from thy spirit? Or whither shall I flee from thy presence?"

19

SUNDAY, APRIL 15, 1956

The traffic is terrible in Los Angeles. It seems much worse than the usual returning-from-the-weekend mess. It is 10:15 by the time I get Marilyn home to the apartment she keeps near Beverly Drive and Olympic.

I say goodbye and tell her I'll call her the next night at seven.

"See ya," she says.

"Next week?"

"Sure." She doesn't seem sure.

I feel embarrassed. "It's just crazy to feel whatever I'm feeling right now, right? I mean, I don't know you."

"Yeah, it's crazy." She shrugs, smiles distractedly, turns and goes inside.

The traffic isn't any better on the way home from Beverly Hills. It feels like rush hour or some kind of holiday; people are milling around on sidewalks and outside houses and shops, talking animatedly to each other. I try the radio in the Oldsmobile, then remember that it isn't working. I turn it off.

Images of Marilyn and Lily and Margaret, and my estranged wife Sophie, way off somewhere in the future, tumble around in my head until I find myself approaching 1833 Shoemaker Drive.

My palms are sweating.

It's a pitch-black moonless night.

The house is dark except for the lamp we always keep on in the window of the foyer. I turn the headlights off, then the engine, and coast carefully, almost by feel down the driveway and into the garage.

I enter through the back, take off my shoes, and climb the stairs to the second floor. There isn't a strip of light under Margaret's door, which means she's asleep.

In my room, I silently close and lock the door behind me. My body feels as if it's been injected with lead. I go to bed and fall asleep immediately.

I wake up, fear clutching my insides.

Margaret is calling my name. I know where she is—downstairs, sitting in Lily's wooden rocker.

I get painfully out of bed, move to the dresser, and open the underwear drawer.

The revolver is gone.

There are no back stairs. I open my door carefully. I'm in my pajamas. I haven't put on my robe. I lock the door behind me, although I can't think why it matters now, and walk soundlessly on the hallway carpeting to the top of the stairs.

It's my nightmare, exactly as it was before I was killed.

She calls my name again: "Richard …"

Fear pushes at me to go back upstairs, but I float over it on wings of righteous indignation and move down to the foyer.

I know what I'm going to do: I stand just around the corner from the passageway to the living room. I call out in a pathetic, faraway voice, pretending I'm still upstairs, "Margaret … would you come up here?"

I don't hear a response. I pitch my voice higher, sadder.

"Margaret …?"

I don't know what I expect her to think. I don't care.

I hear her get up from the rocking chair. I press my back up against the wall around the corner from the passageway.

I hear her footsteps approaching the passageway, then coming through it.

As she reaches the foyer, I slide in behind her, throwing my left hand under her left arm and grabbing her hard behind the neck while swinging my right hand around and gripping her right arm just below the elbow.

The only sound she makes is a long thin squeak.

I lift her against my hip and carry her back into the living room.

I spin her around to face me in the light, squeezing both of her hands in mine.

She doesn't have the revolver. The mahogany box is not next to the rocker. I look around the room, but I don't see it.

I sit her down on the silver brocade settee, near the rocker. "Where's the gun?"

She looks up at me through perfectly round eyes.

"Where's the gun? Goddamn it!"

"Gun?"

"Yes. Your revolver."

"Richard, are you crazy?"

"No, I'm not. I'm not crazy enough to let this happen again. Where's your pistol?"

"How did you know I had a pistol?"

"Never mind. Where is it?"

"It's in my room where I keep it, in my wooden box." She's near tears.

"I thought things had gotten a little better between us," I say. "Why did you call me down here?"

"I don't know. I'm embarrassed to come to your …" Her voice is shaking. "I thought it was the best thing to do. Why did you do that?"

"I don't know … I was scared."

That seems like an answer to her, but she's still breathing heavily and the anger hasn't left her face.

Other things start to flood back into my mind.

"I need to talk to you," she says.

I sit on the settee next to her, feeling cold, dead tired again, and guilty.

"Richard, you're trembling. What is it?"

"I've got a … chill."

She sighs and takes my hand. "Did you catch something on your field trip?"

"I don't think so."

She looks at my hand in hers. "Where's your ring?"

I don't answer; I sweat.

"The alexandrite. I've never seen you without it."

It's Marilyn's birthstone. It was mine to give. Maybe I'll just explain the truth to her in my most charming way. It'll be a little dicey, but my God, it was Marilyn Monroe. Who could blame me? I'll use the Yves Montand defense. He had an affair with her during the filming of *Let's Make Love*. The world sided with his wife, Simone Signoret. Confronted at a press interview, Montand alluded to Monroe having fallen for him, then delivered the only possible argument. It was eloquent. He said, "What can one do?"

Sure. I'll use the French defense.

I look at my ringless hand. "I must have lost it."

"That's too bad." She releases my hand and tries to look at my face, but I turn away. Neither Richard nor Jack have the balls of Yves Montand. When I look back at her, her nerve has apparently dissolved, and she turns away.

"You got a telephone call from a woman," she says.

"Who was it?"

"She wouldn't say. She just asked for you, and I told her you weren't here."

"When?"

"A few minutes ago. A little while."

"What did she say?"

"Nothing. She asked for you, I told her you weren't here, but I said I was your wife, and I'd be happy to take a message."

My heart sinks.

Margaret is studying me. "That was all right, wasn't it?"

"I'm sorry."

"*Why* are you sorry?"

"Because I'm two people now. Forever." Now, she's staring. "I'm two people. But one of them will never be born."

Her eyes widen in alarm again. "Richard, don't. Please don't. Please don't you be insane too."

I think to myself that there are a thousand variations of that possibility. For example: What if I am only Richard Blake and have conjured up—from my own mind—some actor in the future who I imagine has come back and inhabited my body? There are crazy people on the streets of any city, having flights of fancy not very far from that. I wonder if there is any significant difference between "I'm possessed by Satan" and "I'm inhabited by a TV actor from forty years into the future."

"I've been sleeping with Lily."

"I know."

"But I stopped. I never really wanted to."

She blinks. "What does that mean?"

"I'm sorry." She KNOWS? Of COURSE! Lily told her again.

"*Are* you?"

"… Yes, I'm sorry, but I'm more and more confused, Margaret."

"We've got to talk." Two tight creases form above her nose, drawing her eyebrows downward. "I don't know if you know it," she says. "There's been some damage …"

"But what's going to happen? What's going to happen now?" I watch her, hoping she might actually have an answer. "Is that what you wanted to talk to me about? Lily? Did you want to talk about Lily?"

She blinks, looks away, then back at me, smiling sadly. "Yes, that's right," she says. "Lily. I want to talk about Lily—and the unspeakable damage that's been done to her."

I have nothing to say to that.

"But that's not all. Come here, I want to show you something."

Margaret stands as Lily's voice floats through to us from the passageway, "Richard …? Richard …?"

"Oh, God, Lily's up now. You're still shaking, Richard." She raises her voice to speak to Lily, who is coming through the passageway. "We're in here, Lily. I'm going to fix us some tea."

She goes out to the kitchen as Lily glides into the room.

I feel a prickling sensation at the back of my neck.

"Look what I found, Richard."

I turn to face her.

She's barefoot, wearing the thin white nightgown again. "Look what I found." She holds the revolver, looking at it curiously.

I get up as casually as I can and move around the settee toward her. "Give me that."

"I don't think so." She points it at me.

I stop.

"Not now. I'm not going to give it to you now."

I speak very quietly. "Lily, don't touch the trigger."

"Trigger." She looks closely at the revolver. Her other hand is clenched.

I extend a hand slowly to her. "Give it to me."

"You don't come to my room anymore."

"I explained; I couldn't."

"It's a 'bad secret.'"

"It's not a secret anymore, Lily. Put the gun down, and we'll talk."

"You don't come to my room." She narrows her eyes and makes gunfire noises. "Poom-poom-poom." She moves around the room and aims the gun at tables, lamps, vases, and pictures. "Poom-poom-poom-poom-poom."

"Lily …"

"Is Lily being a bad girl?"

"Yes, she is. Now give me the gun."

She stops and faces me again across the room, her hands at her sides. "No. Richard is a bad boy. Do you want to know why you're bad?"

"Why?"

"Because I say so."

"Lily, I'm tired. I want to go to bed."

"You went away and left us. And you danced close with Margaret, and then you didn't come to my room, and now you came downstairs to be with Margaret."

"You don't understand."

"No, I don't." She looks at the gun again. "I have an itchy trigger finger. I heard someone on *The Lone Ranger* say that. Who is that masked man?" She creases her brow like the villain in a television Western. "I'm talkin' to you, pardner."

She raises the gun and pulls the trigger.

Her hand flies back, and she screams as the bullet explodes into the ceiling.

I move quickly toward her. *"Lily, give me that."*

She's too far away. She swings the gun down and around so that it's aimed at me again. "You wouldn't want to stop a piece of lead, now would ya, pardner?"

Margaret rushes back in from the kitchen. Her face is ashen. "What was that?"

I keep my eyes on Lily. "There's been an accident."

Margaret sees and says in a whisper, "Lily, the gun is dangerous."

"I know. You could die from it."

Margaret moves into my field of vision, toward Lily.

Lily turns the revolver toward her.

"I could shoot anybody here, if I wanted, if I got mad. Couldn't I?"

Margaret caresses her with her name. "Lily? Please. Lily?"

"I don't want to get mad. I heard both of you talking before. You were being quiet. You didn't want me to hear."

"We were only talking."

"About what?"

Margaret pauses. "Household matters."

Lily keeps the gun aimed at her sister, but she looks over at me. "Aren't I pretty anymore, Richard?"

"Of course you are."

"But you were downstairs alone with Margaret, in the middle of the night."

"Lily. I want you to stop this," says Margaret.

Lily imitates her, mocking, "*Lily. I want you to stop this.*"

"I'm very serious."

"*I'm very serious.*" Then she says, "*I'M* very serious, Margaret. You think I'm stupid. Richard thinks I'm stupid, but I'm not. Richard, you shouldn't do this to me." Her lower lip pushes out beyond her upper, into a pout. "You love Margaret."

"Lily, please," says Margaret.

"That's not fair." She turns to Margaret again. "Did you tell him?"

Margaret sighs. "No."

"Oh, you should have. It's a household matter. Don't you think so, Margaret?" Her sister doesn't answer her, but Lily insists, "Don't you?"

"Yes."

"You see, Richard," says Lily, "You have responsibilities. You're going to be a daddy." She smiles at the look on my face.

My jaw muscles are trembling. I turn to Margaret. "*Is that true?*"

"We went to the doctor, and he called two days later," Margaret says.

"Why didn't you *tell* me?"

"I wanted to find the right moment."

"She shouldn't have a child. Oh my God, Margaret."

"But she's going to."

"*I'm* here," says Lily. "You shouldn't love Margaret, Richard. You mustn't love Margaret."

"When did you find out, Margaret? Was it before the twelfth?"

"What?"

"When? *When* did you know?"

"Last week."

"What day?"

"Wednesday, I think."

"The eleventh?"

"I think so."

The first time back, while I'd gone out and found my acting job, Margaret got the news. Then, that night, she fed dinner to her husband, watched television with him, let him go to bed with her sister again, then—later, downstairs, executed him. This time—

"What will happen when the baby comes?" says Lily.

She gives us a moment to respond, but neither of us can come up with a word.

"I know you'll take it from me. But you shouldn't. I can take care of a baby." She folds her arms together in front of her and pretends to rock a baby. "See?"

"We see, Lily," says Margaret hollowly.

"You don't. You won't let me keep him, and then he won't have a mother. He won't have his family. Poor little baby." She looks sadly at the infant in her arms. "Poor little baby."

Margaret moves toward her again. "Everything will be fine, Lily. Now, give me the revolver."

Lily levels it at her. "You're the one," she says, clenching her other hand even tighter, into a white fist.

"Give me the pistol," says Margaret.

"We would be a family without you."

"Give it to me, dear."

"A happy little family."

Margaret takes another step toward her.

"Be careful," I whisper.

Lily continues aiming the revolver at her.

Margaret reaches out, only inches away from it. "Give it to me, dear."

Lily focuses raptly on her. "You're the one."

Margaret's hand moves closer. "Lily?"

"Poom. Poom. Poom. You're dead."

Margaret extends her hand toward the gun.

"Margaret!"

She stops and looks at me, then pulls her hand back.

Slowly, Lily turns the gun back toward me, and I have a flash of regret that I haven't used some of the information I've brought back with me about Kentucky Derby and World Series winners. My God, I could have bought some stock in Alcoa or Disney or Sony and guaranteed Jack Cade's future.

I think of the old character actor behind me, drinking the ink.

"Lily has a surprise or two up her sleeve, doesn't she?" She pauses, looking less hurt, more purposeful.

"Please, Lily," I say. "Give me the gun."

"I reckon I could drill you right between the eyes, pardner."

"Lily …"

"But I ain't a-gonna. 'Cause that's the *real* sidewinder."

She swings the gun back around toward Margaret.

She presses the trigger.

Margaret looks at me, no more than mildly startled, and drops.

The revolver is still gripped tightly in Lily's hand. She looks at me and raises her other hand, the fist. She reminds me of the woman standing on top of the mountain, raising the bicycle over her head, about to howl at the moon.

Her eyes examine me.

She beams, lowers her fist, and holds it out to me.

"See?" she says, her eyes flashing. "See? *Whoever you are?*"

She unclenches the upturned fist.

It's the key to my bedroom.

20

They tell me many years later, after I've remembered the events I've described, that Margaret was killed instantly. I don't believe that because when I looked back down at her, she was returning my stare, saying with her eyes, "If only you had been faithful. If only you had made half an effort, this wouldn't have happened."

Margaret had told her neighbor, Amy Jaekel, all her secrets, including the one about her husband's and her sister's affair, which accounted for the icy stares I'd gotten from that woman.

Lily was unprosecutable for Margaret's death, but Richard wasn't. I was booked for first-degree murder, or so I was told later.

What finally saved me was Richard's inability to cope with the weight of all the events in his life during the period of that April 10th through 15th, 1956.

I didn't crack immediately. At first, I defended myself with skill and—pardon my immodesty—finesse. I said that my sister-in-law had come upon Margaret's revolver through negligence on Margaret's part and, in a moment of anger and confusion, had shot her. I knew it wasn't a noble defense, but Lily was going to be put in a home anyway, and her baby would more than likely end up in an orphanage, and there was no reason for me to be sent away too.

But when they told me that Amy Jaekel had accused me of having an affair with Lily, Richard responded that nothing had been his fault, that a man named Jack Cade had taken him away against his will for the weekend previous to the shooting. When I was pressed for the details, I became, as the court termed it, "uncooperative and incoherent," then, finally, silent.

They indicted me for first-degree murder, but my attorney got me off as insane. Later, I would be called a "multiple personality."

I had difficulty talking about all that happened to me during the next four decades because I didn't remember most of it. I spent the time in four state mental facilities. The final one was the institution near Coolidge, which some of the residents waggishly called Coolidge Storage. It wasn't until after I'd been stored there for a while that, with the help of their chief psychotherapist, Dr. Harold Henry, I began to put things together. Dr. Henry was the first one who was willing to tell me anything about Lily. Almost from the beginning, according to Dr. Henry, she hadn't shown any will to live. After her baby was taken away from her, no amount of therapy or drugs was able to bring her out of her depression, and she died a year later.

I heard about it decades after the fact.

Jack and Richard each blamed the other for Lily's death, but they both understood their remorse was pointless, little more than a kind of vanity.

From the moment I realized that my attempt to implicate Lily had collapsed, I began making it as clear as I possibly could that I was in fact two people and not—as I appeared to be—one. This went on for longer than I can remember.

My "breakthrough" happened when I went to Dr. Henry for my session one day, reversed my position, and said that Jack Cade had gone away.

I sat down, facing Dr. Henry, yanked a chunk of hair out of my head and said, "Look. Eight or ten hairs—see? And every one of them comes from the head of Richard Blake. That other one ... that other 'personality'—he's gone now. He's gone forever."

It was a posture I realized it was time to assume.

It made me feel good, that I could do that. If I could drop the other persona, it meant I was *not* schizophrenic—which had been my primary diagnosis.

It was encouraging to think I wasn't crazy.

Even though deep inside me, I was still pretty sure I was.

21

FRIDAY, OCTOBER 11, 1996

I, now as the old Richard Blake, wake up in my rented room and look at the calendar I bought the day I was released from Coolidge. It is exactly the same day—Friday, October 11, 1996—as it was when Jack Cade woke up in a chair in his home to find Sophie staring at the ring on his finger; the day Jack first met Maggie Partridge in La Vieja. Except now there is no Maggie Partridge …

I manage to finagle (without proper ID) a Dodge Dart from Rent-A-Wreck and drive out to La Vieja.

There is no car in the driveway now. A shaggy-haired young man is mowing the lawn next door, in front of the house that used to belong to Amy Jaekel.

I understand that it makes no sense to be here. But what else can I do? I've come where I have to be. I'm here on time.

I have no reason to expect anyone to be home. I ring the front doorbell anyway.

Through the door, I hear someone come into the foyer. The footsteps stop. The door opens two or three inches.

Maggie Partridge peers out.

"Yes?" she says. She doesn't seem to recognize me, but why would she?

Richard Blake is an old man. Maggie Partridge never met him anyway.

"It's me. Jack Cade. You've been expecting me, right?"

"Of course." She continues staring at me. Her expression remains the same. I hear some kind of twittering in the background. Birds? I can't tell if they're inside or out.

"You know who I am?" I say.

"Of course."

Thank God. "I'm so glad to see you."

"Thank you."

I realize she doesn't have any makeup on and her formerly shiny auburn hair is dull and uncombed. She wears a faded dress. She doesn't look well.

"May I come in?"

She opens the door and I go inside, into the foyer. I look up toward the second floor. My knees are shaking. I concentrate as hard as I can on keeping my feet beneath me.

Not appearing to notice, she leads me through the passageway into the living room. I walk slowly, haltingly, behind her.

The furniture from 1956 is gone. The room is spartan but not neat. There are a couple of ordinary-looking easy chairs, an old imitation leather sofa, and a television set with a VCR. An uneven layer of dust covers all of it, including the bare wood floor.

"Won't you sit down?" she says.

I lower myself into one of the chairs. "Thank you."

"Would you like a cup of coffee?"

"No."

"Tea?" She lifts her eyebrows, nodding insistently.

"Yes, well … all right. Thank you." She moves off toward the kitchen.

I notice a newspaper on the table next to me. It's this day's *Los Angeles Times.* I scan it. It hasn't been much of a news day. Carlos Felipe Ximenes Belo and José Ramos-Horta shared the Nobel Peace Prize "for their work toward a just and peaceful solution to the conflict in East Timor"—wherever that is. Vice presidential candidates Jack Kemp and Al Gore debated last night. Neither of them appeared to be a clear winner, according to the *Times* pundit. The O.J. Simpson civil trial is soon to begin. Apparently, Mr. Simpson was exonerated in the criminal one; I remember hearing about that.

My eyes are drawn to the bottom of the page. It's a fluff piece about the latest Marilyn Monroe products. She's not only a movie star who's been gone for over a third of a century; she's now a brand. The latest items are Marilyn cookie jars, and a winery called Marilyn Wines has just released something called *Marilyn Merlot*. I've spent most of my life with a crush on a brand. That probably says something about … *something*.

Maggie Partridge serves me tea and sits on the sofa opposite me. After a lengthy moment of gazing silently at and away from each other, she says, "What are you doing here?"

"I was going to ask you the same thing." I look around the room and notice for the first time that the portrait of Lily is still over the fireplace. I point to it and say, "Lily." She doesn't respond. "Everything has changed so much. I couldn't find out what happened to Rita—my mother." I stare at her, trying to measure her response, but she looks past me with no evident thoughts about what I've said. "I didn't die, obviously. I'm trying to think what any of this may have taught me, but I can't." I surprise myself with an eruption of old man's giggles. "There are worse things than being an out-of-work television actor."

"Are you all right?" She's looking at me with concern—or it could be alarm.

"Yes, I'm fine. Look, I just want to go back and get out of this. I want to undo some wrong things. I met someone the last time back and ended up letting her down. I want to go back and *not* meet her this trip. I don't want to cause her any more trouble than she already has. And I want to stay out of Margaret's and Lily's lives as much as I can. I don't want to do anything more than make it possible for them to create their own fates. I want to work my way back to my original path. I realized when I found there is no record of my mother ever having lived in California that we'd opened too many doors. Can you explain why I could never locate her?"

"No."

"You should be able to. You should be able to account for something like that."

Again, she doesn't say anything and now it seems to me her eyes are unreflective, opaque. She reminds me of most of the inmates at Coolidge.

"What would you like to do now?" she says.

"Didn't you understand? I want to go *back*. You should have known more about this before you sent me off. I hoped I would only be gone a few seconds—like I was the first time, but look at this place. Look at you. It took me all this time to work my way back here, and now something's gone wrong. I dreamed of you being here, and here you are, but this is … all wrong."

The smile remains on her face, but it's clearly strained.

"You shouldn't be here." My tone is blunt; I can see she's afraid. "You don't really know about me, do you? As it is now, Jack Cade never did any testing through the Screen Actors Guild for the Southern California Psychology Group. As it is now, Jack Cade doesn't even exist. *You should NOT be here*."

"Then why did you come? If you didn't come to see me, what are you doing here?"

"I'm lost," I say. "You aren't listed in any of the Los Angeles phone directories. There was an M. Partridge in Orange County, but it wasn't you. I tried every Partridge in Los Angeles, and I couldn't find you. And now I'm scared to death you don't exist any more than Jack Cade does."

She gets up from the sofa and moves with studied control to the television set. She puts a tape into the VCR and turns back to me. Her eyebrows are twisted in anger. "You tell me what this is." She turns on the set and steps back to watch it.

Maggie Partridge appears on the screen. She addresses the camera: "My name is Dr. L.M. Partridge. The experiment I hope to videotape is a result of what I think is a perfect confluence of circumstances: of time, place, and subject."

Partridge turns off the VCR. "Who's that?"

"Pardon?"

She makes a long, low hissing noise and turns the machine on again. "*That.*"

The Maggie Partridge on the screen continues: "Time has now passed. My subject, Jack Cade, has traveled successfully to 1956, and I have now sent him back for the second time. Now it's in the laps of—I hesitate to evoke—the gods. A footnote about this house: *I* am the private party who leases it to the county."

The woman on the television pauses and seems to decide whether she should go on recording or not. "I must add a personal postscript," she says. "While I believe my particular project here is unique, I am firmly convinced that the government has been doing this work for years. I have tried to make my way into their program, but so far, I've been rejected.

"So now I proceed with my own work. It's unlikely that Jack Cade will return, or that I will ever see him again, at least as the person he is now. As for Richard Blake, if he is not killed by Margaret—if he survives—I don't have any idea how that will affect me. But how could I be the same person? The alteration of the lives of three insignificant people in the San Fernando Valley shouldn't have any effect on most of the world, but it's sure as hell likely to have one on me."

My arms feel as if they're rising into the air without my permission—like my body is going to fly away, just drift up into the ether.

Partridge snaps off the machine. "Who is that?"

I'm trembling. "It's you."

"It *isn't.*"

She's standing between me and the fireplace. Over her shoulder is the portrait of Lily.

"Is that the end of the tape?"

"No."

"Show me the rest of it, Maggie."

A short shrill burst. "*That's not my name.*"

"What *is* your name?"

"You *know* what it is. You're not from the hospital. Who are you?"

"The hospital?"

"Of course. You're from the government or something."

"When did they let you out … of the hospital?"

"You know when. Ten years ago. And you know my name. It's Lily. Lily Margaret Partridge." She tries to calm herself. "I was named after my mother and my aunt. Partridge was the name of the people who adopted me."

I try to stand up but can't. "Who was your father?"

It's as if she's taken off a mask, revealing something contorted, an undernourished soul. "My father is an evil spirit; my father is a murderer. He was insane, and they sent him away. I asked about him, but nobody would tell me. They wouldn't tell me about my blood family because my blood family were all insane—except my aunt." She forces a smile. "And me. I'm not insane. I take after Margaret … You see how well I do with your test? You try to scare me and make me give the wrong answer, but you can't because I'm perfectly all right. I watch myself all day long. Every day! And there's nothing wrong with me."

"How did you come to have this house?"

"It was left to me. I remember one of my doctors said, 'Fair is fair. They may have put bats in your belfry, your parents, but at least they left you a house.'" Her look darkens again. "And you're not going to take it away from me now."

"I … don't want … to take your home away from … you." My voice is quivering. "What happened to Mrs. Partridge? Or Mr. Partridge? Or whoever adopted you?"

"You *know* what happened. I only lived with them for … a year maybe, but I kept the name." She points at the television. "That woman is another trick, isn't she?"

"Yes, that's right. She's a trick."

Lily Margaret Partridge looks momentarily pleased—in the singular way only a lunatic can. She turns on the VCR again, and there she is as Dr. Maggie Partridge, Dr. L.M. Partridge, speaking to us.

"Why am I doing this? Because I stumbled onto Jack Cade. Pursuing my work, I stumbled onto Jack Cade. And it was simple. I was given the opportunity to save my father's life. There were drawbacks. Using Jack Cade—as I had to—was unfortunate. But anyone else would have done the same thing, given the chance. I had to save Richard Blake's life. Has there ever been an orphaned girl who wouldn't go to any lengths, take any risks, to find her father? I may not be honored in the scientific community for what I've done, but who in my position wouldn't do the same thing? Aren't we all—all of us—simply looking for our emergence into the light? I only hope that when I meet him, I recognize him. Wouldn't it be ironic if I didn't?"

Lily Margaret stands off to the side, watching me, rather than the image of her other self on the screen. Between and above us hangs the portrait of her mother, looking over us as unconcernedly as she might have in life, blithely unaware of any irony.

When Dr. L.M. Partridge's videotape recording is over, Lily Margaret turns it off, but the television remains on. It's tuned to a vacant channel.

"Where did you get that tape?"

"I don't know. It's always been here."

"Why did you show it to me now?"

"I don't know."

We stare at each other for a very long time.

"Who takes care of you? How do you live?"

"There was an estate for me. My family had a house full of expensive furniture, and there was some insurance. And somebody buys my food."

"And what do you do?"

"Do?"

"What do you do with your life?"

"I wait."

"For what?"

"I don't know."

"Wouldn't you rather be taken care of again?"

Her eyes grow large. "In the home? No. I'm happy here on my own."

"But you're all alone."

"I like being alone. When you leave, I'll be alone, and I'll be fine. I keep busy. I have my parakeets."

Ah. The birds—the *parakeets*. There's a full life.

I hear Margaret say, "Lily. I wanted to talk about Lily—and the unspeakable damage that's been done to her." In some cowled-over fissure deep in my brain, my recycled memory—like a long-lost mountaineering casualty laboring to stay alive—conjures up images of the other L.M. Partridge and of Lily—all of them variations on a theme. I was fascinated by them, hypnotized. In one of those ancient chapters of my history, I remember hearing someone say the universe might have five dimensions, maybe as many as eleven. I feel a sudden longing for the protective walls of the state institution at Coolidge.

Lily Margaret rocks back and forth from her heels to her toes, gazing up at her mother's portrait on the wall, then at the television set, at the fuzzy, snowy nothingness of a channel that's not broadcasting.

"I keep busy," says Lily. "I like being alone."

I get to my feet and slouch toward the passageway.

Still rocking, she begins to hum some old but vaguely familiar tune.

I turn and look back at her one last time.

She doesn't notice. She has no idea she's singing for her father.

22

FRIDAY, OCTOBER 11, 1996 (CONT'D)

"May I help you?" says Mr. Parsons in his high fluty voice.

"I wonder if I might have a few words with you."

He looks me up and down. "Is it about jewelry?"

I can't just blurt out what I'm doing here. "Yes … well, partly."

"Partly?"

"Can we be somewhere private? Your office?"

He measures me again with his eyes. "All right. Come with me." He leads me to the room where we first talked. Parsons motions to the chair Sophie sat in the last time.

I try to sit, miss the target, manage to catch myself, and land awkwardly in the chair.

"Are you all right?"

"I'm fine, thanks. Just a little shaky, I guess."

Parsons clears his throat. "What may I do for you?" He seems too reserved. Maybe he's afraid this old man is going to have a heart attack in his office.

"Could you tell me how much a perfect or near-perfect seven-and-a-quarter carat alexandrite would be worth?"

"That would depend."

"Ballpark."

"May I see it?"

"I don't have it anymore. That's my problem. I … uh, gave it away."

Parsons' gaze darts away and immediately back. "I really couldn't tell you without seeing it."

"Actually, I know its value without asking." I gulp a deep breath. "Do you recognize me?"

"I beg your pardon?"

"We met once before."

"When?"

"Um … well, it was recently. But a … a lot of things have changed since then. Time has a way of doing that, doesn't it?" I aim for a relaxed smile but miss. I muster a weary shrug. "Actually, I'm glad to find you here at all. I stopped a few blocks away at the Beverly Vue Apartments, but I realized I don't know the old boy's name—my wife's patient, I mean. And so I can't find … my … I can't find … Sophie. That's my wife's name—Sophie. And no one I know lives in our house." I realize I'm swallowing back the beginnings of a sob. "I can't find her … anywhere."

He doesn't look surprised at my babbling; not suspicious, only guarded. "I never met you. I have a good memory for faces."

"I was a young man then. And the truth is, I wasn't exactly the person you're seeing now." With renewed fervor, I tell him, "I'm a gemologist too." Parsons tries to interrupt me, but I keep going. "*PLEASE, LET ME FINISH*. You gave me some information about an alexandrite, and then you said I should try to find out where it came from. But I didn't have any luck with that, and now all this time has passed—even though it was only a couple of days ago."

Parson's expression has gone from unreadable to a near scowl, and it strikes me that I might be on the right track.

"I need to know if there's a … a … connection between the alexandrite and the ebony box that began all this." I wipe away some of the tears that have begun to flow down my cheeks. "Allergies."

He picks up the telephone on his desk and says something in muted treble tones.

"You told me Plato said precious stones are living beings. What was your point? Were you talking about me? Do you know who gave me the alexandrite? Did you have the answer yourself all along? I know you think I'm crazy. I know you just told somebody to come in here and get rid of me but please, before they do, try to answer me. For God's sake, give me some help here!"

Parsons' eyes flick back and forth between the door and me.

"I'd begun to think I might not be mad after all, but I need you to substantiate that. I'm desperate, you see."

"Yes, I believe that."

The attractive woman from the first time and a young man with hair that looks like a limp beret open the door and come into the room. The man isn't physically formidable, but he's big enough to handle an old man.

As they lead me out of Parsons' office, I yell, "I know you know what's happening. Why won't you tell me?"

A block south of what was once Morgan's Gifts, I find a dubious, dimly lit workingman's tavern called Doug and Bea's. Behind the bar, a sluggish bartender of indeterminate age wearing a dirty pinstripe dress shirt with a large coffee stain at the crest of his beer belly squints at a newspaper.

There are two customers at four o'clock in the afternoon, sitting at opposite ends of the bar, a woman and a man. The woman is in a nondescript gray polyester dress, too tight for her spreading figure, and has what looks like a self-administered haircut. I estimate by the angle of her slump over the bar that she's been here since the place opened quite a bit earlier in the day.

The man looks to be middle-aged, but I can't tell much more than that because he wears an old Dodgers baseball cap with the brim tipped down over his forehead.

Jack or Richard, or whoever I am as my backside comes to rest on a bar stool halfway between the other two customers, says, "Give me a whiskey, please."

The bartender goes on reading his newspaper.

"Uh … Doug? Are you Doug? May I have a whiskey?"

"Doug passed on eight years ago."

"Nevertheless, I'd like a whiskey—when you have a moment."

"Got till two in the morning, or hell freezes over, whichever comes first." He finishes what he's reading. "What kind of whiskey?"

"I don't know. *Four Roses*. You got that?"

The bartender grunts and pulls a bottle down from a shelf beneath a long mirror that runs the length of the bar.

I sip the first whiskey and am well into the next one before it occurs to me that the aged body I'm dwelling in probably can't tolerate much more. I feel as if I'm about to pass out. I rub my eyes, blink several times, and see that the bartender, who is now washing glasses, has set his newspaper down.

"May I?" I point at the paper. The bartender lifts his shoulders to say it couldn't matter less to him. I pick it up. It's the same edition of the *Los Angeles Times* I saw earlier at Shoemaker Drive. Having trouble focusing, I look at the item about Marilyn again and think about the time I was in a movie with her. I lift the paper so I can see it better.

I catch sight of an elderly man in the mirror, sitting at the bar, chuckling, also holding a newspaper. I don't remember seeing anybody come into this place since I got here fifteen or twenty minutes ago. Anyhow, he appears to be more or less my contemporary, and he's a confused-looking old guy. I consider buying him a drink, until I notice there are still only three customers in Doug and Bea's.

"C'est moi!" I giggle.

The old man in the mirror laughs out loud, then gazes into—I'm not sure where, his mind apparently drifting.

Picking up the newspaper again, I realize Richard is fantasizing about Sophie.

The old man in the mirror scowls.

Richard is having unclean thoughts about my wife. Randy old bastard.

I drift some more, look at the paper again, tap two fingers on the column about Marilyn, and say, "I had a … a thing with her." I glance at the woman, whose glazed focus remains on the bar her head is steadily approaching.

The bartender frowns up at me. "Who?"

"Marilyn Monroe."

He looks me up and down. "Zat right? You and Marilyn, huh? When was this?"

"Oh, a lifetime ago. She thought I was … kind, I guess. And then … And then, we had a … Well, you know …"

The bartender's eyes have narrowed into puffy little slits.

"She used to be every man's dream." I look down, lower the newspaper, and mumble, "Still is, I guess. And for a little while, she was my …" I'm mortified I brought this up and search boozily for the right words to put an end to this conversation. "She was … uh, my … friend."

"Marilyn Monroe was your pal. Rii-iight. And you got it on with your pal, is that what you're telling me?"

"I didn't say that."

He chuckles obscenely.

"You're right," I say. "You don't want to pay any attention to me. I'm just a crazy old … duffer."

The bartender shakes his head and goes back to washing glasses.

I look in the mirror again, the way Jack used to when he was young, trying to locate any signs of depth within his soul. But my eyes aren't as good as they once were, and for a long moment, I have the hazy notion that there's a legion of people in there, looking back at me—male and female, past and present—all trying to sort themselves out. At the same time, I feel, for a moment anyway, a kind of drunken serenity at being lost in something larger.

"You looking at me?"

I glance around me but see no one other than the three characters who were here when I came in. I look at the bartender, still washing glasses. I notice the woman's head is still on its peaceful slow-mo descent toward the bar.

Then, I catch sight of the other customer, the man in the Dodgers baseball cap at the end of the bar, watching me in the mirror.

"Pardon me?" I say to the image.

The man gets slowly off his bar stool. He picks up a canvas bag on the floor next to him by its floppy handles, moves toward me, and sits down again, one stool away.

I notice the man's long, unkempt hair sticking out from under his cap. It doesn't look dirty, and from what I can tell, he looks as if he takes care of himself pretty well. Just another barroom eccentric, I guess. But he doesn't hold himself like the average barfly.

"Lonely being by yourself, isn't it?", he says.

"Who says I'm by myself?"

"Well, I'm the only company you seem to have. Both of them"—the man nods at the bartender and the woman—"are living in their own worlds, in their own peculiar ways. Here, why don't you take a look at this?" He reaches into the canvas bag and produces an ebony box about seven or eight inches square.

I stare at it.

He hands it to me.

I open the front plate and listen to the familiar teensy-weensy-world strains of a generic early rock and roll song. "*Who are you?*" I say. The man looks at his drink, not answering the question. "Do you know *anything*? *Please* tell me. Do you know anything about the alexandrite? I gave it to Marilyn."

"No no no," the man chuckles. "You didn't give it to her. I did." He shrugs. "But I seem to have gotten it back." He holds up his right hand, palm down, swiveling it back and forth. "I don't know when. I don't remember that part." He shows me a shadowy grin. "But I did—get it back. This thing seems to have a life of its own."

Even in the murk of the tavern, there's enough illumination to see the alexandrite he's wearing. It's picking up both the incandescent light in the bar and a thin shaft of daylight slipping in through the dented, splayed blinds over one of the grimy windows.

The stone sparkles, first red, then green.

"Why won't you tell me who you are?"

The man sighs. "Because I'm doubtful you'd believe me. Here. Do you want it back? I think you should have it." He slips the alexandrite ring off and hands it to me. I take it and close my right fist around it.

"Why are you giving this to me?"

"I don't know. Think of me as your personal angel, if you like." He laughs.

"But you've already given me the passport, haven't you? This thing." I look back at the old music box. "This was how I started the journey."

"Oh, you can go ahead and try that, I guess." He shrugs. "But it's probably a red herring. Little doodads like that are almost always red herrings of one kind or another. But we keep hauling them around as if they mean something."

"Then why are you giving it to me?"

"Well, you never know for sure, do you?"

"But I have to try it, don't I?" I say. "The road I've come hasn't worked out—for either … for any of the facets of me. If I can go back, don't I *have* to try?"

He shakes his head. "It's my opinion that the real magic changes all the time. It's hardly ever in the same place twice. You can rarely see it or hold it. And when you can, it never looks or feels the same. It never is the same." He smiles. "Except maybe once in a while, when the fact that it's the same is different."

"Please, tell me who you are."

He seems to look at some point deep inside the space just above my eyes. Then he takes off the Dodgers cap and slowly lifts his face so that it's caught in the beam of sunlight through the window.

He's in his early forties and has obviously been living a hard life. But he seems almost peaceful.

"She said I might run into you!"

"Who said?"

He knows perfectly well who. The thing that now causes me to pass out in Doug and Bea's is not the liquor, it's the shock of recognition.

The man in the baseball cap is Jack Cade.

23

When I come to, he's gone. I've missed the greatest opportunity I imagine I could ever have—to ask myself some hard questions, the ones only I might know the answer to. Like: Who are we? What are we doing here? Where are we? I mean, *really* where are we? Where are we going? Have we gotten any of it right so far? What one change could I make so that my having been here might turn out to be a good thing? Questions like that.

Meanwhile, Richard's presence wouldn't have mattered one way or the other. He would have stood aloof, I imagine, oblivious to my blind probing—to my clumsy speculations on the absence or presence of God. This haunted shell I live in (Richard), this, if I may be forgiven for saying so, pod-person witness to my consciousness, this sad, haunted old man who occasionally speaks my words, does not see out of the same eyes I do.

Whoever *I* am.

APPROXIMATELY TUESDAY, OCTOBER 15, 1996

When I get back to my tiny apartment, I sleep for what feels like no more than a couple of hours.

When I wake up it's the afternoon of the next day (I *think*, although I can't guarantee that). It was fitful sleep, crowded with dreams, only one of which I remember—although I'm left with the vague feeling that all those dreams were the same one, repeating itself over and over, as if I were an especially slow-witted undergraduate student who had to sit through the same lecture a hundred times, until the message I was meant to grasp finally sank in. It struck me that my whole life has been something like that.

At one point in the dream I heard the voice of the guy in the baseball cap (he is me, I've claimed, although—as I think I've said before—I'm no longer sure). I heard him say, "A little low-gear this morning, aren't we, Mr. Cade?" I didn't know why he was being so formal with me. It was as if, despite his teacherly reproach, he was trying to pay me more respect than I'm used to, more than I consider is actually due me. And in a way, I confess I appreciated that extra consideration. It seemed to me the least we all deserve.

"Exactly," he said.

He'd been reading my mind. "What else?" I asked him, but he just looked at me, as if he knew things but didn't know exactly how to tell them to me, or was paying deference to the old man's diminished capacities.

I tried to remember the hard questions I'd wanted to ask him, but I couldn't think of one. So I said, "It seems to me you're expecting me to put my faith in … silence, in the invisible, in nothing more than intuition. What I need to know is, what am I not seeing?"

"Anything, I assume, because you act as if you believe in nothing."

"That's not true. I see what has to be magic all around me, but I don't know what it is or where it comes from."

"So then I'm wrong, you are seeing something—something spectacular."

"Yes, but I don't know what it is, or how to explain it."

"And what you're left with is …?"

"Doubts, thousands of doubts. And fear. I have endless fears."

"I can imagine."

…He shrugged and I studied our images in the mirror behind the bar, wondering which one of us was real, if either of us was.

"What are you looking at?"

"I'm trying to figure out who we are."

He laughed. "You don't look at what conceals the truth to find the truth."

"If I could just make out who you are and what I am and what we're doing together, maybe I'd have a shot at understanding why I got sent on this journey. I mean, I'd like to get back a little control over my life."

He shook his head, took his hat off, then put it on again, but backwards. "This is how the kids wear them these days, huh?"

"What days are these?" I said. "I've lost track."

"It doesn't matter."

"It does to me."

He smiled. "Do you believe the past causes the present?"

"What?"

"What do you think?"

"Does the past cause the present? I don't know, I guess."

"But the past is gone," he said. "How can something that doesn't exist have any bearing on this moment?"

"I don't know. Doesn't the history we all live through change the world?" I realized as I asked it that that was a dense question, the way I'd put it. "I mean it changes the way we look at the world. And how we look at the world is what the world is."

"I don't think so," he said. "And I don't think you'd want to subject that theory to any serious test of logic."

"No, I'm right," I insisted. I didn't like being told I was wrong. "Reality is what we perceive it to be."

"Same with that one."

That made me mad. "Look at the diminishing number of species in the world. If we hadn't been greedy for all that ivory, the elephant population wouldn't be dwindling the way it is."

"That's true," he said. "But listen to the question again: 'Does the past cause the present?' I'm not talking about what we did or didn't do. I'm asking you about time, time itself—time past or any other form of it—I'm saying it has no effect whatever on what is, on right now. Can time undo? Can it restore?" He picked up the LA Times still lying on the bar. "Can time reverse one single occurrence from the so-called past?"

I had no answer. In fact, I was suddenly pretty sure he had me. He was right. And it was disconcerting, to say the least, to realize that the old man I was didn't get to be that way, physically, mentally or any other way, because time did it to me. Time has no tools. Time is not the culprit. I don't even know if there is a culprit. At any rate, it wasn't the past that had turned me into this crotchety old man. So I asked him what seemed like a reasonable question, at least at the time. "What is time?"

I was watching him very closely. A big grin spread over my old self's face. Through a robust laugh, he said, "I don't know. I've got suspicions, but I'm not positive."

"What do you suspect?"

"Well …" He lifted the bill of his cap and scratched the back of his head. "The way it feels to me … is that there probably isn't any such thing—time, I mean. If there was, there wouldn't be any eternity. I mean eternity flat-out eradicates any notion of time. My own personal feeling about time (if I'm allowed a personal feeling about anything) is—fuh-geddaboudit. It doesn't exist. It just seems to me," he went on, "as if for some unknown reason, this is something almost none of us have chosen to look at very closely."

And here he started to fade away.

"No, no, don't go yet," I said. "I haven't learned a single thing."

"Oh, don't worry about that. Eventually you'll know everything. I can't travel your road for you. I seem to be you, but I'm not … exactly—except of course in the sense that everything—time, if you want to go on believing in that, as well as space, and the outer borders of reality itself—are all at the exact center of you."

"So maybe I am you."

He smiled. "Yes, maybe you are."

"Would that make this a magic experience?"

"I prefer to think of it as a holy one. Whenever you encounter yourself it's a holy experience."

He shrugged, smiled, and was entirely without form. Only these words lingered: "The thing you have been looking with is the thing you are looking for."

"What the hell's that supposed to mean?" I called after him.

"Pleasure, like pain, comes and goes," he said. "Joy, rediscovered, lasts forever. It's really cool."

Then there was only silence, and I knew I'd missed my chance again. At first, I felt a sharp disappointment.

But by the time I woke up, I was okay. I felt more or less ready to do whatever I have to.

I take a few moments to mark the passing of the old Richard Blake. Still a little fuzzy in the head, it occurs to me to pee in his shoes, but that doesn't seem very mature, so instead, I tear up his Denny's Early Bird card.

Then, with my mind on the future (in this case—I hope—the past), I place the ebony box next to the alexandrite ring on the counter between the bedroom and kitchenette and open it. I do my best to replicate the conditions of light and sound I remember from the two times Maggie Partridge sent me back, which means silence and only indirect daylight through the windows.

But it's far from silent in my room; I should have known. I can't get into the picture and am unable to transport myself into deep space, or back to anything outside the shabbiness I'm living in. If there are any wormholes in my apartment, they were made by worms.

I work with the ebony box several times for the next two days, but still no luck.

I consider the consequences of what I'm trying to do. If I manage to get back to 1956 again, and do what I want to—not make waves, stay out of Lily's bed—L.M. Partridge will never exist in the form of Maggie, or Lily Margaret, or any other way. Maggie Partridge said she wasn't judging me morally, but wasn't that really a way of telling me, "Please *don't* stay out of Lily's bed—because if you do, it will render me null and void"? Did she take such a risk with her existence, her very survival, because she was hungry for immortality through her work? How does that differ from athletes willing to die pitifully young in order to break some trivial record?

And why didn't the cancellation of Maggie Partridge's existence obliterate this whole experience? Why didn't I, at the moment of the non-conception of Dr. Partridge, find myself sitting in my house in North Hollywood with no memory of any of this? I assume the original Dr. Maggie Partridge gambled that I wouldn't return to a moment when I might make a decision to stay out of Lily's bed and cancel her own existence.

I remember Dr. Partridge's words: "Jack Cade's life can't just arbitrarily end." I wonder if I stumbled across proof of that at Doug and Bea's. On the other hand, I was a drunken old man that afternoon a few days ago. What makes me think I wasn't hallucinating? And if I am out there in that other form, what does that have to do with the man whose body I'm walking around in?

The lunatic is in the hall.

I don't know anything. I haven't for a long time now, unless I count the dawning perception that living and dying terrify me equally.

Long after nightfall, I drive out to La Vieja, park my car down the street, and walk through the darkness to 1833 Shoemaker Drive. I have on a black jacket, a black cap, and easy-fit blue jeans.

I duck behind a hedge at Amy Jaekel's old house, go around to the back, then slide with considerable difficulty through a gap in the wooden fence into the Blakes' old backyard. There are no lights on inside. It's two in the morning. She's probably asleep.

Although it's only the middle of October, it's a cold San Fernando Valley evening. I sit on the ground near the old mesquite tree but far enough away from it that the sky won't be blocked out by its branches. The weatherman said there is a high-pressure area in Los Angeles and as a result, clear skies. I plan to sit in the backyard of Richard Blake's old house and look into the night sky from the exact point in the universe where he lived.

If—predicated on Einstein's curvature of space-time—dreamtime theory is what it's represented to be, and if the universe is five dimensional (or more) as I was told dreamtime connotes, and if I can, with Jack's particular susceptibilities to autosuggestion (and, by now, my experience at it), once again enter into that dreamtime, as I have apparently done before ... I can at least hope I will travel back to April 10, 1956.

Or else, I'm just nuts, and I'm stuck as this old man until I croak.

The night grows colder, the ground damper. I have no success with time transportation but do pretty well imagining myself through the younger eyes of the souls inside me—at least the ones I know about. I see a disoriented old man trying to do something any child knows is impossible.

The lunatic is on the grass.

As I steal away from Lily Margaret Partridge's backyard shortly before dawn and am getting into my Dodge Dart, I look back at the house and see that a light has been turned on in a room on the second floor.

A lonely figure is silhouetted in the window, looking blindly out into the darkness, her parakeets twittering behind her like a feathery Greek tragedy chorus.

Back at my place, in a hot bath, trying to drive the chill out of my bones, I am haunted by visions of Lily Margaret. When I was sitting in the backyard, I was able to feel her upstairs in the house. I imagined her being aware in some animal way of her father sitting out in the wet grass trying to figure out a way to transport himself back to an earlier time. No doubt she couldn't have conceived of this. But maybe she could—maybe that was right down the middle of what her solitary brain could conjure. Maybe she was aware of the inside-out logic of what I was doing and that I was doing it, and she welcomed it. Maybe it had started earlier. Maybe the notion of the cancellation of her existence, and the termination of her pain forever, was squirting around the impenetrable regions of her consciousness all the time father and daughter were having their tête-à-tête, three or four days ago, the second Friday in October of 1996. I giggle, imagining the board of directors meeting when they decided I was no longer mentally ill and that they should release me from Coolidge into the population at large.

In the kitchenette, I stare at the alexandrite, under fluorescent light. Pale green. In bed, I can't sleep. I think of Lily and Margaret. I look at the alexandrite again. I have thought of it as the touchstone to a horror story. The truth is, this unfathomable gem has been the marker for two stories. One emerges out of darkness and fear—the red, nighttime facet. The other, the green daylight façade, reveals a place in me where, if I were to tap into myself and see what I am, I might be surprised. In a good way.

I might find immensity—my home, my garden, my wife, my freedom, my life.

WEDNESDAY, OCTOBER 16, OR THURSDAY, OCTOBER 17, 1996

I wake up shortly after noon with the beginnings of a cold. By evening, it has blossomed into wheezing and sniffling, and I work with the deep space in the ebony box again.

Nothing.

I take my watch and the alexandrite ring off, wash my hands and face, dry off, wrap myself in a blanket, and slump down in front of the television, surfing channels, feeling miserable.

I watch an old *I Love Lucy* rerun. Lucy is dressed up like a man, and Ricky pretends he doesn't know it's her.

I doze off. When I wake up, Lucy and Ricky are on the road to Hollywood. It's an *I Love Lucy* marathon. My cold is brutal. I doze off again.

When I wake up next, they're showing *What's My Line?* I've never seen reruns of that before. I don't have a TV Guide, but I guess I'm watching the Nickelodeon channel on cable. The next time I look up, a white-haired man, nearly as old as I am, is talking to the camera. He says, "The ability to get to the verge without getting into war is the necessary art. If you cannot master it, you inevitably get into war. If you try to run away from it, if you are afraid to go to the brink, you are lost." An announcer says, "Secretary of State John Foster Dulles."

I close my eyes again.

I don't have cable television.

I open my eyes and take a deep breath through my nose. It's entirely unclogged.

My cold is gone.

I reach for my tumbler of Scotch and drain it.

As I put the glass down, I look at my hand.

It is not an old man's hand.

I haven't had a Scotch in decades. "John Foster Dulles?"

I get out of the chair easily and turn from the television to see Margaret standing in front of me, her hands on her hips.

"Please, Richard. We're guests here. Come in and join us this instant."

"I've lost my ring."

"Well, drunks do things like that."

"But I don't care."

24

SATURDAY, DECEMBER 31, 1955

It is somewhere between eleven and eleven thirty P.M. I am at the home of the head of the geology department at UCLA, Dr. H.P. Tandler. I am (according to what's happened *previously*) about to lose my job.

I haven't gone back to the same time, and I remember something about a "Cauchy horizon" and the impossibility of traveling from certain moments to certain other moments, then realize I don't really care. I'm back. I'm close enough. I'm young again.

I give Margaret a kiss that feels to her—I can tell—as if it has passion in it. As a matter of fact, it does—passion and joy. I squeeze her shoulders. "I'm going to go wash my face and come back in and join the group." On my way to the washroom, I turn back to her. "Damn, Margaret. You look fine."

She stares at me, suspicious, stimulated. "Please hurry," she says in an imperious, puzzled tone. Frowning in a funny, sexy way, she leaves the room to go back to the party.

I go into the guest bathroom. In the mirror is Jack's first memory of Richard Blake, even younger—three months, ten days, a few hours, and a couple of nanoseconds, compensating for my distance from the mirror. My eyes fill with tears.

I look at my ringless right hand. The last time I saw the alexandrite, it was on the counter between my bedroom and kitchenette of the apartment over forty years later. It doesn't matter. It isn't the real magic anyway.

I sober up fast. Olga Tandler corners me when I rejoin the others and I listen, engrossed, as she tells me everything she likes and everything she finds "synthetic" about Los Angeles, and I bob my head and smile and agree with all of it, never puncturing her airs with even subtle unkindness, and it occurs to one side of me or the other that somewhere along the way that arrow has been eliminated from our quiver.

At midnight, she kisses me with wet enthusiasm and soon, far from being hostile to me, Dr. Tandler's wife will be my biggest supporter. She stands closer after the kiss, whispering how much we have in common on little puffs of warm moist breath. As Margaret and I leave the party, I imagine Olga Tandler telling her husband what a bright, charming young man that Richard Blake is.

SUNDAY, JANUARY 1, 1956—WEDNESDAY, FEBRUARY 29, 1956

Margaret, Lily, and Richard/Jack take up housekeeping again. Richard doesn't get fired from his job. He quits going to bed with his wife's sister, and I think it's likely Margaret never purchases a revolver.

There is a confrontation a few days later. It seems that my new openness has wiped out Margaret's earlier tendency to let her anger smolder inside her and she is now speaking more directly. After dinner one evening, the three of us are watching television. Lily gets up, yawns pointedly, and says, "Richard, I'm going to bed now."

Trying to conceal a wince, I say, "Sweet dreams, Lily."

But she doesn't leave. She repeats herself. "I'm going to bed *now*, Richard."

After she's gone upstairs, Margaret says, "You've been sleeping with her, haven't you?"

I confess, then, expanding on my contrition, go on to make it the most convincing acting job of my career. I should get a nomination.

Most nights, I come home from school and work at tasks around the house until well into the evening, only stopping to sit down with Margaret and Lily to eat dinner. Later, I join them to watch the last program or two on television before going to bed. I don't think Margaret ever forgives me. Once, she says, "I have to go out for a while. Can I trust you to stay out of my sister's bed while I'm gone?" But our life does finally get back to something resembling functional, even though my habitual unease never goes away.

Once, I see a show on television about a man who had been given the curse of knowing when people are going to die. The man sees Xs on the foreheads of the soon-to-be deceased. A bride and groom turn around after the ceremony to start up the aisle together. Both their foreheads are marked with Xs. A sightseeing bus about to travel through a mountain pass is loading up. They cut to an angle on the passengers boarding the bus. They all have Xs on their brows. Then, one night, the man is alone by himself in a mansion. Outside, a storm is raging. He wakes from a nightmare, knowing he has to go out into the swirling winds and rain. He catches sight of himself in a mirror. In the center of his forehead is an X.

After a few weeks, I begin to take a little time for myself. Sometimes I drive to the ocean on my way home from work and wander the beaches in Venice, Santa Monica, and Malibu. They aren't as crowded in 1956, and there's more public access to them.

On a late afternoon at the end of February, I drive west on Sunset, winding from UCLA out to Pacific Coast Highway, then up to a stretch of beach near the Malibu Pier. The sun is almost set when I get there, but the oceanfront feels friendly, the air balmy and springlike. Seven or eight people wander up and down the wide expanse of beach I've walked out onto.

I sit down and try to enjoy what's left of the sun as it drops from sight, rapidly withdrawing its warmth. I've brought a thermos of coffee from my office and a file with twenty gem plates in it—photographs of exceptional colored stones. I'm going to jot down some impressions and comparisons, but I realize it's already too dark, so I zip up my windbreaker, put a handful of pebbles on the file of photographs to protect it from any sudden gusts of wind, and lie down in the sand.

I'm starting to drift off when a breathless voice above me says, "Hey, mister? Your pictures were blowing away."

I sit up and take the plates from the shadowy figure of a young woman wearing jeans and a bulky Mexican-style cardigan.

"One of them got wet," she says.

"I thought I'd weighted them down."

I unzip my windbreaker and carefully wipe the plate dry on my sweater.

"You'll ruin your sweater."

"That's okay. It'll wash out."

"What are they pictures of?"

"Just some colored stones—sapphires, emeralds."

She nods, starts to walk away, then stops and turns back. "Why would you bring pictures of sapphires and emeralds down to the beach in the dark?"

"I teach geology at UCLA. I was going to make some notes, but I couldn't even see the photographs so I gave up."

She laughs a little breathy noise that's hardly recognizable as a laugh.

Marilyn.

My heart is racing. I don't know what to say. I can't imagine what she's doing here. But I can. She's just arrived from New York and is in preparation to begin shooting *Bus Stop*. She's come down to the late-afternoon Malibu beach to be by herself.

I act calm. "Would you like a cup of coffee? I've got a big thermos of it here."

"I don't know …"

"I don't care who you are."

In the growing twilight, I can tell she's frowning. "You mean you *know*? Just from my voice?"

"Yes."

"That's scary." She thinks it over for a moment. "You're a geology teacher?"

"That's right."

"Okay. I'll have a cup of your coffee."

She sits down in the sand next to me, and I open the thermos. I pour a cup and hand it to her.

"Are you looking for Cherie out here on the beach?"

She flashes a surprised smile. "How would you know that?"

"Your work can't all be fun and glamour. You must have to go through some … grief to find a character."

"It's the other way around. My characters help me find my … pain." She shrugs, embarrassed she's used that word. "I've never been so frightened of anything since I was a little girl. To play this part, I'll have to act. What makes me think I can do that?"

"You've been at it for a while."

"Yeah, but this is different." She pauses. "How do you know about this—a geologist?"

"Oh, I pick up a *Variety* sometimes."

She smiles and looks off toward Japan. "I've been back in New York since near the end of '54. I went there because of a … friend of mine. And I thought I might study and get to be better at what I do so nobody would think I'm a joke, you know?" She makes her voice thinner in a parody of airheadedness. "You know, the dumb blonde, Marilyn? Well, I did study. I did learn." She rakes a handful of sand up against her ankle. "But not enough."

"I think it's twice as hard when it's so important to you."

"I don't even know sometimes if I can do it at all."

"Yes, you can. And never mind what I think—Billy Wilder called you a genius."

She smiles, surprised and embarrassed, then shakes her head. "You're sweet." She takes a sip of coffee from the plastic cup. "The thing is, my friends—sorta friends—in New York expect me to be this … *artist*. I'm sorry, I didn't mean to go on like this."

"That's okay."

She narrows her eyes, as if she's trying to remember something. "And I want to please those people because they're the first ones to take me seriously—as an intelligent person. I don't mean as a brain or anything, but artistically. Some of them think I'm artistically intelligent."

"I think you are."

"Do you?" It's a plaintive, sad question.

"Yes, I do."

"Because even though they say that, I wonder a lot of times if they're sincere. Then I get to a time like this when I'm starting something, and I get so unsure about everything, and I don't believe anything people tell me. It's like being in the dark." She looks around her. "Like this, except all by yourself instead of with someone—like you and I here, talking." She can make out that I'm smiling. "Well, me talking, you listening."

"You're interesting to listen to."

"Not just because I'm …"

"No, not just because of that."

She grins. "You're better than a shrink. Cheaper, too. You should take out an ad in the paper: 'Geologist, objective and everything, available to listen to frightened movie stars.' You'd make a fortune."

"When do you start shooting?"

"Next week."

I can't think of anything else to say that won't sound like I'm trying to come on to her. "I wish you all the luck. I think you deserve it. Can I walk you up to your car?"

"Sure."

It's gotten chilly, and she bundles her thick cardigan around her. We walk up the beach in silence, both of us shivering.

When we get to the highway, she points at a black Thunderbird. "That's me."

I reach out to shake hands with her. "It was very nice to meet you."

She takes my hand and squeezes it. "Same here."

I turn to walk to the Oldsmobile, wishing I could prolong this but not knowing how, when she says, "UCLA is only a couple of miles from Twentieth, you know."

I turn back.

"Would you come by and see me sometime?" She laughs self-consciously.

"I wasn't trying to sound like Mae West. I mean to visit me? On the set?" She says the next very quickly. "We could talk a little, like now." She nods toward the darkened beach.

"Sure." There is no way I could possibly refuse her. *What can one do?* "I'll come by."

"I'll leave a pass at the gate for you." She smiles. "What's your name?"

"Richard Blake."

"Richard Blake." She smiles again, shyly, and gets in her car. "Bye, Richard. Don't forget."

25

MARCH AND APRIL, 1956

Most of the filming of *Bus Stop* is done on soundstages eight and fourteen at Twentieth Century Fox, which is only a ten-minute drive from UCLA. When they're not on location in Idaho or Phoenix, I visit her on a regular basis.

One day, she says to me in controlled, even tones, "I think I'm going insane, just like my mother and her mother." She's just had a fight with one of the other actors.

I tell her about Margaret and Lily—I can't think of a reason not to—and describe Lily's state of mind. Marilyn wants to know what they do out in the San Fernando Valley all day and I say, "Not much. They don't do much."

"That's so sad."

"Yes."

"I love being alone, but …" She laughs, then shrugs it off. "I need to be alone … but you've got to be able to go out into the world when you want to."

"I lead a double life," I say. "My life at home and my life away from it. Actually, that's not quite accurate. I live a quadruple life—minimum."

The day's shooting is over. I stay in her trailer. Feeling a little like the love-struck young man in *Of Human Bondage,* I say I want to tell her something I hope will make her feel less unhappy and ask if she'll listen.

She doesn't say a word, just sits down next to me.

I tell her about Jack and Richard, everything I know how to tell her, everything that's happened, leaving nothing out. She listens to me as if this were no more than an old friend telling her his most recent family gossip. It feels like one crazy person telling another one the deranged details of his disease, and the other one doesn't even raise an eyebrow.

Another day, I talk to her about perceptual filters. It's not the first time I've mentioned the subject. Since we started having our talks, I'm no longer the character in *Of Human Bondage,* but have now morphed into Bottom the Weaver in *A Midsummer Night's Dream,* after he's been turned into an ass and believes that Titania, the beautiful magical fairy queen, is enthralled with him. I'm not saying I mind the feeling. I pour my heart out to her and she … listens.

Nothing I say seems to surprise her until the time I mention Lawrence in *Bus Stop.* "He was a gemologist on a field trip in Utah."

Her reaction comes out like an extended violin note, diminuendo, "But there *is* a Lawrence character." She stares at me, saucer-eyed. "… Or there was. We're probably not going to shoot it because we're short on time. But there *is* a Lawrence. Only he's not a gemologist, he works for the Department of Interior."

"It got changed."

"But the thing is, the only people who know about it right now are Josh, George Axelrod—the screenwriter—and me. Nobody else knows. *Nobody.* I'll probably tell Arthur, but he doesn't know yet." She looks around her dressing room, eyes flashing, her mind apparently racing. "Jesus."

My Bottom the Weaver mind has wandered. "Have you ever heard anybody use the word … damaged? About a person?"

"What do you mean?" She's still trying to make sense out of what I've said about Lawrence.

"They don't use that word about people, not in 1956, do they?"

She frowns. "Why would you ask me that? I don't know. Not that I ever heard of."

I'm remembering my last conversation with Margaret, a lifetime ago, and am not listening to Marilyn. "They say 'damaged' about buildings and houses after tornados … and floods, that sort of thing—but not about people."

"Do you think I'm a damaged … person?"

No, I hear her—the injured kindergartner, Norma Jean. "I think you've been … hurt."

I hear words she will say only months later: "When my emotions kick me on the inside and the world kicks me on the outside, where do I go from there?"

Another day, she says, "I want to—you know, in my life—keep the diamonds and throw away …"

"The kimberlite?" Richard suggests.

"What's kimberlite?"

"Oh, it's just what they call the rock that diamonds are found in—the stuff they throw away; it's mica, magnesium … junk."

"Right," says Marilyn. "I want to get rid of all the junk." She takes a deep breath and studies the look on my face. "You know what's going to happen to me, don't you? Or you think you do."

I want to shout at her to run home and throw away all of her pills, forever, but I don't. "She was always a little in love with death," the armchair psychoanalysts said. What if I rouse that impulse in her now? Abused kids are always snarling variations of "Go to hell" when pressed, and do exactly what you've told them not to. It makes no difference how good or well-intentioned the advice is.

She says, "You won't tell me what's going to happen, will you—whatever you think you know? Because no matter what it is, I don't want to hear it."

"I understand."

"Besides, it's not written in stone, is it?" She forces a smile. "I mean, even if it's good news—my future—if I try, I might be able to make it … even better."

"Of course." I smile broadly, reassuringly, suggesting the sky is the limit, that her future may be glorious.

"Thanks for that." She smiles wistfully and looks away. "But the only future I ever heard of is to get old. If I was someone else, maybe I wouldn't mind so much." She lifts both shoulders, defenseless. "But sex symbols don't get old."

I talk Margaret into enrolling Lily in an occupational therapy course at Cal State Northridge, only a few miles east in the Valley. Lily chooses Beginning Sculpture, which meets on Thursday nights. She has a gift for it, which isn't that surprising. One of her pieces stands on a pedestal in the front yard. Margaret objects, but I insist. The sculpture is made of welded iron (with the aid of a professional iron caster). The figure is disturbing, sexual—a young woman, lost, testifying to the frustrated yearnings of her creator.

Margaret cuts down on her drinking. She doesn't become cheerful, but she's no longer an abiding portrait of gloom. She signs up for a class too, one that meets at the same time as Lily's. It's a survey course in general psychology.

This causes Richard, who is emptying the dishwasher when he hears it, to laugh so hard he drops an entire stack of dinner plates.

Early in the shoot, Marilyn is checked into Saint Vincent's Hospital with bronchitis. She's there for four days, recovers well, and is relatively healthy for the rest of the *Bus Stop* filming.

I pop awake at four A.M. one morning. In a dream, I've heard myself say, "What am I doing here?" I think it's Jack alone doing that dreaming, saying those words. I don't think it has anything to do with being back in time, a forty-year-old man at a moment when, according to the calendar, he should be a baby.

In another dream, I have a son. He looks very much like Jack Cade, but he's a little boy. I've taken him to an amusement park called Raging Waters. I'm standing with him on a stairway leading to the top of "the longest, steepest water slide in the world." Far below, a woman—it could be Sophie, I'm not sure—is looking up at us.

The little boy flicks his tongue along the new braces on his upper teeth. I'm trying to remember if I've sent in my unemployment form. Now my little boy's look reminds me of the question that woke me up, and as I think about it, I realize it's a question that's awakened me many nights: "What am I doing here?" My son looks nervous. When I ask him, he tells me he's fine, but I know in his gut he feels he might die on this godforsaken contrivance in the middle of this boondocks desert at the east end of Los Angeles County.

At the top of the water slide now, a big young man—a ripple-muscled people pusher—says to him, "There ya go," and positions him where he'll start his forty-five-degree (that feels like eighty-nine-degree) descent to a tiny pool far, far below. My little boy looks up at me and his eyes say, "Please, Daddy, what are we doing here?" And he doesn't mean at the top of a water slide.

The guy reaches down and pushes my child off into eternity, then he looks down at me. I say, "What are we doing here? Don't you ever ask yourself that when you're not pushing people?"

He frowns at me, puzzled, and says, "Aren't you an actor? Didn't I see you in a commercial once?"

Then he grins and shrugs, not caring what other me might be coming along for the ride, and pushes me into eternity, too. When I wake up, happy to be anywhere at all, I don't even attempt to make sense out of the dream. There's no point in trying. I don't understand any of it. Never did.

To anyone who's never heard of her (somebody who lives on Mars, for example), the conversations between Marilyn and me might seem to be no more than two career neurotics assuring each other that if they could only make a tiny adjustment here and do a little bit of tweaking there, they would both be completely at peace.

Maybe that's true for me; it's possible. I have at least a prayer of ending up peaceful—out of sync with myself, perhaps, but for the most part peaceful. Marilyn *always* seemed to be doomed. It didn't have to be that way. It was as if, out of our primitive needs, we put a curse on her. We turned her into an icon, then a vessel of our hopes and dreams, and finally a human sacrifice. When she did self-destruct (not even knowing we had—oh, Lord— "enabled" her), we gazed at her with the half-dead look of people attending a public execution, mocking the face of misery we helped her create.

She wanted to live; she said so. She begged us for help. We said, "We worship you." Then we made fun of her and threw her off the cliff like an Incan sacrifice. The pulp press—a mirror to us, whether we believe it or not—egged her on. Later, we cried for her and called her a goddess.

She never understood any of it, not the adoration and certainly not the resentment that amounted to hatred. She wanted more than anything to learn how to survive—to be made well. Her housekeeper said, shortly after her death, "It's my feeling she looked forward to her tomorrows." Marilyn said, "Beneath the makeup and behind the smile, I'm just a girl who wishes for the world." She was being clever, which she was, but the truth behind her frantic sadness—and anyone who came close to being her friend knew it— was that what she wanted more than anything was what most people want: to live in peace and happiness in the world she was born into.

Most of any audience to these scenes between her and me would get up, leave the theatre or hit the remote, and tune in to something believable. There's already too much material on Marilyn—as there is on Elvis, Michael Jackson, and everyone else we treat like public property. We're lucky no one ever overhears us. What Marilyn says would be misinterpreted, misunderstood, and ridiculed as something she wouldn't say, even though every word she speaks, she *speaks.*

I know I could get a copyright on some of the Beatles' songs. I have a couple of notions for screenplays I might call *Rosemary's Baby, Jaws,* and *Star Wars,* but I understand I'm not supposed to do things like that, so I go down to a coin shop one day and make a few purchases. Then I go next door to a fancy hobby shop and buy Mickey Mantle's, Willie Mays,' and Ted Williams' rookie cards, among other select baseball greats. For good measure I throw in early comic book appearances of Superman and Batman. They don't cost much, which is good; I have no reason to expect them to travel anyway.

I've done everything I can think of, but it doesn't make the sick, apprehensive ache in my gut go away.

WEDNESDAY, APRIL 11, 1956

I say goodbye to Marilyn. She hasn't shot today. I meet her at her apartment after my two o'clock class and stay for only a few minutes. I don't feel well.

"I've tried to keep my mind off the calendar," I say, "and now the days are gone."

She answers impatiently, "You're the only one I ever knew who's more screwed up than I am."

"I understand why you say that, but I did know about Lawrence."

She glances around the room like she wonders if it might be bugged. "It's cut anyway. It'll never be shot."

I take her hand. "Don't take them—" I point outside, toward anyone not in the room with us, anyone or anything other than her own best-self voice; not the injured, angry one, but the one that wants to live and be happy "—don't take any of them seriously. They know about one percent of what they say they know. Less."

She puts her hand on my forehead. "You're hot."

"Sometimes it happens when I'm anxious … Listen, I'm sorry but I have to tell you again, I keep getting this distinct message from—sorry to mention him—the other me."

She sighs. "It's insulting you think I'm crazy enough to believe any of that."

"You're right. You don't want to take me seriously, either … I'm sorry."

"If I was to guess, I'd say that's 'Richard' speaking."

"It's not. It's someone who's known you forever—long before you were

Marilyn Monroe, long before ... Don't you feel it, too—a longtime connection between us?"

Now she gazes at me as if she were looking at an injured puppy. "No, honey. I wish I could say I did. But I don't remember anything like that."

"I'm disappointed. I've always felt that. I'd see you on film, or ... any picture of you—mostly film—and I always saw something in your smile, in ... your eyes that I knew was speaking to me alone. And now that I know you, I'm sure of it."

"I don't think it was me you were seeing—I think you were seeing through, you know, that *filter* you talk about. Maybe it was someone you knew before ... or a missing part of yourself, if you're like me. I've always had a missing part." She touches my face with one hand and holds the other up to her own cheek, as if testing to see if we're made of the same material. "Maybe sometimes good things fall apart so better things can fall together."

By the time I get home, I'm feeling lousy and have a fever of 102. Lily is working on a sculpture. "Hello, Richard. Margaret's drinking again. She's in bed. Shall I fix you a Scotch?"

"No, thanks. I'm going to lie down for a while."

I sleep fitfully, dreamlessly, for about two hours. When I wake up, I still feel rotten.

For dinner, I have the burnt roast beef again.

"Margaret burned it," says Lily.

So much for General Psychology. "I'm sure it's good anyway."

"No, it isn't. Margaret burned it."

I stay up and watch the old television shows with Margaret and Lily. We hear the story of the marines on Paris Island again. Grace Kelly gets ready to take the plunge. Joe Friday is stern and thrifty of word but way too articulate for a detective sergeant confronting a "reefer dealer." Ida Lupino goes nuts again as the rats close in.

Margaret doesn't ask me to refill her gin and tonic, but by the way her face has gone slack, I can tell there wasn't much tonic in the large one she's been sipping all evening.

As the eleven o'clock news starts, I say goodnight to them and go upstairs.

I take a shower to try to get my mind back into focus, but can't. I wipe the steam off the big mirror in the bathroom and look at Richard's body for what may or may not be the last time. I wonder if it's possible I'll soon be awakened by Douglas Crossley telling me I'm late for *Hamlet* rehearsal.

I don't look myself in the eye. I'm afraid I might see an X on my forehead.

It's windy outside. I sit like a bent ramrod against the headboard of my bed. I'm terrified of dropping off and waking up to my nightmare.

I'm equally afraid I won't.

THURSDAY, APRIL 12, 1956

I open my eyes and look at Richard's Bulova. It's four A.M.—here and in Kingman, Arizona.

I'm still sitting, slumped now, against the head of the bed.

I've survived my moment again. I have to stay in the year 1956. I feel a flood of deep sadness thinking of Sophie.

I'm alive and out of my time for good. What did I expect? The end of the world never comes when the crazy guy with the placard announcing the apocalypse is waving it at you. It comes while you're sitting on the toilet.

Richard was an old man. Or he had been. He had insisted he was ready to go. It was his time.

"God damn you to hell, Richard Blake."

But Brer Richard, he don't say nothin'.

I fall asleep again. At seven, I get up, call Dr. Tandler's office at UCLA, and cancel my two classes for the day. I tell Margaret I'm sick, go back to bed, and sleep until two in the afternoon.

When I wake up, I can barely move. It's the same sensation I had as I watched Margaret fall to the floor when she was shot, a mixture of grief and exhaustion. I wonder if this is the way old people feel when they reach their final moments, ready to move on—maybe not so much grief-stricken at the end as drained, bone-tired of their years on earth.

I stumble downstairs and drink a glass of orange juice. Margaret says, "I didn't feel very well last night, either. I had the awfullest feeling in the pit of my stomach."

I make sure no one can overhear me, and telephone Marilyn.

She sounds like she just woke up.

"Are you all right?" I ask.

"You're alive."

"Yes."

"Can you come over the hill?" she says. "I've got something for you."

"I don't think so."

"Can we meet someplace? I've got to do press stuff tomorrow."

"I don't know if I can drive. I want to, but I honestly don't know if I can."

After a short silence she says, "I'll mail it to you."

"Could you drive out here? Lily and Margaret are in class at Northridge tonight."

She doesn't answer.

"Marilyn?"

"If you give me directions," she says curtly, "I'll come."

"Are you okay to drive?"

"Yes, I am. I'm not *that damaged*. What time should I come?"

"They leave for class at six thirty and get back about nine thirty."

I give her directions to La Vieja and Shoemaker Drive.

Margaret offers to stay home with me, but I tell her I'm okay and that she doesn't have to. They drive away on schedule.

At nine, Marilyn still isn't here. I continue to have alternating chills and fever.

I sit in a chair near the window the branch of the pepper tree scraped against. I'm wearing a sweatshirt with a sweater over that and am wrapped in a blanket, but I'm still shivering. I'm sure I'm hallucinating; I hear the pepper tree swaying again, as in the other storm.

But it's windless outside, entirely still.

At 9:15, Marilyn's Thunderbird pulls into the driveway. The engine shuts off, the headlights go out, and I hear the car door slam. I get up, leaving my blanket in the chair, and make my way to the front door.

Marilyn, again the shy waif Norma Jean, is dressed in a long navy-blue coat, walking awkwardly toward me. When she gets to the doorway, she reaches up and touches my face.

"You're burning up."

"I'll be all right." I take her inside.

We sit next to each other on the silver brocade settee where Margaret and I sat the night she was killed.

The last thing Margaret said to me before Lily came into the room that night runs through my mind: *I want to talk about Lily—and the unspeakable damage that's been done to her.*

Marilyn looks around at the room I've described to her, at the trappings of Richard's life with Lily and Margaret.

Margaret continued, *"But that's not all."* Then she said, *"Come here, I want to show you something."* At that moment, Lily called out my name. Margaret stopped, turned, and went into the kitchen to fix us some tea.

And now I know what she was going to show me.

"This is for you," says Marilyn. She holds out a hand. "Someone gave it to me—I think, I can't quite remember—a long time ago. I thought you might like it. The stone is red if you look at it indoors, but it's green in the sunlight, and other colors other times. It's my birthstone. Alexandrite." She frowns. "But you already know that, don't you?"

I understand the meaning of what I've just remembered. I have no idea why it took me this long.

The next thing I know, I'm standing beside Marilyn on the front porch. She kisses me goodbye and hurries off to her car. She looks back at me, gives me a little wave, hesitates, then gets in and drives off.

I'm still standing there, looking after her, when Margaret and Lily pull in. The Thunderbird and Oldsmobile passed each other on the road.

I look over at Lily's sculpture on the front lawn, forlorn, longing, eerie. It seems to call out my names through the stillness.

It's almost entirely dark under the portico. I reach out in front of me, placing my right hand on one of the columns.

I imagine—I don't believe I can actually see it in the darkness—a glint of photographic sun flare, a flash of memory, a single red star in a midnight sky; a shaft of clarity shooting through my bewildered consciousness.

The earth trembles.

26

1996 TO THE PRESENT

1833 Shoemaker Drive is a museum now. In it, you can see more than fifty sculptures by the artist Lily St. Carnes. She lives with her sister in New York City—so the literature says.

When I get back, it's still the second Friday in October, but there is no Dr. L.M. Partridge to report my experiences to. She no longer exists. If she does, I wouldn't begin to know where to look for her.

I walk out of the living room, past a surprised museum guard who didn't know anyone was in that room, and head over to Dick's Gas and Hot Food.

If I'd asked the man at the *Los Angeles Times* Information Service, when I spoke to him so long ago, to look up the headline for the afternoon edition of Friday, April thirteenth, the man would have read to me, "Six Killed in San Fernando Valley Earthquake."

I knew if I asked him to read that same headline when I got back this time, the number would have been seven.

The night after Marilyn and I returned from Arizona, encountering all the traffic and the people outside on the sidewalks—shortly before Lily killed Margaret—I turned off the headlights, coasted into the garage, and went in the back door, not looking at the front of the house. Margaret wanted to talk about Lily's pregnancy that night. She also wanted to discuss something else.

I never gave her a chance. I grabbed her, hauled her into the living room, and demanded to know the whereabouts of a revolver she thought was upstairs in her mahogany box and that by then she had no intention of using.

I remember the day all this began, standing beneath the portico at Shoemaker Drive, noticing the steel struts that had been used to reinforce the columns that were damaged, as it turned out, during that quake.

The first April twelfth that earthquake happened, I had traveled abruptly into the future the night before. The second April twelfth, I was in Arizona with Marilyn. But this time, I was standing in the silent darkness, on the porch; looking into the sparkling raspberry red of the alexandrite—as if it were lit from within, a polestar for the lost and weary—when the ground moved and the portico collapsed.

I refuse to go to the Hollywood Health Spa and get on the treadmills with Rita. Before she's finished her first sentence about the shake-up at Paramount, I sit her down firmly and say, "Where was I born?"

"You know where. Kingman, Arizona."

"I checked on that. There was no John Cade Jr. born at Saint Mary's Hospital in Kingman, Arizona, on April 12, 1956."

For once she is speechless.

"What's the story?"

She's defiant. "I didn't think you'd ever have to know. But at least I can tell you now why you've never gotten to be a star."

"What's that got to do with where I was born?"

"Nothing. It's got to do with *when* you were born. I bribed an official at the hospital to … um … fudge your birth record. You were born the next day, on April thirteenth. Friday the thirteenth. I couldn't have that."

I must look stricken because her eyes take on an uncharacteristic look of motherly worry. "I'm sorry, honey."

"It *wasn't* seven minutes later!" I shout. "It was a *day* and seven minutes!"

"What?" She looks even more stricken.

"Nothing … Except now that I say it, I realize it doesn't mean anything.

It might as well have been a hundred and seven years later. Or a thousand."

"What doesn't mean anything?"

If I'd stayed at Saint Mary's Hospital in Kingman, Arizona, fifteen minutes longer, I'd have seen my father bring my mother in to give birth to their baby boy. But that's not the way it was meant to be.

"Time, Ma. Time doesn't mean a thing."

I visit Mr. Parsons at Jewels By Jaxon shortly after I get back from my *trip* but am not surprised that he has no new light to shed. I say thank you and that I'm sorry to take his time again. Then I walk back out onto Rodeo Drive.

I look at the calendar less often now that I'm back, and when I do, I'm never really sure of the date. I've come to expect time to do very odd things. It never disappoints me. When I try to remember my life, it's not exactly my life I'm remembering, but recollections of other lives—all rocketing together into a mind-blowing wash. It's like watching the peeling of an onion in slow-motion rewind. All the layers fly back together and somehow recreate "my" entire life without my ever being able to explain the whole, or even any of the parts. And what I'm left with is a tumble of sensations that feel as if they connect me with … something—but I couldn't possibly describe what that something is, and to try to explain to anyone what happened, or what is happening now, is beyond impossible. I end up unable to think of it as anything other than part of—the immensity.

Sophie and I are still married and living with each other again. She is the big part of *me* coming together. She arouses the same tenderness I feel for the vulnerable and unprotected—not that she's a reed in the wind, unable to take care of herself; she's the very *opposite*—but there is such *total* kindness in her, it makes me feel kindheartedly toward the kindness (or the part of her that values kindness), and I see in her a recognition of the fragility of all of us, and it seems as gallant as anything I've ever seen. I think of Atticus Finch from

To Kill a Mockingbird not liking being spat upon, but able to put up with it because the reason for letting it pass is so vital to our unfolding humanity. It's as if I'm looking at all sides of Sophie now, as if the luxury of seeing out of other eyes for a change has enhanced my comprehensive vision, and I'm able to see a radiance in her I couldn't make out before, or somehow forgot, or lost track of, during all my absences—drifting around in time. Maybe Plato was right, that precious stones are living beings. If so, it's entirely possible it works both ways. That would make Sophie an alexandrite, the glow within her always shifting, her dazzling colors endlessly changing, depending on the light she's in.

I pause briefly and gaze at Marilyn, still smiling imperfectly back at me from the painting in the window of Morgan's Gifts. I remember our last meeting at Marilyn's apartment.

How could she not have felt the same bond I did?

The answer comes to me without even thinking about it. She was busy being Marilyn. She was caught up in that time. Those last minutes alone together in her apartment—when she claimed not to believe there was a longtime connection between us—she was "Marilyn Monroe," the invention she herself didn't, in her heart, recognize, and not the woman, the girl, I'd known most of the times we'd been together.

All those still photos of Marilyn? That wasn't Marilyn.

I walk directly back to the cage. The young man with the oblong head is on duty at Morgan's Gifts.

I smile and give him a friendly hello. I say, "I asked you the other day if you knew who paid for the redemption of my ring. I was wondering if you'd remembered, or if I could talk to the lady who was sleeping over there in the wing chair that day."

The young man stares at me, then at the ring on the hand I'm holding out. "We're not supposed to give out information like that."

"Could you tell me if it was paid for by mail?"

"Dunno."

"If I could just see the envelope, that might help."

"Probably be in the garbage out back."

"Would you mind if I looked through it?"

The young man's face puckers as if he can smell the garbage from where he's standing. "I don't think Mrs. Hightower would like that."

We hear footsteps and look toward the back of the store.

"Hello there." The plump little woman who was drowsing in the wing chair *that* Thursday, October 10, smiles at me. "*I'm* Mrs. Hightower. May I help you?"

"I hope so. I picked up this ring the other day and forgot to find out who paid for it."

She looks puzzled. "Pardon?"

"I'd like to know who pawned and then paid for this ring."

She doesn't even draw breath. "You did."

One night, I walk by another pawnshop, on Ventura Boulevard in the Valley, and see an early, signed photo of Marilyn in the window. She's everywhere, still a brand. This is such a young picture, unlike most of her stills, much more Norma Jean than Marilyn. Her hair is wavier and slightly longer than she usually wore it. It's signed *Best Wishes—Marilyn*. I buy it for more money than Sophie and I can afford. It's not in great shape and the signature isn't authenticated, but to me it shows Marilyn as she is—at her best.

I hang it on the south wall of our living room in North Hollywood. Sophie claims to like it. I'm not so sure. I think she's just being nice.

Probably, before long, the classier angels of my nature will cause me to take the picture down and put it in the attic.

Then, someday, it will end up in the window of some other pawnshop. And someone else can go curl up in dreamtime and travel their own journey.

One night I come into the kitchen and find Sophie starting to cook dinner. I've smelled onions. "Always start with an onion," she tells me her Aunt Libby used to say. I'm in a mindlessly good mood already. I pick her up and sort of dance her around the floor of our small kitchen, which makes her giggle, and since I love the way she laughs, I keep doing it, and before long we've crumpled to the floor with her on top of me, still giggling.

"I've got to take you someplace wonderful, like maybe Italy."

She looks at me skeptically.

"Nope," I say smugly. "We can afford it. I got a job today—that batch of commercials I auditioned for. I just found out they want me."

The truth is I'm not really thrilled with the job, but it's quite a bit of money, and Sophie has always wanted to go to Italy, and now we can do that. And if I don't exactly love this job, who cares? It'll make it possible for me to do something I want to do—take Sophie somewhere she really wants to go. And the job is a pleasant enough way to make a buck; I have no reason or right to complain, despite the fact that it's a personal-hygiene commercial, and not something I really want to be associated with.

Anyway, all I can think now, with Sophie on top of me, is here we are in our house—right now, our hearts beating together—and the idea of living this life in this moment, as completely as we can, for as long as we can, makes me happier than anything I can imagine.

"And when we get home, let's have a baby."

She lifts her head and stares at me. "That's a big commitment."

"I want that."

She smiles gorgeously, sits up, and takes off her sweater.

"The onions are going to burn."

She reaches up and turns off the gas.

Once in a while, I decide to tell Sophie what I've brought away from the experiences I've tried to describe to her, but I usually stop myself.

I do have a few tired bits of wisdom. When I let go of what I am, I become what I might be, that kind of thing. But after you've been curled up—as we all have been, for God knows how long—in warped space-time/dreamtime—even the truisms are no more than clichés. Even John Donne's lovely poem about all of us being connected can't exactly be considered an eye-opener; not by this time, for God's sake. And it's not a news flash that we're always moving in a circle because we're connected. We had the tools to work that one out about the time Eve offered Adam a bite of apple.

One thing I will probably spend my lifetime trying to figure out is how did I know the second I laid eyes on the portico at 1833 Shoemaker Drive, just before my original meeting with Maggie Partridge, that it had once fallen in an earthquake? And more to the point, how did I know with such absolute certainty that it would either subsequently or previously—it doesn't matter in the least—collapse "again"? On me?

But whether I convince myself I've figured that out or I don't doesn't really matter. It's like trying to understand why energy is. The only really important thing I need to digest is that I don't have to go in search of the immensity.

One night I say to Sophie, "We are culturally indoctrinated, re-encoded, to have selective perceptual filters that sift out and discard the lion's share of reality. Most of us fear death, but I'll tell you something: I don't anymore."

"I know," says Sophie. "You've said that."

And that's the end of that conversation.

Sometimes, I open up the subject of immensity, or start to talk about the idea of looking for the light in what is vague and indistinct, but she gives me her patient look, and we end up talking about something else.

It doesn't hurt my feelings. She knows more than I do.

I remind her that she once told me she thought if I were to dig deep into myself, I wouldn't find much good there.

"That's not what I said. I remember the conversation clearly. I said if you tap into yourself, you don't get what you want, you get what you are."

"But you apparently didn't like what I was."

"Not true. It's just that at that moment, we had different ideas about who you are. I think—when you tap deep into yourself—you're my wonderful Jack. At that time, back … *then* … you seemed to think you were … someone else."

She's right, I did.

Still, through every moment of my journey, the duration of which I can even now only guess at, I had the sense of a still-small voice within me telling me that my innate judgment—even though it rarely seemed that way at the time—was better than I'd been brought up to think it was.

Maybe I always knew more than I thought I did.

One night, I'm looking at the picture of Marilyn on our living room wall and am touched for an exquisitely sweet moment by an inkling of déjà vu, tracing out into the darkness over the Santa Monica Mountains, through the shadows of my memories, across the barrier of my intelligence and into the glittering spectacle like a Fata Morgana of the Los Angeles basin. Out of a corner of my mind and through the gloom over the Santa Monicas, I feel a sense of loss and warmth and loss again.

And then I feel her next to me and hear her voice as clearly as when she was still alive to me.

"Your sweetest moments are still ahead of you."

EPILOGUE

Sophie drives her 2008 Toyota Scion over Coldwater Canyon, west on Lexington, south on Whittier, and farther into the unhilly part of Beverly Hills. When she arrives at the high-rise Beverly Vues Apartments, she parks beneath the building, walks up to the elevator on the main floor and into the characterless foyer with the gold-flocked wallpaper. She greets the doorman, who smiles and nods, then she hits the button for the next elevator. When it arrives, she gets in and pushes the button for the fourteenth floor.

When the doors open, she walks several steps to the left down the plushly-carpeted hallway, lets herself into apartment B, takes off her linen jacket, hangs it up in the front hall closet, and goes out onto the balcony that faces west.

A very old man is standing up, hanging onto the railing, looking out toward the Pacific, over what used to be the huge acreage of Twentieth Century Fox.

Without turning around, the old boy says in a surprisingly vibrant voice, "Hiya, darlin.' I'm glad you finally made it."

Sophie smiles lovingly at him. "Hello, Mr. Blake. How are *we* today?"

THE END

Acknowledgments

I am ever grateful for Michael Norell's devoted friendship and invariably perceptive advice.

My thanks also to Bret Easton Ellis, who helped me see the excess of most of my adjectives and almost all of my "wisdom."

To those friends who were kind enough to read various drafts and graciously encourage me to bring this mad story into harmony with itself. They are Betsy Hailey, Don Eitner, John Gallagher, Kevin Cook, Gerry Blanchard, Susan Gleason, Carol Summers, Sara Parriott, and Beverly Vineshaines.

To Pamela Guerrieri, Kevin Cook, Meghan Pinson, and Rhonda Erb for their astute, meticulous editing.

To George Foster, who understands a book in depth before he designs its cover.

To Meghan again, as well as to Sunny Chermé Cooper, for their generous hearts and their evenhanded supervision of a crazy person as they expertly oversaw the big things and the little that go into the preparation and publication of a book.

To my children, Abigail, Charles, and Scott, who always support me in everything I do.

And to Linda, for her patience, her intelligent support, her small-hours comforting. For her love.

About the Author

Rick Lenz is a jack of all trades: actor, artist, and author. He has acted alongside many of the biggest names on stage and screen, and his prismatic roleplaying parlayed over to the pen with a successful string of plays from Off-Broadway to PBS. In 2012, Lenz broke the fourth wall and published an award-winning memoir, *North of Hollywood*, about show business, addiction and recovery, and his checkerboard life in New York and LA. When Lenz is not riding away on his next kaleidoscopic quest, he can be found painting, playing the piano, or reading at home with his beloved wife, Linda.

To see what he's up to now, visit www.ricklenz.com.

Meet the Author

Rick Lenz in conversation with Outrider Literary
North Hollywood, summer of 2015

Q: How did you come up with the idea for this book?

A: About twenty years ago, I did a play on a set much like the living room at 1833 Shoemaker Drive; it had a dark, spooky feel to it. Three women ran the theatre. They were also actresses. They were the original prototypes for Maggie, Margaret, and Lily. Back then, when I wasn't acting, I wrote plays. I soon realized this story needed to open up, to have a broader geography than a play would allow. I knew a lot about Hollywood from being in the movie business as far back as the '60s. The story had to take place in the '50s.

Q: How much of your own life story was placed into the novel?

A: Like most actors, I've been between jobs more often than I've worked. I've always been fascinated at the range of life most actors live "between engagements." Jack had to be an actor.

Q: Do you have an obsession with Marilyn Monroe?

A: I needed a movie that was shooting during the time in question. I stumbled on *Bus Stop* and Marilyn. It soon felt like serendipity. I read and saw everything I could find about her—books, her movies, anything. I once played opposite Susan Strasberg, as Jack does in the book. We talked about

Marilyn at length. She was already planning to write *Marilyn and Me* and was eager to talk about her. I didn't have an obsession with Marilyn when I started *The Alexandrite*. I do now. It was oddly like researching an acting role. I had to get inside her psyche if I wanted to be accurate recreating her on the page. She was one of the most difficult, exhilarating characters I've ever worked on.

Q: Do you have a belief in or have any recollection of past life experiences?

A: No, but I do think we are irrevocably linked to each other, that as Jack says on page one, "Life runs in a circle…" and "If it went out in a straight line, it would take us away from each other." And "That wouldn't work because we are all connected, made of the same stuff."

Q: I would love to know more about the author's own acting career and relationship with Hollywood.

A: I spent my first ten years as an actor almost exclusively on stage. When I did "Cactus Flower" on Broadway, I began to get Hollywood offers. From the start, I loved the feel of old Hollywood. I was not in love with the movie industry. Most of the artists who work in it are great, often brilliantly talented, but the movie industry itself—I think—can quite fairly be called deranged.

Q: Is the character of Jack autobiographical in any way? Are any of his experiences inspired by those of the author's?

A: Except for Hollywood, the ups and downs of being an actor, his eternal quest to find meaning in life, and his abiding love for his wife, both Jack and Richard are fictional…Well, okay, Jack is a tiny bit non-fictional

Q: What or who inspired the character of Lily? Is the story's emphasis on mental illness drawn from something the author has experienced?

A: I had a friend who was autistic, but not so that it prevented her from living a mostly normal life. She was exceedingly gifted musically. I think she was a savant. She is the basis for Lily. Also, during my research, I discovered that both Marilyn and Joshua Logan had what would later be diagnosed as bipolar disorder. In chapter sixteen, Marilyn says, "Anyway, Josh said if he hadn't been the way he was—like me, he meant, I could tell—he would have missed 'the sharpest, the rarest, the sweetest moments of his existence.'"

Those are in fact Logan's words about himself. The complete statement was: "Without my illness, active or dormant, I'm sure I would have lived only half of the life I've lived and that would be as unexciting as a safe and sane Fourth of July. I would have missed the sharpest, the rarest and, yes, the sweetest moments of my existence." Every time I considered revealing each of their on-and-off bipolar struggles, it held back the narrative. Maybe most important: neither of them had what could be called an episode during the shooting of *Bus Stop*.

I came away from my research with not only a new picture of Marilyn, but also a huge respect for Logan's talent and character.

Q: If time travel were possible, is that where you would go? LA in the 1950s?

A: Despite the depression, I think I'd choose New York in the '20s and '30s. American theatre was in the process of being born. It was a very exciting time and place to be an actor or a writer or an artist of almost any kind.

Q: I'd be curious to know where the initial germ of the story started. Was it the alexandrite? Or knowing it was Marilyn's birthstone? Or was it a fascination with the 1950s?

A: Again, I stumbled on alexandrite—more serendipity, I felt. It was a perfect talisman/symbol. I feel about both Marilyn and alexandrite as if they've been anonymous gifts.

Q: Did you actually know Marilyn Monroe? Who do you relate to more, Jack or Richard?

A: Richard was an invention. Jack will sleep next to my wife every night as long as God allows. I didn't know Marilyn, but after my research, I feel as if I do. I do have a friend who studied with her at the Actors Studio in New York.

North of Hollywood:

AN ACTOR'S STUMBLING BABY STEPS TOWARD KINDNESS AND PEACE

Everything makes sense a bit at a time. But when you try to think of it all at once, it comes out wrong.
- *Terry Pratchett*

CHAPTER ONE

I was raised in Jackson, Michigan—population 50,000—a city that lies at the third corner of a triangle with Lansing and Ann Arbor, about forty miles from each. Those towns are home to Michigan State University and the University of Michigan. Jackson is home to the longest-walled prison in the world and the Cascades, the world's second-largest manmade waterfall. It also lays convincing claim to being the birthplace of the Republican Party—it was host to the first official party convention on July 6, 1854. A large pile of rocks on Washington Street marks the spawning ground of the GOP. There is also a plaque, in case the rocks don't ipso facto identify themselves as birth-of-the-Republican-Party boulders.

When it was time for me to spread my wings, I headed to New York because that's where my theatre professors at U of M told me real actors go. They didn't mention anything about real bill collectors, and very little time passed before it dawned on me that "real acting" and show business have a commonality factor that ranges from less-than-you'd-hope-for to zilch. Before I learned that, I once asked an old character actor, didn't he just love being an actor and not having to worry about little hollow people's little petty rules?

He told me I had a paper ass.

* * *

Show business as a career, for those of us whom it chooses—we never choose it; no one lacks that much common sense—is the most enticing siren the gods ever conjured, at least to those with the weakness. The only pathway to her lies between Scylla and Charybdis. Any wayfarer with even minuscule common sense would take whatever evasive action was necessary to avoid that route.

My first acting experience was with a summer stock company, a job I got partly because I fit the costumes. Also, I'd been in a few plays in high school, the result of washing out of football when it became clear I was more than averagely breakable.

I inhaled my first season of stock. It was like the county fair, a magic bottle of emotions and smells, a perfumed medley of canvas and sawdust; hot dogs, popcorn, fresh paint, and old lumber varnished temporarily new. Every day, a genie slipped out of the bottle—this was his only trick and nobody could have asked for better—and blew the pungent winds that signaled the summer rains. The reedy grasses around Clark Lake swirled like an ocean in a typhoon, and I felt a frenzy that made me want to run out across the field, down to the water, and hurl myself into it—except I had a show that night. It was all adolescent longings, and they lingered with me like Erin Bibbin's first kiss hung on the entire walk home after my first and final date with her.

I can still smell that summer. It comes to me in waves when I think of that spot on the lake where the Clark Lake Players lasted for an eternity of twenty-five years. When I think of the water lapping against the dock that extended out alongside the old clapboard theatre building that had previously been a roller rink, and before that a prohibition-era dancehall, I think of my wife's question: "Did you ever feel so good you didn't know what to do with it?"

The Clark Lake Playhouse was above a bar with a jukebox in it. You could hear the constant thrumming of rock and roll even during your loudest scene. I can still hear snatches of dialogue:

"Where were you on the night of August twenty-third?"

"On watch, sir." (Me as a seventeen-year-old navy ensign.)

"And what were your duties on watch?"

"Well, sir ... to watch."

And then from downstairs: "Wake up, little Susie! Wake up!"

You could still hear the buzz of motorboats out on the lake, sometimes even after dark. None of these distractions mattered. It was all too lovely to be even slightly diminished by a trivial encircling din. The romance in the air was so intoxicating that nothing else mattered. The adult camaraderie, the playacting, the beer, and most urgently, the girls. Everywhere you looked there were girls. They paralyzed almost every other perception. It was acceptable to show off shamelessly for them. It was sweet to flirt with them. And they flirted back. It was even more fabulous than that. It wasn't only a mysterious whirlwind of infatuations, not just art for art's sake, not just pretending to be a grownup. It was bigger than all the exhilarating parts of itself. It was magic for magic's sake.

Following my summer stock stint in theatre school at the University of Michigan, I trotted out for my first-year acting class some of the scenes from Broadway comedies I'd done. I found out still later that real actors call all acting "the work." The response to my first anxious classroom performance—I'd wowed 'em in stock—was pretty much the same as it might have been if I'd taken the stage and done what my dog does in the park and for which I plan ahead by bringing along a pocketful of plastic grocery bags. *

About a half hour after sunset on a February evening, I was driving home from Ann Arbor, where I was an undistinguished graduate student, to my first wife, Sarah, and our two baby boys in Jackson. My plan in those days was to teach theatre in college. Nothing else seemed possible. While I was briefly studying pre-med I'd watched my father, an eye-ear-nose-and-throat doctor, pack a bloody nose. I slid down the wall, unconscious. After my dad finished with the bloody nose, he stitched together the gash in my head and told me, "Young medical students faint all the time."

I was looking in a mirror at my stitches for the first time when he said that. I threw up in the sink. He shrugged and his eyebrows, which always spoke the truth even if the rest of him was lying, told me that some part of him had understood all along that doctoring and I would make a sorry match.

Outside my car, a warmer day and then a cold rain had turned the countryside into a vast snow pudding. Now, it was freezing over again and the car was contesting my right to control it. I had the feeling I was not where I was meant to be. I noticed by moonlight the discarded cab of an old road grader that had been abandoned on a defunct utility road, and it struck me that the road grader was as pointless as I believed my life was going to be if I stayed.

A mile farther toward Jackson I saw the slush-covered, rusted-out shell of an old Pontiac. I imagined the man who'd been driving it stopping one day, or maybe one winter night, and getting out. It could have been a night like the one that was shaping up now. The Pontiac had just frozen up and quit. He said to hell with it, and hitched a ride straight to New York City. I pictured him living in a penthouse overlooking Central Park, telling his new friends how he had once been imprisoned in an Andrew Wyeth winterscape until one day he found he'd had it with the bitter cold and scraping ice off his windshield with the base of a tire jack, and he finally got smart enough to make his way out of that frigid hell and come to this civilized place, to live the way elegant people should.

And all the well-bred guests warm their hands by the fire and their insides with Hendrick's martinis. They laugh with captivating suavity and one of them says, "By Gad, sir, you are a character. A Pontiac. By Gad, sir." (Apparently Sydney Greenstreet is on the guest list.) And everybody smirks and chortles until they're contented as puppies wedged in and warming themselves in all the comforts of mom.

Then it hits me, in my case anyway, that's not a soothing thought—that being tucked in with Mom is a lot like being outside in a freezing cold Pontiac.

"By Gad, sir," says Sydney. "You are a character."

It dawns on me: This is an improv.

"Which character are you, by the way?"

Improv is torture when you fear there is only one perfect answer for each question. At any rate, I don't know the answer to this one.

"By Gad, sir." Sydney is frowning now, has a distinctly menacing look. "You seem to be in the wrong movie."

* * *

This story is about celebrity and non-celebrity and, from a very personal point of view, everything in between. It is about the stumbling progress of my life, and about Hollywood, and how I feel about both. Sometimes I feel cheerful, sometimes dark. I try to apply light therapy as I go—light is my preference—but there is no way I can make the dark parts go away (yet) at my personal whim.

One more thing: There will be no descriptions of anyone's tits—for example, Jacqueline Bisset's—which by the way I have seen, nor will I say anything directly bad about Lauren Bacall. Were I to describe Jackie Bisset's breasts or anything physically about her, it would be insufficient and redundant anyway. If you've never seen them, I suggest renting the *The Deep* and taking a look for yourself. As for Lauren Bacall, she's a complicated lady and it would be stupid and in poor taste for me to give you an appraisal of her personality based on my limited experiences with her. It wouldn't be fairly representative.

Besides, I really do hate being unkind.

* * *

In *Cactus Flower*, my first Hollywood movie, I played opposite Goldie Hawn, who became pretty much my best friend for a while. It was the first big part in a movie for both of us. Walter Matthau and Ingrid Bergman were in it, too. Walter told me he'd had a crush on Ingrid for years, and since he was the muscle in getting the film made, being very hot at the time, he insisted she play the role.

Ingrid talked to me at length about *Casablanca* because I was married at the time to Claude Rains' daughter (whom I'd played opposite in Buffalo in a stage production of "You Can't Take It With You"). I told Ingrid that Claude never saw Casablanca because he didn't like watching himself on film—had a phobia about it. She was surprised, but then acknowledged that she, too, was usually uncomfortable watching herself. (I think it's an unnatural experience for anyone.) She still spoke with wonder about the success of *Casablanca*. She had almost no relationship with Humphrey Bogart away from the set—their involvement was exclusively professional. She also expressed awe that the film worked as well as it did. She said that as they were shooting it, she had no idea where the story was going, that nobody really did. She was completely baffled as to whom she was supposed to care about most, Victor Laszlo (Paul Henreid's character) or Rick Blaine (Bogie's).

I had very little firsthand knowledge about movie stars, but I speculated that Ingrid was different from the rest. She was in her very early fifties. I was twenty-nine. It didn't matter; she was incredibly sexy. Like Walter Matthau, I developed a crush on her. It was hard to be around her and not fall under her spell. She was elegant in a kind, centered way with something friendly to say to everyone. But also, one of her secrets, both on screen and in person, seemed to be the ability to make men fall in love with her—with the possible exception of Humphrey Bogart. I think she knew she had that gift, and I wondered if she wasn't turning it on just a tiny bit for me. (I got the idea she wasn't particularly attracted to Matthau.) She was especially kind to me, I thought.

One day, Gene Saks, the director, called cut on a shot in which she and I were dancing. He said, "Rick, your hand is covering Ingrid's face."

I had ruined Ingrid Bergman's profile! I was going to be sent to would-be movie-actor-failure hell. But she smiled sympathetically at me and petted the back of my head; she knew these things happened. Now I was positive she was very fond of me.

Seeing me at the premiere in New York several months later, she said, "Hi, Nick."

A year or two before this, I'd done the Broadway version of "Cactus Flower" with Lauren Bacall, who terrified me because she reminded me of my mother and who later told John Wayne—when I was in *The Shootist* with them—that she'd "discovered me." Wayne glowered at her and said, "Aw, shut up, Betty." (Her real name is Betty Persky.) He was "a little ill"— so they said at the time—and I guess not in the mood for Hollywood nonsense. I got along fine with him, although protocol called for me not to volunteer much chitchat. He asked me what my politics were—I think because I had long hair, a pretty good giveaway in those days. I told him I wasn't political. He studied me for a couple of seconds, then smiled and shrugged.

Goldie and I remained friends for a few years, but we drifted apart. Her career went better than mine. So I started to ask her for parts in her movies. After that, it didn't take long for her to stop returning my calls. She and I have the same birthday, different years. I'm older by six.

Occasionally, we exchange cards.

One time, my late friend John Ritter did a staged reading of one of my plays, opposite Sharon Gless. I invited Goldie and she wrote me a note, saying she was sorry she couldn't come, that she was out of town. That was as close as we ever came to seeing each other since the unforgettable day that she and Julie Christie and I played tennis on Boris Karloff's court.

* * *

I'm lost. I don't know what movie I'm in. It could be *Star Wars*. It's as if I'm in a George Lucas spacecraft, careening around in a kaleidoscopic wash of ceaselessly merging space and time, illogically sequenced, tumbling moments of my life. I hang still for an instant, then whoosh, I'm shot into the next moment, each time increasingly sure nobody I encounter knows my name—or anything about me, which in the business I've chosen to spend my life is catastrophic. Sometimes these moments are happening to me right now. Sometimes they're merely memory. I never know until I get there.

I pray all of this is no more than a nightmare, that I'll wake up before I crash, but it doesn't happen. The harsh reality hits me that I've become one of those Hollywood people catalogued in the entertainment industry, because I'm over fifty and not famous, as old-to-dead. I'm like a drowning man, watching his life in fast-forward—except there isn't the slightest sense of chronology.

* * *

I watch the Academy Awards with friends. *Brokeback Mountain* is nominated in several categories, and gay cowboy jokes are sprinkled through the opening of the ceremony. Jon Stewart, the host, introduces a montage—film clips that can be taken as sexually ambiguous, featuring cowboys of past Westerns taking off their coats, their chaps, opening their vests for the showdown; handling and caressing their guns. Then, near the end of the montage, they show a shocked and terrified frontier newspaperman as John Wayne in *The Shootist* inserts an immense Colt .45 into my mouth. All I remember about that scene was trying to keep my teeth from getting broken. My reaction to having a large, metaphorical penis stuck in my mouth in front of hundreds of millions of people on Academy Award night is that I'm thrilled. It's the largest audience I've ever played to.

About two weeks after that scene was filmed, I arrive in Carson City, Nevada, to do more work on the movie and find out that Wayne has been feeling worse than a little ill. He's been in the hospital with pneumonia for several days. "If shooting lasts much longer," the wardrobe guy confides, "he may not make it."

But I know better. I live in this culture. He's John Wayne.

My last scene with him is an exterior. It's the continuation of the gun-in-my-mouth scene.

He's shaky. When he hits me with his pistol hand on the back of my neck, he also hits me with the pistol. After we're wrapped for the day, I go to the hospital where they put two stitches in the back of my head.

Two weeks later, I'm on the Warner Brothers lot. I have one last scene with Harry Morgan. It's early in the morning, at least a couple of hours before I'll be shooting with Harry. I'm alone on an idle backlot street, sitting in a canvas chair with my name stenciled on it. I'm watching some extras at the end of the street, just sitting around, staring. One of them is in a telephone booth. Others are lined up, waiting to make their calls. They're spending these moments of (what seems to me) their virtually vacant today—trying to get themselves booked for a vacant tomorrow.

I hear a familiar voice, behind me.

"Did you know [director Don] Siegel used a double for me while I was sick?"

I swivel my head around and look up dumbly at John Wayne. I can't make myself say a word. People come to Wayne, not the other way around.

"A couple long shots in this thing are going to show some other guy being J.B. Books."

He's remembered the pistol slap and is telling me he wasn't himself that day.

"Anyway," he growls at me, "sorry about that." He briefly directs his gaze toward the back of my head. "I only ever did that once before."

He shows me a barely perceptible shoulder shrug, turns, and with his distinctive hitchy saunter, moves off toward his trailer.

I should have saved those stitches. I wonder what they'd bring on eBay?

Sometime after I've shot that exterior outside of the widow's house (the widow is Bacall's part) in Carson City, I run into Ronnie Howard at a blackjack table in the Orchard Casino in Carson City. He's charming and affable and we chat about not much of anything. Then, out of nowhere, I'm surprised and gratified when he promises me that if he should ever have any success as a director, he will use me in all his films.

I still have a five-dollar chip from that casino. It's probably worth five dollars today.

* * *

Cognitive dissonance is the basis of most good acting. It means that you come to believe what you find yourself doing. You take a job working for a political party, and you come to believe in the cause. You are an actor playing love scenes, and you find yourself falling in love with the actress you're playing opposite. You are in an easy chair, in a warm pool of light. The rest of the house is in darkness. You're reading an especially scary mystery novel. You hear a noise from somewhere upstairs. You get up. You move slowly to the bottom of the stairway. You look up. Your anxiety builds. You hear the noise again. It sounds less like the squeaking you originally would have called it and more like moaning. You start up the stairs.

If you are any good, you should now be literally terrified.

If you hang around Hollywood long enough, cognitive dissonance becomes your genetic instruction. Your psyche gets bent into the shape of your eight-by-ten.

At first you say, "Not me."

I was given a sobriety test by the side of the road early one morning in Beverly Hills. When I was called on to say my ABCs, I got hung up around P or Q and failed. And I was sober. It was the pressure of the moment. It was real life that was the problem—my instinctive cognitive dissonance. It's a great acting tool. It can also work against you.

When I was ten years old, I used to play with a boy named Dixie Thorpe. He was nine. I have no idea where he got that name. I don't think his family was from the South. One day, Dixie's mother took us to Crispell Lake, one of the hundred or more swimmable lakes that pepper Jackson County, Michigan. Crispell was about a half mile across, and the area around it hadn't been built up much. We were going to swim at the small county park.

Dixie changed into his bathing suit first and got down to the edge of the lake before I did. As I came out of the bathhouse, I saw a group of four or five boys in the water around the end of the swimming dock. Dixie and I didn't know these kids well. They went to a different grade school. They were a little older than us and the few times we'd run into them, they'd always harassed us with preadolescent taunting for no other reason than they could, and because each of them wanted to prove to his buddies that he was a tough guy.

Dixie had never been to this lake before and wasn't a strong swimmer, but I was. It was a pretty shallow lake, so no one seemed to be worried. I was almost down to the water when Dixie reached the end of the dock. I saw him look hesitantly down, apparently working up the courage to go in. The boys standing in the water jeered and yelled at him, "Dive in, pantywaist. What are you scared of?"

Dixie was a gutsy kid. He wasn't scared of anybody. I liked that about him. It made me feel gutsy, too; confident, just like Dixie.

As I reached the lake, he backed up a few steps. The boys, standing shoulder deep in the water, continued to goad him.

I felt something leaden in the pit of my stomach. I ran out onto the dock, yelling, "Dixie! Don't!"

But by then he was sprinting full tilt toward the water. He threw himself off, head first, launching himself into an awkward jackknife dive.

He seemed to hang in the air forever.

He hung on in the hospital for a week before he died. I never saw him again.

The boys had been standing on their knees.

* * *

Whatever punishment they got came from their parents. However much it was, it was surely not as much as they've had to live with their whole lives.

I should have seen what might happen to him before I did. I didn't feel guilty—not exactly. I suppose the right word is angry. I was older than Dixie. I'd been swimming at that park before. I knew how shallow the water was. I shouldn't have let it happen.

For a while, I tried to shut him out of my mind, to forget he'd ever existed. But it didn't work. In a sense, I've seen him grow up. At every crossroad of my life, I've imagined the benchmark moments that never happened to Dixie. In some small way it feels as if I've looked at the world through Dixie's eyes.

About twenty years ago, the anger started to fade. At the same time, I feel Dixie's presence more than ever. He doesn't speak to me, but he has quietly forgiven me.

Maybe guilt is the right word.

Anyway, whenever I do something that feels like it's the decent thing to do, or the kind thing, he sort of pats me on the back. It's hard to explain.

Darkness.

Every theatre goes dark sometime. There are always other stages, other shows.

Not for Dixie.